PRAISE FOR AMY CLIPSTON

"*Breaking New Ground* is a beautiful story of heart, hope, and healing. You'll feel the warmth and emotion of this book long after the last satisfying page."
—JENNIFER BECKSTRAND, *USA TODAY* BESTSELLING AUTHOR OF *THE AMISH QUILTMAKER'S UNCONVENTIONAL NIECE*

"Amy Clipston once again entertains us with a story that reaches all the way to the heart."
—VANNETTA CHAPMAN, *USA TODAY* BESTSELLING AUTHOR, ON *BUILDING A FUTURE*

"Clipston kicks off the Amish Legacy series with a heartwarming romance . . . It's a tender romance, precisely the kind that Clipston's fans expect."
—*PUBLISHERS WEEKLY* ON *FOUNDATION OF LOVE*

"Amy Clipston has once again penned a sweet romance that will have her readers rooting for a heroine who deserves her own happily-ever-after. Crystal Glick is a selfless, nurturing woman who has spent her life caring for others—to the detriment of her dream of a family of her own. Duane Bontrager is a much older widower with three nearly grown sons. Readers are in for a treat as these two overcome one obstacle after another to be together. The real stars of the show, however, are Crystal's nieces and nephews. They're enchanting. Grab a cup of coffee, a piece of pie, *Foundation of Love*, and settle in for a lovely Clipston story."
—KELLY IRVIN, AUTHOR OF *THE BEEKEEPER'S SON* AND *UPON A SPRING BREEZE*

"A heartwarming story that works as both a standalone romance and a satisfying series installment."
—*PUBLISHERS WEEKLY* ON *THE COFFEE CORNER*

"Clipston always writes unique and compelling stories and this is a good collection of light reading for evenings."
—*PARKERSBURG NEWS AND SENTINEL* ON *AN AMISH SINGING*

"Amy Clipston's characters are always so endearing and well-developed, and Salina and Will in *The Farm Stand* are some of my favorites. I enjoyed how their business relationship melded into a close friendship and then eventually turned into so much more. *The Farm Stand* honors the Amish community in the very best of ways. I loved it."

—SHELLEY SHEPARD GRAY, *NEW YORK TIMES* AND *USA TODAY* BESTSELLING AUTHOR

"This series is an enjoyable treat to those who enjoy the genre and will keep readers wanting more to see what happens next at the Marketplace."

—*PARKERSBURG NEWS AND SENTINEL* ON *THE FARM STAND*

"Clipston begins her Amish Marketplace series with this pleasing story of love and competition . . . This sweet tale will please fans of Clipston's wholesome Amish romances."

—*PUBLISHERS WEEKLY* ON *THE BAKE SHOP*

"Fans of Amish fiction will love Amy Clipston's latest, *The Bake Shop*. It's filled with warm and cozy moments as Jeff and Christiana find their way from strangers to friendship to love."

—ROBIN LEE HATCHER, BESTSELLING AUTHOR OF *WHO I AM WITH YOU* AND *CROSS MY HEART*

"Clipston closes out this heartrending series with a thoughtful consideration of how Amish rules can tear families apart, as well as a reminder that God's path is not always what one might expect. Readers old and new will find the novel's issues intriguing and its hard-won resolution reassuring."

—*HOPE BY THE BOOK*, BOOKMARKED REVIEW, ON *A WELCOME AT OUR DOOR*

"A sweet romance with an endearing heroine, this is a good wrap-up of the series."

—*PARKERSBURG NEWS AND SENTINEL* ON *A WELCOME AT OUR DOOR*

"*Seasons of an Amish Garden* follows the year through short stories as friends create a memorial garden to celebrate a life. Revealing the underbelly of main characters, a trademark talent of Amy Clipston, makes them relatable and endearing. One story slides into the next, woven together effortlessly with the author's knowledge of the Amish life. Once started, you can't put this book down."

—SUZANNE WOODS FISHER, BESTSELLING AUTHOR OF *THE DEVOTED*

"With endearing characters that readers will want to get a happily ever after, this is a story of romance and family to savor."

—*PARKERSBURG NEWS AND SENTINEL* ON *A SEAT BY THE HEARTH*

"[*A Seat by the Hearth*] is a moving portrait of a disgraced woman attempting to reenter her childhood community . . . This will please Clipston's fans and also win over newcomers to Lancaster County."

—*PUBLISHERS WEEKLY*

"This story shares the power of forgiveness and hope and, above all, faith in God's Word and His promises."

—*HOPE BY THE BOOK*, BOOKMARKED
REVIEW, ON *A SEAT BY THE HEARTH*

"This story of profound loss and deep friendship will leave readers with the certain knowledge that hope exists and love grows through faith in our God of second chances."

—*KELLY IRVIN, AUTHOR OF THE BEEKEEPER'S SON AND UPON A SPRING BREEZE, ON ROOM ON THE PORCH SWING*

"A story of grief as well as new beginnings, this is a lovely Amish tale and the start of a great new series."

—*PARKERSBURG NEWS AND SENTINEL* ON *A PLACE AT OUR TABLE*

"Themes of family, forgiveness, love, and strength are woven throughout the story . . . a great choice for all readers of Amish fiction."

—*CBA MARKET MAGAZINE* ON *A PLACE AT OUR TABLE*

"This debut title in a new series offers an emotionally charged and engaging read headed by sympathetically drawn and believable protagonists. The meaty issues of trust and faith make this a solid book group choice."

—*LIBRARY JOURNAL* ON *A PLACE AT OUR TABLE*

BREAKING
NEW GROUND

OTHER BOOKS BY AMY CLIPSTON

CONTEMPORARY ROMANCE
The Heart of Splendid Lake
The View from Coral Cove
Something Old, Something New

THE AMISH LEGACY SERIES
Foundation of Love
Building a Future
Breaking New Ground

THE AMISH MARKETPLACE SERIES
The Bake Shop
The Farm Stand
The Coffee Corner
The Jam and Jelly Nook

THE AMISH HOMESTEAD SERIES
A Place at Our Table
Room on the Porch Swing
A Seat by the Hearth
A Welcome at Our Door

THE AMISH HEIRLOOM SERIES
The Forgotten Recipe
The Courtship Basket
The Cherished Quilt
The Beloved Hope Chest

THE HEARTS OF THE LANCASTER GRAND HOTEL SERIES
A Hopeful Heart
A Mother's Secret
A Dream of Home
A Simple Prayer

THE KAUFFMAN AMISH BAKERY SERIES
A Gift of Grace
A Promise of Hope
A Place of Peace

A Life of Joy
A Season of Love

YOUNG ADULT
Roadside Assistance
Reckless Heart
Destination Unknown
Miles from Nowhere

STORY COLLECTIONS
Amish Sweethearts
Seasons of an Amish Garden
An Amish Singing

STORIES
A Perfectly Splendid Christmas included in On the Way to Christmas
A Plain and Simple Christmas
Naomi's Gift included in An Amish Christmas Gift
A Spoonful of Love included in An Amish Kitchen
Love Birds included in An Amish Market
Love and Buggy Rides included in An Amish Harvest
Summer Storms included in An Amish Summer
The Christmas Cat included in An Amish Christmas Love
Home Sweet Home included in An Amish Winter
A Son for Always included in An Amish Spring
A Legacy of Love included in An Amish Heirloom
No Place Like Home included in An Amish Homecoming
Their True Home included in An Amish Reunion
Cookies and Cheer included in An Amish Christmas Bakery
Baskets of Sunshine included in An Amish Picnic
Evergreen Love included in An Amish Christmas Wedding
Bundles of Blessings included in Amish Midwives
Building a Dream included in An Amish Barn Raising
A Class for Laurel included in An Amish Schoolroom
Patchwork Promises included in An Amish Quilting Bee

NONFICTION
The Gift of Love

BREAKING
NEW GROUND

An Amish Legacy Novel

AMY CLIPSTON

ZONDERVAN®

ZONDERVAN

Breaking New Ground

Copyright © 2023 by Amy Clipston

Requests for information should be addressed to:
Zondervan, *3900 Sparks Dr. SE, Grand Rapids, Michigan 49546*

Library of Congress Cataloging-in-Publication Data

Names: Clipston, Amy, author.
Title: Breaking new ground / Amy Clipston.
Description: Grand Rapids, Michigan : Zondervan, [2023] | Series: The Amish
legacy series; 3 | Summary: "In the third installment of Amy Clipston's
beloved Amish Legacy series, Korey Bontrager and Savannah Zook pretend
to date, only to find themselves unexpectedly falling in love"--
Provided by publisher.
Identifiers: LCCN 2022046302 (print) | LCCN 2022046303 (ebook) | ISBN
9780310364399 (paperback) | ISBN 9780310364436 (library binding) | ISBN
9780310364412 (epub) | ISBN 9780310364412
Subjects: BISAC: FICTION / Small Town & Rural
Classification: LCC PS3603.L58 B74 2023 (print) | LCC PS3603.L58 (ebook)
| DDC 813/.6--dc23/eng/20220926
LC record available at https://lccn.loc.gov/2022046302
LC ebook record available at https://lccn.loc.gov/2022046303

Zondervan titles may be purchased in bulk for educational, business, fundraising, or
sales promotional use. For information, please email SpecialMarkets@Zondervan.com.

Printed in the United States of America

23 24 25 26 27 LBC 5 4 3 2 1

In loving memory of Margaret E. "Maggie" Halpin. Maggie—you fought a valiant fight to the very end. I will forever miss your love and friendship. I'm so grateful to be able to count you among my "sisters."

GLOSSARY

ach: oh
aenti: aunt
appeditlich: delicious
Ausbund: Amish hymnal
bedauerlich: sad
boppli: baby
bopplin: babies
bruder: brother
bruderskinner: nieces/nephews
daadi: granddad
daadihaus: small house provided for retired parents
daed: father
danki: thank you
dat: dad
Dietsch: Pennsylvania Dutch, the Amish language (a German
    dialect)
dochder: daughter
dochdern: daughters
dummkopp: moron
Englisher: a non-Amish person
fraa: wife

1

freind: friend

freinden: friends

froh: happy

gegisch: silly

gern gschehne: you're welcome

Gude mariye: Good morning

gut: good

Gut nacht: Good night

haus: house

Ich liebe dich: I love you

kaffi: coffee

kapp: prayer covering or cap

kichli: cookie

kichlin: cookies

kinner: children

krank: sick

kuche: cake

liewe: love, a term of endearment

maed: young women, girls

maedel: young woman

mamm: mom

mammi: grandma

mei: my

naerfich: nervous

narrisch: crazy

onkel: uncle

Ordnung: the oral tradition of practices required and forbidden
     in the Amish faith

schee: pretty

schmaert: smart

schtupp: family room

schweschder: sister

schweschdere: sisters

sohn: son

Was iss letz?: What's wrong?

Wie geht's: How do you do? or Good day!

wunderbaar: wonderful

ya: yes

THE AMISH LEGACY SERIES FAMILY TREES

Crystal m. Duane Bontrager
|
Tyler (mother—Connie—deceased) m. Michelle
Korey (mother—Connie—deceased)
Jayden (mother—Connie—deceased)

Cecily (deceased) and Lee Zook
|
Savannah
Tobias ("Toby")

Dorothy m. Eddie (Edwin) Blank
|
Levi
Dean

Michelle m. Tyler Bontrager

A NOTE TO THE READER

While this novel is set against the real backdrop of Lancaster County, Pennsylvania, the characters are fictional. There is no intended resemblance between the characters in this book and any real members of the Amish community. As with any work of fiction, I've taken license in some areas of research as a means of creating the necessary circumstances for my characters. My research was thorough; however, it would be impossible to be completely accurate in details and description since each and every community differs. Therefore, any inaccuracies in the Amish lifestyle portrayed in this book are completely due to fictional license.

CHAPTER 1

KOREY BONTRAGER'S HEARTBEAT ACCELERATED AS HE STOOD on the rock driveway under the rapidly darkening sky and stared up at the familiar two-story home with the small front porch. The house was quiet with only a single lamp burning in the front window, and the early April air around him was cool and held the hint of animals. While his pulse pounded in his ears, the only sounds he heard were the rumble of traffic on a distant highway and a dog barking on a nearby farm.

He dropped his two duffel bags on the ground with a thud and then studied the modest brick home. This was the house where he had been born and raised with his two brothers—one younger and one older. And this was the home he'd fled fourteen months ago after he and his older brother had a falling out. No, it was more than a falling out. It was an estrangement.

His mouth dried as emotions swamped him—sadness, guilt, betrayal . . . and hope.

But this house was more than that. It was his history. His best and worst memories had been born and grown there. Many of them remained, and his most precious were of his mother.

Korey closed his eyes and envisioned his mother—his

beautiful mother—and his heart squeezed. His mother had passed away nearly four years ago after a battle with cancer, and to Korey's dismay, his father had remarried two years ago.

He set his jaw as he thought about how Crystal, his stepmother, had moved into their house and into his mother's place, and that familiar resentment that had hung over him like a dark cloud filled his chest. He took a deep breath and tried to breathe away the tightness in his chest like Sherman, his elderly friend and neighbor in Ohio, had taught him.

He still couldn't understand how his older and younger brothers stood by and accepted his stepmother as if she hadn't rocked their family to its very core. It had been too soon for *Dat* to move on, but they acted as if it were only natural.

Korey rubbed his hand over the stubble on his chin and turned his attention and his flashlight beam toward the barn, then to the cinder-block building beyond it where his father stored his supplies for his roofing company. Both buildings looked the same as in his memories of working with his father and brothers. He had once believed that his father's business would be his future, and he had never considered leaving the roofing business. But everything changed fourteen months ago when he went to work with a cousin in Ohio and left his family behind.

Korey's stomach clenched as his flashlight beam illuminated the new two-story house that sat at the back of his father's property with its small front porch and fresh white paint. A soft yellow light glowed in an upstairs window. Thoughts of his older brother, Tyler, and their fractured relationship assaulted his mind. It was Tyler and his betrayal that had chased Korey from Pennsylvania to Ohio. Korey and Tyler had always had their differences since they were children. In fact, their squabbles were a normal part of their day-to-day while working together on their father's roofing jobs, but this had been different.

When Korey and Michelle had broken up after more than a year of dating, it had become apparent to Korey that Tyler had feelings for her. Soon after the breakup, Tyler started dating Michelle, and Korey couldn't stand the sight of them together, which was why he had arranged to move to Ohio to get away from them. But while leaving had helped to heal some of Korey's wounds, he was startled to feel that familiar resentment and anger within him. And even though he knew deep in his heart that he and Michelle weren't meant to be, he still couldn't dismiss the betrayal that his older brother not only dated her but *married* her. Tyler had certainly broken the unspoken code between brothers.

Korey closed his eyes and slowly breathed in through his nose as he recalled the conversations he'd shared with Sherman. And then Sherman's words that had pushed Korey to purchase the tickets and make the fourteen-plus hour trip from Sugarcreek, Ohio, back home to Bird-in-Hand, Pennsylvania, filled his mind: *"You're hiding from your problems here. Family is God's gift to us. Don't forsake your family."*

He opened his heart to God and sent up a silent prayer: *Lord, soften my heart toward my brother and my father. Help me close this distance I feel between my family and me. My heart can't stand to be separated from them any longer, but I need your help to forgive them and move on. I can't do this without your guidance.*

Then Korey hefted his bags onto his shoulders and started up the path toward the front door of his father's house. His shoes crunched along the rock path as the beam from his flashlight guided his way.

When he reached the top step, the front door swung open,

and Korey's younger brother, Jayden, grinned from the doorway. "Well, look at what the cat dragged in! The prodigal son has returned."

Korey dropped his bags on the porch and chuckled as his younger brother enveloped him in a warm hug. "Hey, Jay."

Dat stood behind Jayden with a wide smile on his face. Except for more gray peppering *Dat*'s dark hair and beard and a few more wrinkles around his mouth and dark eyes, he looked the same.

"*Sohn.* You're finally here." *Dat*'s voice seemed to croak. "We've been watching out the window for you. Your taxi must have snuck up on us."

Korey cleared his throat against a sudden thickness. He had missed his family more than he'd realized.

"*Dat.* Hi." Korey stepped into the house and hugged his father.

"It's so *gut* to finally see you." *Dat*'s voice was hoarse as he patted Korey's back. "Are you hungry, *sohn*?"

"No, *danki*. I grabbed a sandwich at the train station."

Jayden lifted Korey's bags. "Did you bring your rock collection?" he teased.

"Ha." Korey rolled his eyes. "Give them to me."

"Nope. I got it." His younger brother slipped in the front door and into the family room.

Korey followed him and was grateful to find it just as he recalled with the same sofa, two wing chairs, and a recliner, along with a coffee table, two end tables, and two propane lamps. It was still home. *His* home.

Dat rubbed Korey's shoulder. "You've been gone too long, *sohn*. We've *all* missed you."

Korey swallowed a sarcastic snort. Surely Tyler was grateful to get Korey out of the way so he could become *Dat*'s business partner. Korey's absence also enabled Tyler and Michelle the opportunity to enjoy planning their wedding and building their house without his interference. No, they certainly hadn't missed Korey at all. In fact, everyone had moved on without him. He tried in vain to swallow his resentment.

"Crystal wanted to stay up to see you, but she was too tired," *Dat* continued. "She told me to tell you that she'll make your favorite breakfast in the morning—chocolate chip pancakes—to celebrate your return."

Korey clamped his lips together. It was obvious Crystal was going to welcome him home, despite his past behavior. Korey had gone out of his way to be unpleasant to her when she and *Dat* were first dating, but then he had turned his sarcasm to silence after they were married. Embarrassment covered Korey. He would try to accept his stepmother somehow. *Help me, Lord.*

"We have church in the morning," *Dat* said. "Will you join us?"

Korey nodded. "*Ya.* Of course." He jammed his thumb in the direction of the stairs. "Has my room been converted into a sewing room or something? Or do I still have a bedroom?"

"Of course you still have a room, Korey." *Dat* fixed him with a look. "It's just as you left it."

Relief twined through Korey. "Thanks."

"We'll see you in the morning then." *Dat* rubbed Korey's arm.

"*Gut nacht, Dat.*"

Jayden took a step toward the stairs and a smirk overtook his face. "It's been so long since you've been home. Does it look familiar to you? Would you like me to show you the way to your room?"

"That was so funny that I forgot to laugh." Korey frowned and gave him a playful punch in the arm. "I remember the way." He chuckled. He had missed his younger brother, the loyal peacemaker who never took sides despite how often he and Tyler bickered.

Korey took one of the bags off of Jayden's shoulder, and Jayden waved to *Dat* before grabbing a Coleman lantern from the coffee table and heading to the stairs.

They climbed the steep steps and then walked into Korey's room, where they both set his bags on his double bed in the center of the room. Korey peered around, finding his same dresser, desk, chair, and bookshelf.

His bed was made with a blue and gray quilt that he recalled his mother creating many years ago. His heart squeezed as he thought of his mother sitting in her sewing room, working on the quilt.

I miss you, Mamm.

Then he imagined Crystal in his room, preparing for his return. It had been so kind of her to take the time to make the bed for him. Did he even deserve her thoughtfulness after the way he'd treated her? He pulled in a deep breath through his nose as guilt pummeled him.

"So, how was Ohio?" His younger brother's question pulled Korey from his thoughts.

When Korey looked over, he found Jayden sitting backward on the desk chair. Jayden pushed his hand through his thick sandy-blond hair before resting his elbows on the back of the chair.

Korey shrugged as he unzipped a bag and began pulling out his clothes. "I spoke to you on the phone while I was there and shared the highlights." He chose a few hangers from the closet and started hanging up his trousers. "I told you that working in the RV factory was okay. I enjoyed getting to know *Mamm*'s cousins better."

"*Ya,* I know."

Korey hung all of his trousers in the closet and then moved on to his shirts.

"You said you were active in youth group there."

"I was." Korey took care of his shirts and then began loading his socks into a nearby drawer. "I already mentioned that I made a lot of *freinden.* Everyone was very welcoming."

"Were there any *schee maed*?"

Korey shrugged as he pushed the sock drawer closed.

"Did you date at all?"

Korey stopped working and studied his brother. "Are you serious?"

"Of course I am." Jayden gave a little laugh. "Does that mean you're confirming that there weren't any *schee maed* there?"

"There were plenty, but I wasn't looking." Korey shook his head. As if he would ever trust another woman with his heart! Korey was better off alone.

He finished putting away his clothes and then gave his younger brother a sideways glance. Jayden rested his chin on his palm and watched Korey with an intense or possibly suspicious look.

"Spill it already," Korey said with a sigh. "What do you *really* want to ask me, Jay?"

"Are you going to stay here now that you're back?"

"*Ya,* most likely." *We'll see how it goes with Tyler . . .*

"Are you going to come to work with us at the roofing company?"

"I'm hoping *Dat* will agree to it."

Jayden rolled his eyes. "Of course he will. I'm still working with Ty's crew, and it's going well. Ty is great at keeping us on schedule." He snorted. "I'm sure you remember how he was before you left, always working on a business plan to increase our jobs and keep us working."

A muscle twitched in Korey's jaw. Tyler had been determined to take over the company, always keeping *Dat* focused on how great his business plans were. Tyler insisted he wasn't trying to push Korey out of the way, but he was able to run his own crew, and now—

"Did you like working in the RV factory more than roofing?" Jayden's question transported Korey back to the present once again.

Korey's eyes darted up to where Jayden watched him. "No. I actually prefer roofing. I like being outside."

Jayden smiled. "That's *gut.*"

"Why?"

"Because we're all glad you're back. We missed you."

Korey lifted his chin. "Everyone missed me, huh?"

"Are you really going to start that again?" Jayden's lips turned down in a frown. "You have to know by now that Ty never meant to hurt you. He *has* missed you. You're our *bruder.*"

Korey held up his hand. "I don't want to argue with you, Jay."

"*Gut.*" Jayden stood and cupped his hand to his mouth to cover a yawn. Then he picked up his lantern. "Are you going to ride to church with me tomorrow since you'll need to buy a horse and buggy?"

Korey nodded. "Of course."

"Great. Well, I'll see you in the morning. Don't stay up too late."

"I won't. *Gut nacht,* Jay."

His younger brother crossed to the doorway and then tapped the woodwork. "I'm glad you're back." He disappeared into the hallway. A few moments later, Korey heard a door open and then click shut.

Korey finished unpacking his bags, changed for bed, and climbed under the sheets and quilt. He flipped off his lantern and rested his arm on his forehead as he stared up at the ceiling through the dark.

Tomorrow he would have to face his former community, and while he was eager to see his old friends, anxiety still churned in his chest. Would his former friends accept him back? Or would Korey feel like the odd man out if they had moved on with their lives? Would he have any friends left here at all?

Korey's stomach knotted. Tomorrow he would have to face his older brother and his bride for the first time since he'd left. He slammed his eyes shut and sent up a prayer:

Lord, please help me bridge this giant chasm dividing me from my family. Help me mend my broken relationships.

Then he waited for sleep to find him.

The following morning Savannah Zook stood by the Hertzler family's barn and buttoned her white sweater. The early April morning air was cool, and she shivered, regretting not wearing a coat. Birds sang in the nearby trees while the colorful flowers in Mary Hertzler's garden danced in the light breeze.

"I can't wait for the youth gathering today," Macy Yoder, Savannah's best friend since first grade, gushed. "I'm hoping that Keith will finally ask me if I want a ride home." Her pretty face lit up with a grin, and she hugged her arms to her chest and twisted back and forth as if imagining riding in her crush's buggy.

Savannah was certain Keith already had noticed her best

friend, and she was also convinced he would ask her to ride home with him. Since Macy's eyes were as green as the lush summer grass and her hair resembled the color of sunshine, Savannah was surprised none of the young men in their district hadn't already asked her to be their girlfriend.

Willa Mast grinned and grabbed Macy's arm. "Oh, wouldn't that be wonderful? Then we could all go on group dates together, right, Jodie and Gail?" she asked their other friends who stood nearby. "Then we'd all have boyfriends!"

"Well, not all of us." Jodie Bender looked pointedly at Savannah.

Gail Hostetler shook her head. "I'm sure Savannah wouldn't have any problem finding a boyfriend if she'd just show some interest."

"*Ya*, that is the whole problem, Savannah. You act like you're too aloof to date." Willa clucked her tongue. "You have to make an effort and actually talk to the guys instead of behaving like you're better than they are."

Savannah swallowed a groan. All her friends talked about was dating, but she had much more important things to worry about. She scanned the nearby groups of young folks for her younger brother, Toby. She finally spotted him standing near their cousin Dean. Her heart fell as she took in Toby glancing around awkwardly before kicking a pebble with the toe of his shoe while Dean talked to his friends. Dean laughed with his buddies, but Toby looked as if he felt like a stranger or more like an outcast. And the sight nearly broke her heart.

If only Toby could find a true friend . . .

"There has to be *someone* you like, Savannah," Willa said.

Savannah turned her attention back to her group of friends.

They all stared at her as if something was wrong with her, and it made frustration boil in her chest. "Why are you all looking at me as if I'm *narrisch*?" she asked.

Jodie and Gail shared a look before Jodie nodded at Savannah. "There has to be a young man who has caught your eye."

"There isn't." Savannah shook her head. "I'm not interested in dating. You all need to accept that. You all want to have boyfriends, but I don't."

Willa looked confused. "Why not? We're all twenty-four, and it's time we start thinking about having a family. Don't you want to get married?"

"I have other priorities." Savannah pivoted to look at her brother again.

Toby was all she had, and she was all he had. She had to make sure he was okay before she even considered settling down and having a family. Besides, she couldn't think of one young man in her district or her youth group with whom she had anything in common. They seemed to be living carefree lives, and she couldn't relate to that.

Willa lifted her chin. "Well, I'm ready to get married. I just hope Tommy asks soon."

"Me too," Jodie said. "I'm very happy with Peter."

Gail gave a dreamy sigh. "I feel the same way about Ike."

Savannah held back the urge to roll her eyes. She pushed the ties to her prayer covering over her shoulders and longed for the church service to start so she could escape this ridiculous conversation. Was it nine o'clock yet?

Just then, Willa's eyes widened as she looked at something over Savannah's shoulder. "Oh my goodness. You won't believe who just climbed out of that buggy."

Savannah and her friends turned toward where Willa had focused her attention.

"Who are you talking about?" Macy asked.

Gail grabbed Savannah's sleeve. "Korey Bontrager is back!"

Savannah pulled her sleeve out of Gail's hand as she watched Korey help Jayden unhitch his horse from his buggy.

"I heard he ran to Ohio after Michelle started dating his *bruder*," Jodie said.

Gail grinned. "And then she *married* his *bruder*!"

"Well, I heard Korey didn't treat her well," Jodie countered.

Willa held up her finger. "And I heard she liked Tyler all along and just used Korey to get to him."

"It has to be difficult to see his older *bruder* with Michelle," Macy mused. "I mean, they're living on his *dat*'s land, and Korey will have to see them every day. Can you imagine that? It has to be dreadful for Korey to look at his *bruder*'s *haus* every day and think about how he could have had that with Michelle if he'd just treated her better."

Her friends collectively murmured an agreement.

Jodie shook her head. "Poor guy."

Savannah watched Jayden lead his horse toward the barn while Korey glanced around, his expression anxious as he turned his straw hat in his hands. His dark eyes seemed unsure as he placed his hat on his thick dark hair. He looked as if he wanted to be anywhere other than at the Hertzler farm on a church Sunday.

Her heart went out to him, even though she'd never known him very well. Although they had grown up attending the same one-room schoolhouse and in the same church district, Korey had been a year ahead of her in school. She recalled sitting in front of him at school and occasionally sharing a passing conversation, but she didn't know much about him.

Still, Savannah could almost feel the angst that was reflected in Korey's expression. Wasn't it obvious to her friends that the man was apprehensive about his return home?

She faced her friends, suddenly irritated with them and their gossip. When would her friends grow up? "Maybe we should stop making assumptions about Korey and what happened between him and Michelle and also him and his *bruder*. After all, it's none of our business. And don't forget that gossip is a sin."

Willa frowned. "Savannah Zook, you are no fun."

The other women laughed.

"So, let's talk about Keith," Jodie told Macy. "How can we get him to ask you to ride home with him after the youth gathering?"

While her friends turned their attention back to helping Macy get a boyfriend, Savannah released an impatient sigh and focused on Korey as he walked toward the stable with his younger brother. Curiosity filled her, but as she had told her friends, it was none of her business.

Still, as she took in the uncertainty clouding Korey's face, she wondered what had driven him to leave his community and what had motivated him to come home.

CHAPTER 2

KOREY'S STOMACH ROILED AS HE STROLLED BESIDE JAYDEN from the stable and took in the members of his congregation milling around near the Hertzler family's barn, waiting for the church service to begin.

Uneasiness wrapped around his chest and squeezed as he scanned the sea of faces. Although he recognized nearly every person in the crowd, he felt like a stranger in the community where he'd grown up. He pondered if he should have stayed in Ohio, but wise Sherman's words filled his mind once again, and he squared his shoulders. He'd felt God calling him home. Now he simply needed to find a way to fit in again.

He reflected on how well the morning had gone so far. When he'd entered the kitchen, he'd been greeted by the delicious aroma of chocolate chip pancakes and coffee, along with his stepmother's smile that had been as bright as the sun streaming in through the windows.

Breakfast had been both delicious and pleasant while he'd enjoyed the scrumptious food and answered his family's questions regarding his time in Ohio as well as his long trip back to Pennsylvania. Korey felt welcome in his home, and he was grateful.

And to make the morning even better, Korey had been relieved that he'd managed to avoid seeing Tyler before he and Jayden left for church. But that had only delayed the inevitable. Korey couldn't avoid his older brother at church. The congregation consisted of approximately a hundred members, and Korey would run into him for sure.

He tried to tamp down the dart of nerves in his stomach. He had to be strong.

When doubt overcame him, Korey slowed his gait. Maybe he should have slept in and prepared himself to face Tyler when he came home after church.

"It's so great to have you back, Kore," Jayden said, his feet picking up speed. "I'm sure everyone will be thrilled to see you. People ask about you all the time."

Korey swallowed, falling behind his younger brother.

"I guess you'll go to buy a horse and buggy tomorrow." Jayden stopped and faced him, his light-brown eyebrows drawing together. *"Was iss letz?"*

"Nothing." Korey shrugged.

"You made it home!" Dwight Smoker, Korey's best friend, rushed over to him and shook his hand. "Jayden had told me that you were coming, but I was afraid you'd change your mind."

Korey took in his best friend's dark beard, a reminder that he had married Kendra more than a year ago. "Dwight. *Wie geht's?*"

"I'm doing fantastic." Dwight's smile lit up. "Kendra is expecting, and we couldn't be more excited."

Korey couldn't imagine becoming a parent, especially at twenty-five, but he was happy for his best friend. "Oh my goodness. Congratulations."

Just then a crowd of young men gathered around Korey and Dwight, and they began tossing questions to him.

"Welcome back, Korey!" someone called.

Korey nodded. "Thanks."

"How was Ohio?" someone inquired.

Korey rubbed his clean-shaven jaw. *"Gut."*

"Are you here to stay?" another asked.

Korey shrugged. *"Ya,* I suppose."

"Did you bring a *fraa* with you?" another called, and everyone chuckled.

Korey shook his head.

"I don't see a beard, so I guess not!" someone announced, and the laughter grew even louder.

When Korey turned, he found Tyler standing nearby and watching him, his face holding a hesitant expression. Korey stilled and the muscles in his shoulders tightened. The moment of truth had now arrived, and he had no choice but to address his older brother.

Wading through the crowd of onlookers, Korey ambled over to him. Although Tyler had been born only fourteen months before Korey, he looked different and somehow older than twenty-six. Perhaps the dark beard he grew since marrying Michelle made him appear maturer.

Korey's hands clenched into fists as that thought hit him square in the chest. Tyler was now Michelle's *husband,* and he wore that evidence on his face for the world to see.

"It's so *gut* to see you, Kore." Tyler reached out as if he were going to hug Korey but then shook his hand instead. *"Dat* said you were coming home, and I was so relieved to hear it. We've missed you."

Korey nodded. "You have a nice *haus*."

"Thank you. We like it."

We. Korey's pain sat on the tip of his tongue, but he held it back.

"So, how have you been?"

Korey shrugged. "Okay. You?"

"*Gut*." Tyler smiled and rubbed his hands together. "Really *gut*."

They stared at each other, and an awkwardness stretched between them like a giant chasm, or perhaps even an ocean. Would Korey ever find a way to be close to Tyler? Was that possible after all of the hurt and betrayal that had broken their relationship? Korey studied his brother and wondered how they could ever move past what had come between them. Only God could make that happen. Yes, it would be a divine miracle.

"So . . ." Tyler gave a nervous laugh. "How was your trip home?"

Korey opened his mouth to respond and then noticed movement out of the corner of his eye. It was finally nine o'clock, and a line of people began filing through the barn for the church service.

Tyler pointed to the barn. "I guess I'll see you after the service."

Korey frowned. Tyler would sit with the other married men in the congregation. Another reminder of how Tyler had moved on without him. And Dwight would be in the married men's section as well. Would Korey have any friends to sit with during the service?

"You can sit with me," Jayden said as if reading Korey's mind while he patted Korey's arm.

Korey turned to his younger brother, and relief unraveled some of the stiffness in his neck and spine. For a moment, he'd forgotten Jayden was still standing beside him. "Thanks."

After waiting their turn, Korey and Jayden traipsed into the barn and found a place on a bench in the unmarried men's section of the congregation. Korey picked up the hymnal beside him and ran his fingers over the worn cover as he scanned the married men's section. His eyes found Tyler and *Dat* sitting with other married friends. Jonah Chupp, Tyler's best friend, also sported a beard, evidence that he had married Charity, Michelle's best friend, while Korey had been in Ohio.

For a moment, Korey felt as if he'd been left behind while his friends had moved on, getting married and moving over to sit with the married men. Perhaps if he had stayed in Pennsylvania, he would have found a wife and a secure future too.

He shook off the thought. What was he thinking? He wasn't ready to get married. He wasn't even ready to share his heart. In fact, he couldn't even imagine dating.

At the same time, staying in his father's house wasn't his idea of the best situation for his return to the community. He would have to figure out a way to find enough money to build a house of his own or find one to rent—possibly one far enough away from Tyler and Michelle that he wouldn't have to sit in church with them every other Sunday, their relationship in his face while he worshiped the Lord. Instead, Korey would try to join a new church district and start a new life, leaving his past hurts behind him.

But running away like a coward wouldn't help him repair this broken relationship with his brother. Korey released a long breath through his nose.

When his eyes moved to the married women's section of the congregation, he found his stepmother sitting beside Michelle. Crystal smiled as she spoke to a woman beside her. She was a patient woman, always seeing the bright side of life, no matter what trials she had faced. She and *Dat* had worked through the rocky start of their relationship when Korey and Tyler had struggled to accept her into their family. And the ever-present smile on her face was proof that Crystal was happy with the life she and *Dat* had managed to build. Korey had to work on letting her into his heart, but it was so difficult after losing *Mamm*.

A memory of seeing his mother sitting in that section beside Michelle's mother hit him hard and fast, and his heart lurched. Oh, how he missed her! So much had changed in the past few years. He closed his eyes for a moment and worked to slow his galloping heartbeat.

When he opened his eyes, Korey's gaze moved to Michelle. She whispered something to Charity, her best friend, sitting beside her. Michelle looked the same as he remembered with her pretty face, bright blue eyes, and light-brown hair. Yet she also had a different air about her, much like Tyler did. She looked maturer and more settled in her life.

Michelle turned to Crystal and said something, and Crystal's green eyes sparkled as she touched Michelle's arm. It was apparent that the two women had grown close since Michelle joined their family. A strange jealousy twisted through his gut. The close relationship between his stepmother and Michelle was just another reminder of how his family had moved on without him.

But you chose to leave...

When the song leader started the first line of the opening hymn, Korey dismissed his confusing thoughts and turned his attention to worshiping the Lord. He would worry about his situation with his brother later.

"How does it feel to be back?" Dwight asked while sitting across from Korey during lunch.

After the service ended, Korey helped the men convert the benches into tables for the noon meal. The congregation ate in shifts with the men enjoying lunch first while the women served it, and then the women eating after the men were done.

Once the benches had been set in place, Korey and Jayden found a place to sit, and Tyler, Jonah, and Dwight joined them across the table.

Korey placed lunch meat and cheese on a piece of bread and folded it in half. "It feels . . . strange."

"It will get better," his ever-positive younger brother insisted. "Soon it will be like you never left."

I doubt that. Korey nodded anyway.

Jonah lifted a pretzel. "Tell us about Ohio. How did you like your work?"

"It was very different than working on a roof." While they ate their sandwiches, Korey talked on about working in the RV factory and about the friends he'd made.

"It sounds like you enjoyed your time there," Tyler commented after Korey finished his story.

Korey nodded, not sure what to say to his older brother.

"*Kaffi?*" Savannah Zook asked as she stood behind Korey, holding a coffee carafe.

Korey handed her his cup. "*Ya. Danki.*"

He peered up at her while she filled the cup. Although Savannah had been a year behind him at school, he couldn't remember having more than a brief conversation with her while they were in the schoolhouse or on the playground. She'd always seemed confident and sure of herself, the complete opposite of other young women in their church and school district. Savannah had always been outspoken and unafraid to speak her mind, especially when anyone mistreated her younger brother, Toby.

Savannah handed him his cup and then filled Jayden's, Tyler's, Dwight's, and Jonah's cups before moving on down the table.

"Are you going to come to the youth gathering with me today?" Jayden asked Korey. "It's going to be at the Esh family's farm."

"I don't know."

"You could always ride home with Michelle and me instead of going to the youth gathering," Tyler offered. "Then we could all visit and get caught up."

Korey hesitated. While he wasn't interested in going to the youth group gathering just yet, an awkward ride home with his brother and his ex girlfriend sounded like torture.

"I'll stay home from the youth gathering and join you. It will be like a family reunion," Jayden offered as if sensing Korey's misgivings.

What would Korey do without his younger brother? He felt himself relax once again. "Okay."

The conversation turned to the discussion of work. Korey remained quiet while his brothers detailed their roofing jobs on this week's schedule. He could only imagine how many jobs his brothers had completed together while he'd been gone. Surely their bond was closer than ever, and that thought sat heavy on his heart.

Korey finished his sandwich and a few pretzels and then felt the urge to exit the barn and breathe in some of the early spring air. "Excuse me," he muttered as he climbed off the bench.

Jayden looked concerned. "You okay, Kore?"

"*Ya.* I'll be right back." Korey made his way past the rows of tables, nodding to familiar faces before stepping outside.

His shoes crunched along the rock path as he walked away from the conversations swirling behind him in the barn. He sucked in a deep breath, inhaling the aroma of flowers mixed with the familiar scent of animals as he turned his gaze toward the clear blue sky.

When he heard voices, he twisted toward the Hertzler family's two-story, brick home while Savannah and her best friend, Macy, strolled up the path. Savannah carried a coffee carafe, and Macy balanced a tray with pieces of pie on it.

"I mean, I think he likes me. He seems to. At least he smiles every time he sees me," Macy was saying, her face animated.

Savannah nodded while frowning.

"But then I also saw him talking to—" Macy met Korey's gaze and stopped speaking, her cheeks turning pink. "Oh, hi, Korey."

He nodded and stepped off the path, giving them room to pass on their way to the barn.

As Savannah followed Macy and stepped past him, her toe hit a rock, and she teetered.

"Whoa!" Korey's hand shot out, and he grabbed her arm along with the carafe before she fell.

Savannah gasped as she righted herself.

Korey released her arm. "You okay?"

"*Ya.*" She took the carafe from him. "*Danki.*"

"*Gern gschehne.*"

She studied him for a moment, and he cleared his throat, feeling as if she were scrutinizing him. He could only imagine what she thought of him. Surely the rumors were still rampant about what happened between him and Michelle.

Then Savannah suddenly hurried off toward the barn, where Macy stood in the doorway, looking confused.

"What happened?" Macy asked her.

"I almost tripped," Savannah announced before they disappeared into the barn.

Korey sighed and scrubbed his hand down his face, once again wondering if coming home had been the right choice. He didn't feel a part of his community anymore. Maybe he should have stayed in Ohio and built a life there.

But then how would he repair the issues with his family if he'd stayed away? As hurt as he was, he'd missed his family. He'd yearned for his heart-to-heart talks with his father, and he'd missed the camaraderie he'd always shared with Jayden.

And deep down, he wanted to have Tyler in his life again. He longed for them to feel like brothers instead of enemies or strangers.

Help me, Lord.

When footsteps sounded behind him, Korey turned as Michelle emerged from the barn with an empty tray tucked under her arm. He set his jaw at the inevitable awkwardness.

His ex-girlfriend met his gaze and stopped in her tracks, something unreadable flickering over her face before she offered a tight smile. "Korey. Hi."

"Michelle." He crossed his arms over his chest.

"How are you?"

"Gut."

She paused for a beat, and a wave of awkward silence rolled in. Memories of when they'd been happy together tumbled through his mind. He recalled laughing with her at youth gatherings and holding hands while riding home in his buggy.

But that felt as if it had been a hundred years ago. So much had changed since then. They were both different now—no longer the people they'd once been. And all that was left now was pain.

"You look well," she finally said.

"You too."

She balanced the tray in her hand. "I need to run along and get some more pie. I'll see you later."

"*Ya.*"

Michelle gave him another manufactured smile before she continued toward the house.

Korey ran his tongue over his teeth and once again hoped he'd somehow find the strength to assimilate back into the community.

Savannah and Macy walked out of the Hertzler family's kitchen together after eating lunch and helping clean up the barn and the kitchen.

"Are you going to the youth gathering today?" Macy asked as they meandered toward the field of buggies.

"*Ya,* I just need to go home to get changed and pick up the cookies I baked yesterday."

"Okay. I'll see you there." Macy gave her a wave and then hurried off toward her parents' horse and buggy.

Savannah's steps picked up speed, and she approached Toby as he hitched his horse to his buggy. "Are you going to the youth gathering?" she asked him.

"No." He kept his back to her while he worked.

"You should go."

"Why?" He faced her. "Because you need a ride, right? You can ride with Dean." He nodded toward where their cousin stood talking and laughing with a group of his friends.

Savannah folded her arms over her waist. "That's not why I want you to go, and you know that, Toby. You need to come and spend time with your *freinden*."

"*Mei freinden?*" He looked incredulous. "Please, Vannah. No one likes me. They ignore me when I'm around. It's like I'm invisible." He lifted his straw hat and pushed his hand through this thick dark hair, the same dark hair Savannah had inherited from their father—their deadbeat father who had abandoned them after their mother had died giving birth to Toby when Savannah was five years old.

"That's not true, Toby. People do like you. You just have to try talking to them. Be more outgoing, and everyone will interact with you. You just need to come to the youth gathering and have fun."

Toby finished hitching up the horse and then spun toward her, his face crumpling with a frown. "Everyone thinks I'm stupid."

"You're *not* stupid," she said, her heart breaking.

"Look, Vannah, you need to face the fact that I'm not going with you to the youth gathering." His deep blue eyes, which mirrored her own, flashed. "I'm going to go home, and you can ride with Dean like you always do. So stop nagging me about it."

"You and Dean are both nineteen, which means you should spend time with him and his *freinden*."

"Dean is nice to me because he has to be. We share a room and we're family. That doesn't mean we have to be *freinden*, especially since I don't fit in with his *freinden*."

"You can make *freinden* if you try. You can hang out with me and *mei freinden*."

"It's not the same." Toby looked past her shoulder at something behind her. Then he gave a solemn nod.

Savannah spun, and she flinched when she found Korey standing by Jayden's buggy and watching them. Embarrassment crept up her neck. Surely Korey hadn't been standing there the entire time and overheard her painful conversation with her brother. And if he had, why did she keep running into him? Wasn't once today enough?

Korey nodded at her, and she returned the greeting before facing her younger brother again.

"Let's go home, and we'll talk about this later, Toby."

"You're not my *mamm*, Vannah. So, stop acting like it."

She gritted her teeth and climbed into his buggy as Toby's frustrated words floated through her mind. No, she wasn't Toby's mother; however, after all she and Toby had been through, she was responsible for him, no matter what he said. And she wouldn't ever take that responsibility lightly, no matter how much it irritated Toby.

Because *Mamm* would want her to care for him in *Dat*'s absence. It was her sisterly duty.

CHAPTER 3

"Why didn't Toby come to the youth gathering today?" Macy asked Savannah as they sat on a hill watching a group of their friends play volleyball.

Savannah ripped out a blade of grass and wrapped it around her finger, keeping her attention on the volleyball players who leapt through the air, striking the ball back and forth over the net. "He said he was tired and wanted to go home and rest."

"That's too bad."

Savannah frowned. One day she'd convince Toby to join her and her friends at a youth gathering—with God's help, of course.

Gail, Jodie, and Willa climbed the hill, chatting and grinning as they made their way over to Savannah and Macy.

"What are you two doing up here all by yourselves?" Gail asked as she plopped down on the grass beside Savannah.

Macy tented her hand over her eyes, blocking the bright afternoon sun. "We were just talking."

Savannah pulled another blade of grass and wound it around her finger. She scanned the volleyball teams and found her cousin Dean serving the ball. Her chest pinched when she remembered how Toby insisted he didn't fit in with Dean and his friends. She recalled how Toby had always stood on the outskirts at school.

At times she contemplated if Dean had pushed Toby away, but Dean wasn't mean-spirited. Her cousin was always kind to Toby, and she'd never heard him utter a cruel word toward him. At the same time, Dean had remained silent when the bullies had teased Toby at school. While she longed for Dean to defend Toby, she also understood how peer pressure worked. Also, Savannah was frequently punished for her outbursts, and she was certain Dean hadn't wanted to stay after school to clean the classroom as she had so often done.

Savannah tossed the blades of grass onto the ground and swiped her hands down her teal dress, brushing away the dirt that had landed there. She had to find a way to convince Toby to come to the youth gatherings and mingle. He needed friends. It wasn't healthy for him to be alone. Every time he insisted he was stupid, her worry for her younger brother wrapped tighter around her heart. He wasn't stupid, no matter what the bullies at school had drilled into his head.

"Savannah?"

"Huh?" She looked up and found her friends standing over her, watching her with curious faces. "I'm sorry. Did you say something?"

Macy laughed. "*Ya*, we said we were going to play volleyball."

"We need to get down there before it's too late to join the game." Willa touched Macy's arm. "Look, Mace! Keith is talking to our boyfriends." She pointed to where her boyfriend, Tommy, talked with Peter and Ike, Jodie and Gail's boyfriends. "We should all go play volleyball together."

Jodie rubbed her hands together. "*Ya*, that's a *gut* idea!"

"Go have fun." Savannah waved them off. "I'll stay here."

Despite her friends' protests, Savannah remained on the hill while they trotted down toward where the four men stood at the volleyball net. She rested her elbow on her bent knee as they approached the men.

While Willa, Jodie, and Gail struck up conversations with their boyfriends, Keith and Macy also gravitated to each other, and soon they were playing volleyball on the same team.

Savannah smiled as Macy and Keith laughed together during the game. Macy's bright expression told Savannah what she already knew—that Macy was excited to have Keith's attention. And Savannah was happy for her. She wanted the best for Macy.

Savannah's gaze moved to another volleyball game where her cousins, Dean and his older brother, Levi, and Levi's girlfriend, Iris, continued to play. She tried to imagine Toby with them, also enjoying the game, and once again she felt sadness overtake her. Instead, she envisioned Toby at home, napping in his room. While Savannah prayed that her brother would take part in their youth group, she worried that he would spend the rest of his life alone.

Her greatest fear was that he wouldn't fall in love, get married, and have a happy life, which was why she vowed to always take care of him, no matter what. Toby was her first priority, no matter the cost to her own happiness.

Savannah set her chin on her palm while the games played out at the volleyball net. When Macy's team won, she and Keith high-fived and laughed before heading toward the snack table.

Popping up to her feet, Savannah brushed her hands down the skirt of her teal dress once again and then descended the hill and headed toward the snacks.

Macy turned toward Savannah and made a beeline toward

her, taking Savannah's hand and pulling her away from members of their youth group. "Did you see me playing volleyball with Keith?" she asked, her pretty face lit up with a smile.

"I did. It looked like you two were bonding."

"We were." Macy leaned in close. "Savannah, he asked me to ride home with him. I'm so excited I could burst!"

Savannah hugged her. "I'm so *froh* for you." And she was.

"Are you okay?" Macy's smile dimmed.

"Of course I am. Why?"

"You didn't join us to play volleyball. *Was iss letz?*"

Savannah shook her head. "Nothing is wrong. I just wanted to sit."

"Well, if Keith asks *mei dat*'s permission to date me, then you'll be the only one in our group without a boyfriend. I don't want you to feel lonely."

"I won't be lonely, Mace."

Her best friend looked unconvinced.

"Honestly, it's fine. You just concentrate on getting to know Keith. I'm *froh* the way things are."

Macy searched Savannah's eyes. "You don't mean that."

"I do."

"You don't want a boyfriend?" Macy asked, and when Savannah shook her head, she looked aghast. "Why not?"

"It's not a priority for me now, but you don't need to worry about me." She peered over Macy's shoulder to where Keith watched them, looking eager. "I think Keith is waiting for you."

Macy's smile was back. "Really?"

"*Ya*, really." Savannah nodded toward him. "Go talk to him. We'll chat later."

As Macy hurried off to meet Keith, Savannah folded her

arms over her waist. She had a feeling that Macy would soon be Keith's girlfriend, and she hoped that Macy would enjoy her time with him.

But deep down, Savannah also feared that she was growing apart from her group of friends while they moved on with their boyfriends. And despite the brave face she wore every day, Savannah would be lonely.

Korey was perched on a wing chair across from the sofa where Tyler, Michelle, and Jayden sat. He picked up his mug of coffee and tried to ignore the anxiety that rolled through him while Michelle and Tyler held hands and Tyler talked on about a roofing job he was working on at a motel over in Millersburg.

Michelle seemed to glow as she hung on Tyler's every word, her blue eyes sparkling with love for him. And Tyler's eyes were soft and warm as he regarded his wife with that same affection apparent in his expression. Marriage looked good on Michelle and Tyler.

Korey pursed his lips. He wasn't jealous of Michelle and Tyler since he knew in his heart that he hadn't been the man for Michelle. But at the same time, he felt out of sorts, awkward, and alone. Once again, he felt left behind.

"How's your cheesecake, Korey?"

The question yanked him from his thoughts, and he turned to his stepmother sitting on the wing chair beside him. Crystal's smile was friendly and eager.

"It's *appeditlich*." He lifted the small plate with the half-eaten piece of chocolate chip cheesecake as if to toast her. "Perfect."

Crystal nodded toward the sofa. "Michelle made it for you."

"Oh." Korey turned back toward Michelle, who gave him a pleasant smile. *"Danki."* He felt flustered by her gesture.

"Gern gschehne. Crystal and I thought you might want to have some of your favorites when you arrived home, so we each planned to make something that you like."

"That's right," Crystal chimed in. "Tonight I have lasagna ready to put in the oven, and Michelle is bringing the garlic bread."

Dat grinned from his recliner. "I'm grateful for all of the wonderful meals they are planning for you."

While Korey chewed another piece of the moist cheesecake, he once again took in how close Michelle and Crystal had become. Michelle was truly part of the family—perhaps she was closer to his *dat* and Crystal than he ever would be. Had he been replaced?

But Korey was aware that this estrangement he was experiencing was his fault. He had been the one who had decided to leave. He had done this to himself, and now he had to figure out how to undo the damage.

And then another thought struck him: what would their family have looked like if *Mamm* hadn't died? Would Korey have even dated Michelle? Would they have decided to break up, and would she have run to Tyler's arms before marrying him? And if so, would *Mamm* and Michelle be the ones planning the family meals together?

But if *Mamm* were still alive, then Korey never would have left. He wouldn't have felt the need to separate himself from his family because *Dat* wouldn't have married Crystal in the first place.

Korey's heart ached when he thought of his mother and the memories of her in this house. He could still hear her humming while she baked, and he could envision her beautiful smile as she laughed at one of *Dat*'s silly jokes. He closed his eyes, losing himself in memories of his precious mother.

"You okay, Kore?" Jayden asked.

Korey cleared his throat. "*Ya.* I think I'm still tired from the long trip."

"It will take you a few days to recover, but we're sure glad you're here," *Dat* said.

Crystal lifted her mug of coffee. "That is true."

"*Danki.*" Korey took another bite of the cake while Tyler continued talking about work. He glanced around the room, taking in the members of his family, and he wondered how long he'd feel like a stranger in his own home.

Later that evening, Savannah climbed the porch steps of the two-story white house where she and Toby had come to live after their father abandoned them nearly nineteen years ago.

She turned toward her aunt and uncle's store, Blanks' Bulk Foods, a long, one-story white cinder-block building that sat next to the house. Tomorrow morning Savannah's alarm would awaken her early, and she and Toby would eat breakfast before going to the store, where they worked full-time.

Since their cousin Dean had chosen a career in construction, building houses, and his older brother, Levi, owned his own home and built kitchen cabinets for a living, neither of them worked at the store.

Savannah used to wonder what it would feel like to work somewhere else. She would imagine working at a gift shop in the touristy section of Bird-in-Hand, where she would interact with folks who came to visit Amish Country. She would also lose herself in thoughts of watering flowers at a garden center or baking cookies and other treats at a bakery or selling vegetables at a farm stand. But then she'd remind herself that the store was all she knew and was where she belonged with her family—her aunt and uncle. Besides, by working at the store she could keep an eye on Toby.

When Savannah reached the back door, she yanked it open. She had ridden home from the youth gathering with Dean, who was stowing his horse and buggy in the barn. She stepped into the mudroom and kicked off her shoes. When she entered the kitchen, she was surprised to find her aunt Dorothy sitting at the table, flipping through a cookbook.

"How was your day, Savannah?" Her aunt looked up from the cookbook.

With her kind brown eyes and warm demeanor, *Aenti* Dorothy always seemed to go out of her way to make Savannah and Toby feel welcome and loved. She had never spoken ill of Savannah's father, but Savannah often contemplated what *Aenti* Dorothy thought about her father's leaving them.

She also pondered what would have happened to her and Toby if *Onkel* Eddie, Savannah's mother's brother, hadn't taken them in.

"It was *gut*." Savannah sat down at the table across from her aunt. "Macy rode home with Keith Troyer."

Her aunt smiled. "Is that right? Does she like him?"

"Very much. I have a feeling they'll be dating soon."

"That's exciting." A curious expression overtook her aunt's face. "Is there a young man that has your eye?"

"No." Savannah shook her head.

"Well, you're twenty-four now, only a year younger than Levi. You should be dating too." *Aenti* Dorothy leaned forward, excitement sparkling in her dark eyes. "In fact, I have a feeling Levi is going to ask Iris's *daed* for permission to propose soon. After all, he has his own *haus* now, and they've been dating for a few years. I would imagine we'll be planning a wedding soon." Then she patted Savannah's hand. "Who knows? You could be next."

"Oh, I don't think so." Savannah ran her fingers over the wood tabletop. "What did Toby do today?"

"I haven't seen him all afternoon. I assumed he was napping."

Savannah stood. "I'd better get to bed. I'll check on Toby and then take a shower." She started for the stairs leading up to the bedrooms, her flashlight guiding her way.

"See you in the morning," her aunt called after her.

"Gut nacht." As Savannah climbed the steep steps, her footfalls echoed in the stairway.

When she reached the hallway, she found a warm yellow light glowing under the doorway that led to the large bedroom Toby shared with Dean. Since her aunt had converted Levi's room into a sewing room after he'd moved out, her brother still shared a room with Dean.

Savannah knocked on the door and hoped Toby was still awake.

"Come in." Her brother's voice was muffled.

She pushed the door open and found him stretched out on his bed, his long legs touching his footboard. "How was your afternoon?"

"Quiet."

"I missed you at the youth gathering."

"I'm sure you're the only one who did."

She scowled at his self-deprecation.

"Is that all you needed, Vannah?"

"I wanted to make sure you're all right."

"I'm fine. You don't need to baby me anymore. Besides, we both have to get up early in the morning, so you really should get to bed." He rolled over and faced the wall.

She sighed. "*Gut nacht,* Toby."

After showering and changing into her nightgown, Savannah climbed into bed and flipped off her lantern. She looked up toward the dark and then closed her eyes and opened her heart to God: *Lord, please help me be the best sister I can to Toby. All I want is for him to have a happy life. Lead me on a path to help him find friends. And help me prove to him that he's not stupid. Help him learn to love himself and appreciate the gifts you have given him.*

Then she snuggled under her quilt, hoping she could put her worries out of her mind and sleep.

Later that evening, Korey filled a glass with water from the sink and took a long drink. He peered out the kitchen window toward his brother's house sitting at the back of his father's property and wondered if he would ever have a home of his own. Would he fall in love and get married? Or would this loneliness follow him the rest of his life?

"There you are," *Dat* said.

Korey spun and faced his father, standing in the doorway and holding a lantern. "*Dat.* You startled me."

Dat set the lantern on the table. "I'm sorry." He sat down at the table and then pointed to the chair across from him. "Have a seat."

Korey joined him at the table.

"I was wondering if you plan to come work for me again."

"I had hoped I could." Korey rubbed the stubble on his chin. "If that's okay with you."

"Of course it is. Why wouldn't I want you to work for me? You're *mei sohn*."

The taut muscles in Korey's back released as relief flooded through him.

"I'm assuming that you're planning to purchase a horse and buggy tomorrow."

"*Ya*, I sold everything in Ohio and I have the cash." Korey's gaze moved to the doorway as Crystal entered the kitchen. "Hi, Crystal."

She smiled as she drifted to the counter and retrieved a cup from the cabinet before pouring herself a glass of water.

"I'll have my driver take you out tomorrow for your horse and buggy," *Dat* continued. "And you can start working for me on Tuesday. We're busy, so I'm grateful to have you on my crew. We're working on a roof at a store out in Paradise right now."

"Great," Korey said.

Crystal faced them and leaned against the counter. "Korey, since you'll be out tomorrow, would you mind stopping by the store for me?"

"No, I don't mind at all."

"I appreciate it." She picked up a piece of paper. "I have a shopping list here."

"I'll take care of it," Korey said.

Dat smiled. "*Danki*."

Korey said good night to his *dat* and Crystal and then headed back up to his room. He stopped in Jayden's doorway and peered in at his brother, who was sitting up in bed, reading a book. "*Gut nacht*."

When Korey turned toward his bedroom, Jayden called him back.

"Next week you need to come to youth group with me," Jayden told him.

Korey folded his arms over his chest. "I'll think about it."

"There's nothing to think about. Just come. It will help you feel a part of the community again. Don't you want to reconnect with your *freinden*?"

Korey sighed. "*Ya*, I do."

"Well, that's the best way to do it."

"All right," he conceded. His younger brother was wise beyond his twenty-one years. He tapped the doorframe. "See you in the morning."

As Korey padded into his room and changed for bed, he tried to imagine easing into his community once again.

CHAPTER 4

THE FOLLOWING AFTERNOON, SAVANNAH STOOD AT ONE OF
the front registers and handed Esther Fisher her receipt. *"Danki*
for coming to see us."

"You have a *gut* day, Savannah." The middle-aged Amish
woman pushed her full cart toward the store exit.

Savannah helped the next customer, an Amish man with a
long white beard and thick glasses, and then stepped away from
the counter to look for her brother. He had been stocking shelves
when her aunt and uncle disappeared into the back office to handle
some paperwork. But as customers swept into the store, she hadn't
seen where he had gone.

She peeked down the first couple of aisles and found each of
them empty. She heard her brother laughing at the far end of the
store, and she picked up her pace as curiosity nipped at her.

When she came to the last aisle, she stilled. Surprise gripped
her when she found Korey grinning while Toby talked to him.
Her jaw set as memories of the bullies at their school hit her hard
and fast. She could still hear the boys and girls taunting Toby and
laughing at him while he struggled with reading aloud or calculat-
ing math problems on the blackboard.

But she couldn't recall a time when Korey or his brothers had been cruel to Toby. At the same time, she didn't know him well enough to trust him. She hovered at the end of the aisle, lurking behind a display of disposable baking pans while she eavesdropped on their conversation.

"So, Toby," Korey began, "what are your favorite kinds of pancakes, then?"

Her brother hesitated. "I guess blueberry."

"Blueberry? Huh."

"What does that mean?" Toby chuckled.

"Nothing. I just think that chocolate chip pancakes are the best."

"They're *gut*, but I also like strawberries and cream pancakes."

"Hmm," Korey seemed to consider this. "I suppose they're pretty *gut*, but what about cupcake pancakes?"

Toby gave a groan. "Oh, that sounds so sweet. I'll have to try them. Now you're making me hungry."

"I agree. I might need to get pancakes for lunch now. That restaurant that serves breakfast all day is right down the street." Korey laughed again.

Curiosity overtook her. Why was Korey Bontrager making small talk with her brother? Did he have an ulterior motive?

Unable to resist standing by any longer, Savannah marched down the aisle toward him, feeling her face contort with a deep scowl. "What's going on here?"

Korey jumped with a start and pivoted toward her. "Savannah. Hi. We were just discussing pancakes."

"Pancakes?" She divided a look between the two men.

Toby expelled a frustrated sigh. "*Ya*, pancakes. Everything is fine here, Vannah."

"Okay." Savannah turned her attention toward Korey. "May I help you find something, Korey?"

He rubbed the back of his neck. "I sure hope so. Crystal gave me a list, but I don't know this store."

"Give it to me." She held out her hand, and Korey placed the list on her palm. "Let's get a shopping cart."

After retrieving a cart from the front of the store, Korey pushed it while Savannah guided him through the aisles. They made their way to the soups and added a few cans to the cart.

When they reached the cereal aisle, she placed two boxes in the cart. "When did you get home?" she asked him.

"Saturday night." He leaned on the cart.

"How was your trip home?"

"Long." He pointed to the list, clearly not willing to discuss his return to their community. "What else is on there?"

"Pancake mix, syrup, flour, sugar, brownie mix," she read.

They continued on their way, and he grabbed the pancake mix from a high shelf. More questions about what led Korey away from the community and what had brought him home bubbled up to her lips. While she wasn't one for gossip, she was curious about how he was doing.

"How did you like Ohio?" she asked as they moved to the baking supplies.

Korey found the flour and sugar. "I liked it well enough."

"Are you glad to be back?"

"*Ya.*" He gestured toward the list in her hand once again. "What else do I need?"

They gathered the rest of the items, and then Korey steered the cart up to the register, where Savannah began ringing up his groceries. His posture was rigid, and his expression was hesitant, as if he hoped she wouldn't ask him more questions about his time in Ohio. She recalled how uncomfortable he looked at church, and she wondered how he was adjusting to being back home. But it was none of her business, as she'd told her nosy friends.

"Korey!" *Aenti* Dorothy exclaimed as she joined them at the front of the store. "So *gut* to see you."

He smiled. "Hi, Dorothy."

"We're all so glad you came back."

"*Danki.*" He pulled his wallet from his back pocket.

Aenti Dorothy sidled up to him at the counter. "I'm sure your *bruders* are glad you're back. The three of you are awfully close, right?"

"Sure." Something Savannah couldn't decipher glimmered in Korey's expression as he fiddled with his wallet.

Savannah studied his deep-brown eyes, recalling the rumors her friends had shared on Sunday. Surely he and Tyler couldn't be close after Tyler had married Michelle. After all, Korey had left soon after Tyler and Michelle had started dating. Tyler's relationship with Korey's ex-girlfriend must have caused a rift between the brothers, which had to be painful for his entire family.

Yet Savannah would never know the truth. Even though she and Korey had grown up in the same church district and attended the same school, she didn't know him well enough to read his expression.

Still, she pondered how deeply the brothers' relationship was fractured. She couldn't imagine feeling alienated from Toby.

"It's looking like it's going to be a *schee* day," Korey suddenly said. "Spring is here."

Aenti Dorothy and Korey continued making small talk about the weather while Savannah finished ringing up and bagging his groceries. After she told him the total, he handed her a stack of bills, and she gave him his change and receipt.

"Thanks for helping me with my shopping," he said, pushing his wallet into his pocket.

"You're welcome."

Korey turned just as *Onkel* Eddie and Toby emerged from the back of the store and waved at him. "Have a great day. I'll see you at church."

Both her uncle and her brother nodded before Korey pushed the shopping cart toward the exit and disappeared out the door.

While her aunt and uncle began restocking the candy display at the front of the store, Savannah walked over to where Toby placed bags of cat food up on the shelf. "Why were you and Korey discussing pancakes?" she asked him.

"It's no big deal." Her brother hefted another large bag onto the shelf. "He told me that he needed to find the pancake mix and then he asked me about my favorite kind of pancakes. I told him blueberry pancakes, and he said he liked chocolate chip the best. That's it."

When a young Amish woman pushed her cart full of groceries with a toddler sitting in the seat toward the counter, Savannah returned to the cash register to help her.

As she rang up the items, she continued pondering Korey and his family situation. She sent up a quick prayer, asking God to help the Bontrager family heal, and then she focused on her task at hand.

"How is the construction going over on that *haus* in Ronks?" *Onkel* Eddie asked Dean after supper later that evening.

Dean picked up his glass of water. "It's going well. We're almost done framing it. It's going to be huge—five bedrooms, four bathrooms, a formal dining room, and a three-car garage."

Onkel Eddie snorted. "That's an awfully big *haus*."

Savannah carried their dishes to the sink and began filling one side with soapy water.

"I guess that house will take a while to build." *Aenti* Dorothy gathered up their utensils and set them on the counter.

"Oh *ya*. I enjoy the work, though, *Mamm*," Dean told her.

Savannah peeked over at the table, where Toby sat studying his lap, and her heart squeezed.

Toby looked up at their uncle. "I'll take care of the animals." He pushed his chair back and stood.

"*Danki*, Toby."

Then her brother disappeared out the back door.

Savannah washed and dried the dishes, then set them in the cabinets before she swept the kitchen. While she worked, her uncle and cousin continued discussing the house construction, and her aunt wiped down the table and counters.

After her chores were done, Savannah grabbed a sweater and stepped onto the porch and breathed in the cool April evening air. She found her brother slouching on the porch swing, staring out toward the dark barn with his face clouded by a scowl.

She sank down on a rocker beside him as worry threaded through her. "Do you want to talk about what's bothering you?"

Toby licked his lips. "I just wish I could be more like Dean." He kept his blue eyes focused on the barn as if it held all of the answers.

"What do you mean?"

"I don't like working in the store." He moved on the swing, and it shifted under his weight. "I'd rather do something like he's doing."

"You can do whatever you want, Toby. If you want to work in construction, then you can do it."

He met her gaze, aiming a searing look at her. "No, I can't. You know I have trouble reading and understanding numbers. I could never measure the wood or interpret the plans. The foreman would laugh me off of the site before I even got started."

He turned his attention to the toes of his boots. "I'll never be able to do anything other than work in the store. No one would hire me because I can't even complete a job application without help."

"Toby, I could help you—"

"I don't want your help!" he snapped before popping up to his feet and stomping into the house, leaving her alone on the empty porch.

Savannah sighed and ran her hand down her face. Her one goal was to see her younger brother happy, but she had no idea how to make that a reality. If only she could find a way to help Toby.

"Lead me to the answers, Lord," she whispered.

"*Danki* for going to the store for me today, Korey," Crystal said while the family ate beef stew that same evening. "It was such a tremendous help."

Korey swallowed a bite. "*Gern gschehne.* I stopped by Blanks' Bulk Foods."

"Oh *ya*?" *Dat* lifted his glass of iced tea. "How are Eddie and Dorothy doing?"

"Fine. I talked to Toby and Savannah too." Korey considered how Savannah reacted to him when she saw him talking to Toby. Her nearly permanent, suspicious scowl had taken him by surprise. She acted as if Korey had done something wrong by simply speaking to her younger brother.

But he shouldn't have been shocked at how Savannah had treated him. He recalled how she always watched over Toby in school and shielded him against the mean kids. It seemed that Savannah was still as overprotective of Toby as she had been back then, even though he was nineteen now.

Crystal clucked her tongue. "Those poor *kinner*. I just recently learned about how their mother died in childbirth and then their *daed* took off. So *bedauerlich*." She shared a sad expression with *Dat*.

"It's not our place to judge, but I still don't understand how Lee Zook abandoned his *kinner* like that." *Dat* frowned. "I could never even imagine doing that. I would always worry about *mei kinner*, wondering if they had enough food to eat and if they were warm on cold nights. It seems unnatural for a parent to just walk away like that."

"*Ya*, I agree. Dorothy and Eddie are wonderful to have taken them in and raised them. They are a blessing. It's so hard to lose a parent, and those two lost both of theirs," Crystal said.

Grief took hold of Korey as memories of his mother filled his mind once again. He tried to imagine how Savannah felt losing both of her parents at such a young age, but he couldn't even begin to fathom the depth of her bereavement. It was no wonder Savannah kept such a close watch over her younger brother.

"How's that motel over in Millersburg going?" *Dat* asked Jayden.

Jayden wiped his mouth with a paper napkin. "We'll be done tomorrow. Tyler thought we would have it done today, but he sometimes overestimates how fast we can work."

Dat chuckled while Korey cringed.

Then Korey silently chastised himself. He had to find a way to stop reacting each time his older brother's name was mentioned, but he couldn't stop resentment from overtaking him.

"What's next on your agenda after that motel job?" *Dat* asked.

Korey turned his attention to his bowl of stew while Jayden talked on about his crew's schedule. He ate a few bites of stew and then buttered a roll.

"Are you ready to get back to roofing tomorrow, Korey?" *Dat* asked.

Korey swallowed a bite of the roll. "*Ya.* You just tell me what time you want to leave."

"We'll leave at the usual time in the morning," *Dat* began before discussing their schedule.

They finished supper and the men helped Crystal carry their plates, utensils, and glasses to the counter.

"*Danki* for supper," *Dat* told Crystal before kissing her cheek.

Jayden tapped Korey on the arm. "Help me in the barn."

"All right." As Korey followed his brother outside, he felt his body relax for the first time since he'd returned to Bird-in-Hand. It was good to be home. He was ready to get back to work on his father's roofing crew.

Wednesday afternoon Savannah sat at the kitchen table and read a novel while eating a turkey and cheese sandwich for lunch. She enjoyed the quiet time alone after working in the store all morning. She and her family members always took turns going home to eat during the day so that they were sure to have enough coverage at the store to help customers.

When the back door opened, Savannah looked up from her book as Macy hurried in carrying a ziplock bag of cookies. "Macy. *Wie geht's?*"

"I couldn't wait to come see you. Your *aenti* told me that you were in here having lunch. I have so much to tell you." Her best friend dropped onto a chair across from her and set the bag of cookies on the table in front of her. "I made chocolate chip *kichlin* yesterday. Have one."

Savannah opened the bag and pulled one out. "*Danki.* So, what's the latest news?"

"Keith asked me to be his girlfriend Sunday night!" she squealed.

"Macy! That's fantastic. Tell me everything."

"Well, he took me home, and then asked to see *mei dat.* I waited in the kitchen while he talked to him in the *schtupp.* Then we walked out to his buggy again, and he asked me to be his girlfriend. After I said yes, he kissed my cheek." She gave a dramatic sigh. "I've never been so *froh* in my life, Savannah. I think I'm in love."

"Whoa." Savannah held up her hand as if stopping her. "Don't you think it's a little too early to say love?"

Macy frowned. "I really like him, Savannah. He's just so handsome and sweet."

"That's great. I'm really happy for you, but I think you should take your time getting to know him before you decide it's love, okay? I don't want you to get hurt."

Macy waved off Savannah's advice. "Fine. Now we need to find you a boyfriend so we can double-date."

Savannah took a bite of the delicious cookie while irritation filled her. When would her friends drop this subject and just let her be? She didn't need a boyfriend, no matter what they said. She swallowed. "These are fantastic. *Danki* for sharing." She needed to change the subject and fast. "So, is Keith going to pick you up Sunday for the youth gathering?"

"Oh *ya*. He also called me last night to see how my week was going. He's just so nice, Savannah."

They ate cookies and talked about their friends until Savannah said she had to get back to work. After cleaning up the kitchen together, Savannah and Macy made their way down the rock path to the store.

Savannah hugged her friend. "*Danki* for coming to visit me."

"I'll see you Sunday!" Macy waved before heading down the path toward the road.

Savannah found her aunt at the front counter ringing up a customer. She waited nearby until she was done. "I'm back from lunch. You can take your break if you'd like."

"*Danki*. What did Macy want?" *Aenti* Dorothy asked as she glided out from behind the counter.

Savannah shared Macy's story about how Keith asked her to be his girlfriend.

"*Gut* for her." *Aenti* Dorothy smiled. "Maybe Keith has a *freind* for you."

"I'm in no hurry." Savannah took her place behind the counter, grateful to see an Amish woman with a full shopping cart of groceries headed her way.

Aenti Dorothy touched her arm. "You're young, and you should

55

be dating and having fun, *mei liewe*." Then she started toward the door. "I'll be back soon."

"Take your time." Savannah smiled and greeted the customer and then turned her attention toward ringing up her items.

While she worked, she hoped she could find a way to stop her friends and family members from nagging her about dating. She would think of something.

CHAPTER 5

KOREY CLIMBED OUT OF THE BACK SEAT OF HIS FATHER'S DRIV-
er's pickup truck Friday evening. Every muscle in his body
screamed out in pain from working on a roof at a large home in
Ronks, but he enjoyed the work outside and breathed in the fresh
spring air. He especially appreciated the opportunity to spend the
day with his father. He also liked the other two members of the
crew, and the four of them seemed to work well together.

The week had flown by, and Korey had managed to avoid seeing his older brother despite their proximity. Every day he looked
toward Tyler's house and expected to find him out on the porch
or stowing his horse in the barn that Tyler shared with *Dat*. Korey
had tried to prepare himself for an encounter and another strained
conversation, but so far, he hadn't encountered him. While Korey
was grateful not to have the extra stress, he also dreaded when he
would have to interact with Tyler. He prayed daily for patience and
guidance for how to handle his relationship with his older brother.

"Let's take care of our supplies," *Dat* said as they moved to the
back of the truck.

Korey helped his father unload the tools and store them in
the cinder-block building next to the barn. They worked together

in silence, and soon the task was complete. He and his father were walking toward the house when a gold Dodge diesel truck rumbled into the driveway.

Dat waved at the truck. "Tyler and Jayden are home."

Korey's stomach clenched as his brothers climbed out of the pickup truck.

"Hey!" Tyler climbed out of the passenger seat. "Supper at *mei haus*. Crystal and Michelle are cooking together tonight."

Dat looked surprised. "Really?"

"*Ya*. I was running late this morning, and Michelle walked over to ask Crystal if she wanted to all eat together tonight."

"That sounds fun." *Dat* tapped Korey's shoulder. "Let's get cleaned up, and then we'll head to Tyler's. You haven't seen his *haus* yet. Now you'll finally get a tour."

Korey pressed his lips together as he followed his father up the porch steps and into the mudroom where they shucked their jackets and removed their work boots.

When they entered the kitchen, his father faced him and gave him a sympathetic expression. "I know this is hard for you, but I have faith in you. You will get over your anger and resentment and accept your *bruder* and his *fraa*. I know you can do this, Korey, because I believe that's why you decided to come back home."

Korey swallowed against his dry throat. To the very bottom of his core, he wanted to believe his father, but he still doubted his capacity to forgive. He took in the empathy in his father's dark eyes, and he was touched by his father's faith in him. *Dat* had more faith in him than Korey had in himself, and he was humbled by it.

Jayden appeared behind Korey and tapped his arm. "Come on, Kore. Let's clean up. They made something *appeditlich*, and I'm starved."

His younger brother hastened through the kitchen toward the stairs.

Korey turned back to his father. "I'll do my best." His voice was hoarse.

"That's all I can ask, *sohn*." *Dat* rubbed his hands together. "I'm hungry too. Let's go."

A strange feeling overcame Korey as he followed his father and Jayden up the porch steps leading to the front door of Tyler's house. *Dat* opened the front door and entered a small family room.

While *Dat* disappeared toward the kitchen doorway, Korey glanced around at the sofa, end tables, coffee table, love seat, and wing chairs. His body vibrated with a mixture of resentment and anxiety. Tyler had everything now—his own roofing crew with employees, a home, a wife, a future. Korey was still stuck in the same place he'd been before he left for Ohio—living in his father's home and working on his father's roofing crew.

But was it Tyler's fault that Korey had chosen to leave home? In some ways, yes, but in others, no. Korey had done that himself. He'd left, despite his family's pleas for him to stay.

"Would you like a tour?" Jayden asked.

Korey shook his head. "No, it's okay."

"Well, I'll tell you about it then. The utility room is over there, off of the kitchen. They have a bedroom down that hallway and a bathroom. The stairs are over there, and upstairs they have two more bedrooms and a bathroom. It's really a nice-sized *haus*. They won't have to worry about adding on anytime soon."

"Uh-huh." Korey's nostrils flared. "They are quite blessed."

"Let's go see what's for supper," Jayden said as he took off toward the kitchen.

Korey remained cemented in place while he imagined Tyler and Michelle enjoying their house together as a married couple. Pain grabbed him by his throat and shook him, and he closed his eyes, attempting to pull in air through his nose.

Lord, please soften my heart toward my brother and Michelle.

When he opened his eyes, he found Tyler standing in the doorway, watching him with a hopeful expression.

"I'm glad you're here," Tyler said.

Uncertain how to respond, Korey stared at him.

Tyler made a sweeping gesture toward the kitchen. "Would you like to come and sit down? Michelle and Crystal made chicken and dumplings."

Korey continued to watch his brother while trying to calm his raging emotions—anger, betrayal, despondency, and confusion.

"Please, Kore." Tyler folded his hands as if praying. "I want you to join us and be a part of the family again."

Korey took a step toward him. "Okay," he murmured.

When Korey joined his family in the kitchen, he took a seat beside Jayden. He scanned the table and found his family watching him with apprehension shining in their eyes. Perhaps they were waiting for him to lose his temper as he had so often done before he'd left home.

But Korey held back his angry words and forced a smile. "It all smells fantastic," he managed to say before everyone seemed to relax.

After a silent prayer, they began filling their plates with chicken, dumplings, and rolls.

Korey kept his eyes trained on his plate while Jayden, Tyler, and *Dat* fell into an easy conversation about work. Once again, Korey felt left out, wondering what to say to them.

"How was your first week back at work with your *dat*, Korey?" Crystal asked.

When he heard his name, Korey's head popped up, and he turned toward his stepmother beside him. "It was *gut*."

"Did it take you a while to get back into roofing, Korey?" Michelle asked from the other end of the table. "Or did you remember how to do the job?"

Korey studied his ex-girlfriend, and the familiar hurt rolled over him. Michelle's smile faded, and she cast her blue eyes down toward her supper.

Guilt drifted over Korey. If he was going to try to mend the brokenness with his family, then he had to at least answer when he was spoken to.

"It came back to me really quickly," Korey said. "Once I picked up a hammer, I remembered what I was supposed to do."

Michelle's blue eyes snapped to meet his gaze. "Oh, that's *gut*." Her smile returned.

Korey turned to Crystal. "Supper is superb."

"*Danki*, but it was Michelle's idea to have everyone over."

"Oh." Korey looked at his sister-in-law again. "It's fantastic."

"I'm glad you like it."

Korey joined in on the discussion of work while they finished supper. Later Michelle brought a plate of brownies to the table for dessert while Crystal made coffee.

After dessert, Korey followed his father and brothers out to the porch while Crystal and Michelle cleaned up the kitchen. Korey took a seat on a rocking chair and looked out toward his father's house while the sun began to set, sending glorious hues of pink, orange, and yellow across the sky.

His brothers and father continued their discussion of work while Korey lost himself in thoughts of his future. He contemplated what it would feel like to own his own home. And if he had one, would he want to live on his father's property or move to another church district and start a new life with a new congregation?

He allowed those questions to settle over him and decided he would start saving money for his own house. After all, he was twenty-five now, and it was time to start acting like an adult. He couldn't live with his *dat* and Crystal forever; at least he hoped he wouldn't have to.

"So, Kore, did you date anyone in Ohio?"

Korey angled his body toward his older brother, who watched him with curiosity. "No."

"You should settle down." Tyler smiled. "You'll be glad you did."

Korey stared at Tyler. Had his brother just bragged about marrying Korey's ex-girlfriend? Was he trying to start an argument with him?

"You can build a *haus* too," Tyler continued as if reading Korey's earlier thoughts.

Dat nodded. "You could build a *haus* here, Korey. And you too, Jayden. I'd love to have you all here. I have plenty of land."

Korey rested his left ankle on his right knee and pushed his rocking chair into motion.

"Tyler is right about dating, Korey," *Dat* said. "You need to get back into the youth group. You should date and then settle down."

"I remember when you all were nagging me about that," Tyler chuckled.

Korey's slow, simmering fury built as he eyed his older brother. "But I don't think any of us meant for you to date my ex-girlfriend," he seethed.

"Whoa." Tyler held up his hands in defense. "I didn't mean anything by it."

"All right, all right," *Dat* began, a hint of warning in his voice. "Don't start arguing again."

Korey kept his focus out toward his father's house while his brothers and father discussed friends in the community. He gripped the arms of the rocker and worked to stop his heart from pounding with anger. He had to be civil. He couldn't let his father down, no matter how much Tyler irritated him.

Later Crystal and Michelle joined them on the porch, and they continued their discussions about people they knew.

"Well, I think it's time to head home," *Dat* said as he stood. "We have work tomorrow morning." He took Crystal's hand. "*Danki* for having us for supper, Michelle and Tyler." He flipped on his flashlight with his free hand, and they started down the stairs together.

"We'll see you both soon," Michelle called after them.

Jayden said good night and then followed *Dat* and Crystal toward the house.

Korey nodded at Michelle and took a step toward the stairs.

"Please wait a minute." Tyler held up his hands, stopping him. "Look, Kore, I want us to start fresh. I never meant to hurt you."

Korey sucked in a deep breath through his nose. "It's going to take time before I can trust you again."

"I-I understand." Tyler's expression fell. "I'll give you all the time you need. Please don't give up on me, okay? You're *mei bruder*."

Korey gave him a solemn nod and then jogged down the steps.

He flipped on his flashlight and trudged down the path leading to his father's house. He found Jayden sitting on the porch steps when he arrived home.

Jayden stood as Korey approached. "You're coming to the youth gathering with me on Sunday, right?"

"I guess so."

"Why wouldn't you go?" Jayden asked.

"My best friend is married now and expecting a child. I feel like I've been left behind."

"No one left you behind, Kore. Everyone is different. Just because Dwight is married doesn't mean you need to be."

Korey nodded. Once again, his little brother had a point.

"So, you'll come then, right?" Jayden smiled.

"I don't know. It will be so awkward being there without Dwight. I really don't know anyone else at the youth gathering. It would be uncomfortable for me."

Jayden looked offended. "Am I invisible?"

"No, Jay, you aren't," Korey chuckled.

"So come with me and make *freinden*. The gathering is in Paradise. There will be a lot of folks there from other youth groups too."

"I'll think about it."

"*Gut.*" Jayden patted Korey's arm as they walked into the house. "We'll get you back on the social scene in no time, and maybe you'll have a girlfriend too."

"Don't push it." Korey studied his younger brother. "And what about you? Why aren't you dating?"

"Because I'm not in a hurry."

"Well, neither am I."

"I respect that," Jayden said, and Korey smiled.

Savannah sat near the volleyball nets Sunday afternoon. She looked out over the games and was surprised to see Korey and Jayden playing on the same team as her cousins Dean and Levi. Korey wore mirrored sunglasses, and she couldn't help but notice they looked good on him.

Then she shook herself. Why on earth was she watching Korey Bontrager? But for some reason, she couldn't tear her eyes away from him. She was impressed with his athletic ability as he skillfully jumped up and spiked the ball.

She smiled when he and his team won, and he traded high fives with his younger brother and her cousins before they started another game.

She was so engrossed in watching the game that she jumped with a start when Macy and their friends appeared and sat down, surrounding Savannah.

"We have news, Savannah," Macy said, and their friends nodded.

Savannah felt a pang of suspicion. "What's up?"

"I've been talking to Keith," Macy began, "and he said he has a cousin he wants you to meet."

Savannah felt her brow furrow. "What do you mean?"

"Keith has a cousin who is going to come and meet you at the youth gathering next week," Macy said.

Jodie grinned. "We're so excited."

"If it works out, then we'll all have boyfriends," Gail added as Willa clapped.

Savannah shook her head "Oh, no, no, no. I don't need anyone trying to play matchmaker for me."

"It will be fine," Macy insisted. "Keith has promised me that Jerry is nice, respectful, and good-looking."

Willa lifted a finger. "He sounds perfect for you."

The other three nodded in agreement as a sour feeling filled Savannah's stomach.

"Hold on now." Savannah held up her hands. "I appreciate your concern for me, but I am not interested. Please tell Keith not to bring his cousin. I'm perfectly fine on my—"

"No way, Savannah," Jodie interrupted. "You're not going to talk us out of this."

Willa shook her head. "We want you to start dating."

"I agree." Macy took Savannah's hands in hers. "Trust me on this, okay? I would never deliberately lead you wrong or hurt you. You know that."

Savannah swallowed. "I do trust you, but I'd rather meet someone on my own."

"Yeah, right," Gail snorted. "We all know how stubborn you are."

Jodie guffawed. "That's why you're alone!"

Savannah frowned, offended. When Macy gave Savannah a pleading look, she decided to drop the subject, but she was irritated with her meddling friends. They didn't respect her enough to listen to her.

"So, Macy," Willa said. "Tell us all about Keith."

"You two are so cute together!" Jodie gushed.

"I'm so *froh*." Macy gave a dreamy sigh.

Their friends were riveted while Macy began talking about Keith, and Savannah listened for a few moments. Then, still hurt by how her friends had ignored her pleas not to set her up with a man she didn't know, she decided she needed a break from them.

Savannah excused herself and headed over to the snack table. She hoped a drink would thaw her frustration with her friends as she picked up a cup of lemonade and took a long draw.

"Are you okay, Savannah?"

She spun and found Korey standing beside her. She wished she could see his eyes behind those mirrored sunglasses since she couldn't be sure if he was teasing her or if he was truly concerned for her well-being. "I'm fine."

"You sure?" He seemed to study her. "You look upset."

She blinked. So it seemed he was truly concerned, and that surprised her. "*Ya*, I'm okay."

He nodded but remained silent.

"Would you like some lemonade?" She handed him a cup.

"*Danki.*"

"I saw you playing out there." She wanted to kick herself as soon as the words escaped her lips. Oh, she hoped he didn't think she was flirting. "Did you play a lot of volleyball in Ohio?"

He nodded. "*Ya*, I did."

"Oh." She ran her finger over the rim of her cup and searched for something to say.

"Is Toby here?"

She hesitated for a moment. "No."

"Where is he?"

"Why do you want to know?" She eyed him with suspicion.

"I was wondering why he wasn't here with you and your cousins."

"He-he didn't feel up to coming."

Korey frowned. "That's a shame. I would have liked to see him. He could have played with Jay and me."

She watched him. She was confused by his interest in her

brother, but she didn't see any sign of a lie or of mockery in his face. If only he'd remove those sunglasses!

"Savannah, why are you looking at me like I'm the biggest jerk on the planet?"

"Are you making fun of *mei bruder*?"

Korey's lips twisted into a deep frown. "I would never make fun of your *bruder*. I genuinely enjoyed talking to him at the store on Monday. I would have liked seeing him today too."

Her mouth dropped open with surprise.

"Hey, Korey!" Dean called as he, Keith, and Levi sauntered toward them. "Are we going to play some more? Or are you going to stand here, drink lemonade, and talk?"

"I thought we'd take a break for a few minutes," Korey said.

"I'll let you get back to playing," Savannah said as she took that opportunity to slip past Korey and head back toward her friends.

CHAPTER 6

KOREY WATCHED AS SAVANNAH WALKED AWAY, AND FOR SOME reason he was disappointed. He longed to talk to her and find out why she was so incredulous every time he asked about her brother. He found her both confusing and intriguing.

"So, I asked Macy Yoder to be my girlfriend last Sunday night," Keith said.

Korey took another sip of lemonade. While he recalled that Macy was best friends with Savannah, he didn't know her very well either.

"That's cool," Dean said, and Levi agreed. "I was talking to a *maedel* named Patience earlier." He nodded toward a group of young women standing near the back door of the house owned by the Stoltzfus family, who was hosting the gathering. "I want to talk to her some more."

Levi grinned at his younger brother. "That's great. It's about time you started dating."

"What about you, Korey?" Keith asked. "Are you seeing anyone?"

Korey shook his head. "I've only been home for a week. I need to sort out my life before I even consider finding a *maedel* to date."

"So tell us, Korey," Dean began. "What's it like seeing your *bruder* married to your ex-girlfriend?"

Keith snorted. "That has got to be awkward."

Korey shifted his weight on his feet.

"I'm not sure if *awkward* is the right word," Levi added.

Korey pointed toward the volleyball net. "How about we go play another game?"

When no one responded, Korey dropped his empty cup into a nearby trash can and started toward the volleyball nets. He looked up toward the hill and spotted Savannah peering down at him. He smiled and nodded, and she nodded in return as her pink lips tipped up.

And he noticed that she had a pretty smile that reminded him of sunshine, warm and inviting.

Later that evening, after singing hymns with the youth group in the Stoltzfus family's barn, Savannah collected her empty container that had held her peanut butter cookies and then switched on her flashlight as she walked outside with her friends. She zipped her sweater and breathed in the cool evening air as she looked up at the stars twinkling in the dark sky.

"Oh, there's Tommy!" Willa faced them and grinned. "I'll see you all next week." Then she hurried off toward her boyfriend waiting by his buggy.

Jodie hugged each of them and said good night before running off to meet her boyfriend, Peter.

Savannah scanned the sea of horses and buggies illuminated by lanterns and flashlights for her cousin Dean.

"Just think, Savannah," Gail said. "Next week you'll have a date to take you home too."

Macy grinned. "That's right. I'm certain you and Jerry will hit it off, and then all of us will have boyfriends."

Savannah rolled her eyes. "There's more to life than dating."

"Right." Gail chuckled. "You're just saying that because you don't have a boyfriend. Your tune will change when you have a boyfriend of your own. Have a *gut* week." She took off toward Ike.

Macy bumped her shoulder against Savannah's. "Don't be so negative."

"I'm not negative. I'm just realistic."

Macy pulled Savannah against her for a side hug. "I'll see you soon."

"Have a *gut* week."

While Macy went off to meet Keith, Savannah weaved through the knot of horses and buggies in search of Dean. She padded up to his horse and buggy, where he stood talking to Korey and Jayden. Both of the Bontrager brothers held lanterns. Savannah was grateful Korey had removed his sunglasses from earlier in the day, and she was happy to actually see his eyes.

For a moment, she found herself comparing the two Bontrager brothers. While they both were tall, fit, and had similar angular jaws, Korey's eyes reminded her of the color of milk chocolate while Jayden's were hazel. Korey's hair was also deep brown, and his younger brother's hair was sandy blond.

Korey met her gaze and smiled, and she felt her cheeks warm. She hoped he hadn't felt her staring at him.

"Well, I guess we'd better head home," Jayden said. "It's getting pretty late."

Dean shook Jayden's hand. "See you at church on Sunday."

Savannah opened the passenger side door and hopped up into her cousin's buggy before flipping on the lantern he kept on the floor.

Korey appeared and leaned in the door. "Tell Toby I said hello, all right?"

"*Ya.* Of course." She was dumbfounded by how genuine he seemed when he asked about her brother. Did he actually consider Toby a friend?

"*Danki.*" He tapped on the door. "Have a *gut* week at the store."

"You too." She did a mental head slap. Why had she said, *You too*? She worked at a store, but he was a roofer! She sounded like a *dummkopp*! She'd never tripped over her words with a man before. Why did Korey have this sudden effect on her?

Korey grinned and then spun to face his brother. "Hey, Jay. I'll follow you home." Then he sauntered off toward his horse and buggy.

Savannah looked out across the field and spotted her cousin Levi and his girlfriend, Iris, both holding flashlights while climbing into Levi's buggy to start their journey to Iris's parents' farm.

Dean settled into his seat and guided the horse toward the road. They were silent, and the *clip-clop* of horse hooves and the whirr of the wheels filled the buggy as Dean's horse followed a line of their friends' buggies all starting their journeys toward home.

"Do you know Patience Herschberger?" Dean suddenly asked.

Savannah angled her body toward him. "Vaguely. I spoke to her when we were setting out the desserts for everyone. I think she lives in Ronks."

"That's right." Her cousin kept his eyes on the road. "I'm going to go visit her this week after work."

"Oh. That's nice."

"Do you think you can get a ride home from someone else next week?"

Savannah blinked. "I-I guess so."

"*Gut.* I'm going to ask her if I can take her home."

Savannah swallowed a sigh. She knew this day would come, but she didn't think it would be so soon. While she was happy that Dean was interested in dating, she wouldn't have a ride home unless Toby came to the youth gathering.

She could always ask Macy if Keith could give her a ride, but she didn't want to be a third wheel. Surely Macy wouldn't appreciate Savannah's having to tag along and interfere with their alone time when she and Keith could talk on their way home.

Savannah thought about Jerry, the man who was supposedly coming to see her next Sunday. While she wasn't interested in being set up on a blind date, she at least hoped that Jerry would be a nice person. If so, she hoped he might offer to give her a ride home so that she wouldn't have to be a third wheel in one of her friends' boyfriend's buggies.

She'd figure it out somehow. At least she hoped so.

⁓⁓⁓❧⁓⁓⁓

"How did it go tonight?" Aunt Dorothy asked when Savannah stepped into the family room. Her aunt was relaxed in her favorite wing chair reading a devotional.

Savannah sat on the sofa across from her. "Well, *mei freinden* are setting me up with Keith Troyer's cousin. He's coming to the youth gathering next week."

"That's fantastic! You never know where it might lead. After all, I met your *onkel* through *freinden*."

"I don't know . . ." Savannah picked at the hem of her black apron.

"*Mei liewe*," her *aenti* began, "don't be so skeptical. He might be a nice young man, and you might decide to get to know him better."

Savannah forced a smile. "Maybe." Then she sat up straight. "Dean met someone today. He's planning to visit her this week and give her a ride home next Sunday."

"Oh, that's *wunderbaar*! What else do you know about her?"

"Her name is Patience Herschberger, and she lives in Ronks. She's very *schee*. She has blond hair and blue eyes, and she seems very sweet."

Aenti Dorothy beamed. "Oh, I hope it works out for Dean."

"I do too." Savannah cupped her hand to her mouth to shield a yawn. "Excuse me. I suppose I should get to bed. I'll see you in the morning."

When Savannah climbed into bed, she closed her eyes as memories of her mother filled her mind. She envisioned *Mamm* reading to her while they sat on a rocking chair on the porch of her former house. And she recalled her mother singing while hanging out laundry.

She could still see her mother's beautiful face with her deep blue eyes and her gorgeous smile. Her light-brown hair hung to her waist when it wasn't hidden under her prayer covering. And her voice was so sweet and warm.

"If only you were here now, *Mamm*," she whispered. "I would tell you about *mei freinden* pressuring me to date, and I could ask you for advice. And you could tell me how you met *mei daed*." She sniffed as tears welled up in her eyes.

"We could talk about dating, and you could answer my questions. How do I know when I've met the right man? How do I know if I'm in love? How do I know when it's time to get married? A *mamm* is supposed to answer these questions and guide her *dochder*."

Savannah wiped her eyes. "Toby needs you too. I can see how lost he is at times. He's so unhappy, and he has such low self-esteem. I do the best I can, but he's right—I'm not his *mamm*. If only God hadn't decided it was your time . . . We both need our parents."

Savannah's thoughts moved on to her father, and her stomach clutched. She had been daddy's girl, riding on his back and laughing and playing with blocks on the family room floor. She would never understand why he left. Had Savannah done something wrong? Or had he decided he didn't want to be a father without his wife by his side?

She wiped her eyes again and shifted onto her side. While she was grateful for her aunt and uncle, she would never stop missing her parents.

"Heal my heart, Lord," Savannah whispered. "And help me be a better *schweschder* to Toby."

⸺⸙⸺

Tuesday morning Korey sat back on his heels, lifted his sunglasses, and swiped the back of his arm across his sweaty forehead. He slipped his sunglasses back over his eyes and peered across the roof of the bank and sighed. The mid-April sun was hot as he worked with his father and two other crew members.

Thoughts of Savannah had swirled in the back of his mind since Sunday night. He kept replaying their conversation by the snack table, and he found himself pondering her situation, wondering what it was like to grow up without her parents and living with her aunt, uncle, and cousins.

He also longed to know more about Toby and why he chose to skip the weekly gatherings instead of spending time with the other youth in their community.

After hammering another shingle in place, Korey turned toward his father. *"Dat."*

"Ya?" Dat looked up, tenting his hand over his dark eyes.

"Do you remember when Savannah Zook's *mamm* died and her *daed* left?"

Dat nodded. *"Ya,* I do. It was so *bedauerlich."*

Korey sat facing his father. "What happened?"

"Well, let's see." *Dat* also sat down, and he looked as if he were recalling it in his mind. "Her *mamm's* name was Cecily, and she was so excited about her second child."

"What happened to her?"

"Toby was born at home like most Amish *kinner,* and something went wrong. I don't know what it was. We don't normally discuss those private things, but whatever happened was serious since she passed away. From what I understand, Lee did the best he could, but he was lost without his *fraa.* He tried to make it on his own for a while, but he left before Toby turned a year old. From what I understand, no one knows where he went."

"Did he ask Dorothy and Eddie to take them?"

Dat shook his head. "I don't think he directly asked them. He had a *maedel* helping him during the day while he was at work. Dorothy did her best to help him, but Dean is only a couple of months older than Toby. She had her hands full too. I heard that Lee brought his *kinner* over to Dorothy and Eddie and said his helper asked for a few days off. Then Lee left Dorothy and Eddie a message on their voice mail during the night and said he had left and wasn't coming back. I don't think he told anyone where he was going."

"Why did he choose Dorothy and Eddie?"

"Eddie was Cecily's *bruder*. I think they are the *kinner*'s only family here."

Korey nodded slowly, and his heart broke for Savannah and Toby. He couldn't imagine their grief. Surely Savannah remembered her parents, even though Toby hadn't even had a chance to know them.

Then Korey recalled how mean the kids were to Toby in school. They called him stupid when he struggled to calculate math problems or read aloud. He could still envision how Savannah's face would turn as red as a ripe tomato when the other students called Toby names or laughed at him. Many times she had to stay after school to help clean as a punishment for losing her temper or yelling at the bullies. Of course the bullies would receive punishment too. Still, Teacher Rosemary would remind Savannah to let her handle it, but Savannah always defended Toby, no matter what.

"Why are you asking about Savannah and Toby?" *Dat* asked, interrupting Korey's thoughts.

Korey rested his elbow on his bent knee. "I talked to Savannah at the youth gathering, and I've been thinking about her situation. I'm curious about her."

"Are you going to ask her out?" *Dat* grinned.

"Oh no," Korey scoffed. "I don't need the complication of a girlfriend right now."

"If you find the right girlfriend, she won't be a complication. Instead, she'll be a confidant and the best *freind* you've ever had."

Korey picked up his hammer. "We should get back to work."

As he positioned another nail, Korey considered his father's advice about having a girlfriend, but he didn't need one. He had enough to worry about with his issues with his older brother.

Right now, Korey was focused on finding his place in the community and in his family. Besides, he doubted he'd ever trust anyone again after what happened with Michelle. How could he know if a *maedel*'s feelings were genuine or if she was really falling for another man instead of him?

Korey couldn't handle another heartbreak like that. And staying single was the best way to avoid getting hurt again.

CHAPTER 7

Thursday morning Savannah rang up groceries for a young *Englisher* woman who looked to be in her midtwenties with pink highlights in her long, sunshine-colored hair. Savannah tried her best not to stare at her unusual hair color as she told the woman her total.

The woman handed her a stack of bills.

"Thank you for coming in today. Please come back to see us soon," Savannah said, giving the woman her receipt and change.

As the woman pushed her shopping cart toward the exit, Savannah's eyes swung to Toby standing at the end of an aisle talking to an older *Englisher* woman.

The woman handed Toby a bag of noodles, and Toby's eyes widened with panic as his mouth worked, but no words passed his lips.

Oh no! She had to help Toby and quick!

Savannah's heart started to pound as she hurried over to her younger brother.

"I-I-I," Toby stammered before pushing the bag of noodles into Savannah's hands and trotting toward the back of the store.

The woman stared after him, her gray brows drawing together with confusion.

"Excuse me," Savannah said to the woman, her words coming in a rush. "May I help you?"

The woman frowned, shaking her head. "Oh dear. I didn't mean to upset him. Is he okay?"

"What did you ask him?"

"I forgot my glasses, and I can't read the ingredients. Does this have gluten?"

Savannah's hands shook as she read the ingredients to the woman, working hard to keep her anxiety out of her voice.

"Thank you so much." The woman took the bag of noodles from Savannah's hand and set it in her overflowing cart. "I'm ready. Would you please ring me up?"

Savannah tried to mask her frown. "Of course." She wanted to check on her brother, not help this woman! But she had to be respectful. Her aunt and uncle constantly reminded her and Toby that they valued each customer, no matter how exasperating the person might be.

While ringing up the items, Savannah kept peeking toward the back of the store, hoping to see her brother emerge. Worry threaded through her when he never reappeared.

After the woman paid, Savannah moved out from behind the counter just as her uncle walked over to her.

"*Onkel* Eddie, would you please take over the register? I need to check on Toby."

"*Ya*. He's in the stockroom."

Savannah rushed to the back of the store toward the stockroom, where a hammer pounded. She found Toby fixing the wooden supports on a shelving unit that had been broken for months. She stood by watching him, stunned for a moment.

When Toby stopped hammering, he turned toward her,

his handsome face flashing with irritation. "I'm *so* stupid that I couldn't help that woman. She asked me to read the ingredients to her, and I just froze."

"You're *not* stupid, Toby." She pointed to the shelf. "You just fixed the shelf that *Onkel* Eddie has been talking about fixing for months." She touched the supports that Toby replaced. "And you do really *gut* work. I never realized how skilled you are."

He snorted. "Don't patronize me, Savannah. I'm a dunce. I'm useless. I'll never be as *gut* as Dean and Levi."

"That's not true, Toby. We're all different."

Shaking his head, Toby stomped off toward the loading dock.

Savannah hugged her arms to her waist as a wave of sadness swept through her. If only she could find a way to help her brother see just how special he was.

⁓⁓⁓⁓⁘⁓⁓⁓⁓

"Who fixed the shelves in the stockroom?" *Aenti* Dorothy asked later that evening while walking toward the front of the store.

Savannah looked up from sweeping. "Toby did."

"And he did a fantastic job." *Onkel* Eddie flipped the Open sign to Closed. "*Danki*, Toby. I'd been meaning to look at that for months, but I always got busy with another project and then forgot about it."

Toby shrugged while straightening a round display of greeting cards. "It's no big deal."

"It *is* a big deal," Savannah corrected him. "We're proud of you."

Toby speared her with a look. "Knock it off, Vannah," he grumbled. "I can't stand it when you patronize me."

Savannah's shoulders slumped as she returned to sweeping. While she knew she sometimes tried too hard to be Toby's champion, she didn't know how else to prove to him that he was worthy of praise. In fact, he was just as worthy as everyone else.

Sunday morning Korey took a seat between Toby and Jayden in the Miller family's barn. The late-April air in the barn was warm and held a hint of the smell of animals mingling with the scent of hay. Korey spotted Dean, Levi, and Keith sitting one row in front of him in the unmarried men's section.

Then Korey turned toward Toby. "How was your week?"

"Just another week at the store." Toby shrugged. "Yours?"

"*Gut.*" Korey opened his mouth to respond but then stopped when he heard Dean mention Savannah. While he wasn't one for gossip, curiosity got the better of him, and he stilled.

"*Ya,*" Keith said. "My cousin Jerry is going to meet us at the youth gathering."

Korey leaned forward, tapping Keith on the shoulder. "Hey, Keith. I don't mean to listen in, but what did you say about your cousin Jerry?"

"Hi, Korey. It's no problem." Keith craned his neck over his shoulder. "Macy keeps insisting that Savannah needs a boyfriend. She says that Savannah is too serious and doesn't have any fun. So I offered to introduce her to my cousin Jerry. He's a brick mason and lives over in White Horse. He's going to meet us today over at the Kanagys' farm for the gathering."

Toby's eyes widened with shock. "You're setting *mei schweschder* up with someone?"

"Ya." Keith shrugged. "He's a nice guy. I think they'll get along perfectly well."

Toby shook his head. "I don't think she'll be interested."

"Why not?" Korey asked.

"I heard her tell *mei aenti* that she's not interested in dating right now."

"Well, she might like Jerry," Dean quipped. "He's a hard worker and has a great sense of humor."

Keith nodded. "Macy keeps saying Savannah would be much happier if she had a boyfriend. She insists that if Savannah met someone, she wouldn't be so uptight. She said that Savannah rarely smiles anymore, and she's worried about her. I think meeting someone nice might do her some good and change her perspective."

Korey peered over to where Savannah frowned while Macy and Willa talked animatedly on either side of her. Curiosity filled him as he considered what Toby and Keith said about her. Why would Savannah not want to date when all of her friends had boyfriends?

It seemed like all of the young women were focused on dating, getting married, and starting a family. Korey clearly remembered when he was dating Michelle, and she constantly nagged him about getting married. He'd never imagined that a young woman would not want to date. Korey tilted his head while studying Savannah. She seemed different from all of the other young women in the church district. He found her so intriguing, and he longed to know more about her.

When he glanced over at the married men's section, he found Jonah, Dwight, and Tyler talking and smiling. Korey recalled how close he and Dwight were before Dwight married Kendra and before Korey left the community.

But now Dwight was married, and it was obvious he was close friends with Tyler as well as Tyler's best friend Jonah. Jealousy slithered through Korey's gut. He had no idea how to bridge the enormous chasm between him and his older brother. He pressed his lips together.

"You all right, Korey?"

He looked over at Toby, who seemed to study him.

"Ya." He cleared his throat. "So, you said things are *gut* at the store?"

Toby frowned. "It's the usual." He hesitated as if contemplating something. "What about you? Where are you working right now?"

"We actually just finished up a job reroofing a bank."

"Really? Where?"

Korey shared the details of the job and then talked about what project was on his schedule for the upcoming week. Toby seemed to hang on his every word as if roofing were the most interesting trade he'd ever encountered.

When the song leader started singing the first line of the opening hymn, Korey opened his hymnal and cleared his throat. He felt someone watching him, and he looked up, surprised to see Savannah's bright blue eyes focused on him.

He gave her a smile and nod, but she continued to stare with an unreadable expression on her pretty face. Then she dipped her chin and turned her attention to her hymnal.

Korey once again wondered why she was against dating, and he suddenly felt determined to find out the answer.

After church, Korey, Jayden, and Toby converted the benches into tables before choosing a spot to sit together for lunch.

"Korey!" Dwight hurried over and climbed onto the bench across from him. "We haven't talked in a while. How's work?"

"*Gut.* I've been working on *mei dat*'s crew. How's farming?"

"The usual. There's always so much work to do."

"How's Kendra feeling these days?"

"She's doing great. I can't believe how fast her due date is coming. She's due at the end of June, and we're already more than halfway through April." Dwight nodded as a young woman placed a plate of bread and lunch meat on their table.

"That's exciting."

"Married life is fantastic, Korey. You need to consider it."

Korey chuckled. "*Ya*, well, I think it will be a while for me."

While Jayden discussed work with a few friends beside him, Korey listened as Dwight talked on about his farm and how happy he was to be married to Kendra.

After finishing a sandwich, Korey turned to Toby. "Are you going to the youth gathering today?"

Toby shook his head while chewing a few pretzels.

"Why not?" Korey asked.

Toby lifted his cup of coffee. "I would feel . . . awkward."

"Why?"

Toby hesitated.

"Well, you could hang out with Jay and me, right Jay?"

"Huh?" Jayden spun to face him. "What, Kore?"

"I told Toby that he could hang out with us if he came to the youth gathering today."

Jayden smiled. "Of course you can. We'd be glad to have you on our volleyball team."

"Absolutely," Korey agreed, hopeful that Toby would say yes.

"I'll think about it," Toby said and then sipped his coffee.

Korey grinned before popping a pretzel into his mouth. *"Gut."*

"Are you excited to get to the youth gathering?" Willa asked Savannah later that afternoon while they helped clean up in the Miller family's kitchen.

Savannah shrugged as she set a stack of serving trays in Fannie Miller's cabinet. *"Ya."*

"I'm sure you must be anxious to meet Jerry," Jodie gushed while scrubbing a handful of utensils. "You are going to just love him! Right, Macy?"

Savannah glanced behind her, grateful none of the other women were listening to their conversation. "Would you please keep your voice down? Not everyone needs to know that I'm being set up on a date."

"What's the big deal?" Macy asked. "My parents met through *freinden.*"

Gail nodded. "Mine did too."

"Who knows? Maybe we'll all be engaged by the fall," Jodie sang.

Gail snorted. "Let's just hope that Savannah likes Jerry. It seems like she's awfully difficult to please."

Jodie and Willa chuckled while Macy gave her a sympathetic look.

"That wasn't very nice," Macy chided, and their friends busied themselves with cleaning up the kitchen.

Savannah set her dish cloth on the counter. "I'm going to go see if I can find Toby." She started for the door, her irritation flaring. She didn't appreciate being the butt of her friends' jokes.

"Wait." Gail touched Savannah's arm as contrition flickered across her face. "I'm sorry. That was mean. I sincerely apologize. Please don't go."

Savannah folded her arms over her waist. "I don't like being picked on."

"I know, and I'm very sorry." Gail frowned. "Please forgive me."

Savannah took in the apologies on her friends' faces and sighed. "Fine." Then she returned to drying dishes.

"Toby!" Savannah hollered her brother's name as she jogged toward him after the kitchen was clean. "Toby! Wait up!"

He stopped walking and spun to face her. "I thought you were going to ride with Dean to the youth gathering."

She worked to catch her breath. "I am, but I wanted to talk to you. I saw you and Korey talking before church and during lunch."

"So?" He shrugged.

"What did you talk about?"

"Nothing really." Toby rubbed his clean-shaven jaw. "He asked me about work, and he told me about the roofing jobs he completed last week. Then he asked me to go to the youth gathering and said I could hang out with him and Jayden."

Savannah's heart lifted. "Are you going to come?"

"No."

Her smile fell.

"I'll see you at home tonight," he said.

Savannah's heart sank as her brother turned and headed to the stable to fetch his horse.

"Hey, Savannah!" Macy yelled. "Are you ready to meet Jerry?"

Savannah swiveled toward her best friend. "Sure," she said as dread filled her.

When she arrived at the youth gathering, Savannah walked with Macy and Keith to where a group of young people were gathered near the volleyball nets.

"There he is," Keith announced as he approached a young man with light-brown hair. "Jerry! I'm so glad you made it." He shook his cousin's hand.

Savannah smoothed her black apron.

Macy poked her arm. "Go say hello and introduce yourself."

"I'm not a kid." Savannah shot her best friend a look and then held out her hand to him. "Hi. I'm Savannah."

Jerry met her gaze and seemed to assess her with his gray eyes. He was average height, slightly shorter than Keith, and he had a pleasant smile. "I'm Jerry."

He gave her hand a half-hearted shake before releasing it.

Macy took Keith's hand. "Well, you two get to know each other. We're going to play volleyball." She winked at Savannah and then steered Keith toward a nearby volleyball net.

Savannah clasped her hands together while trying to think of something to say to this stranger. "I work in my aunt and uncle's store. What do you do?"

"I'm a brick mason." He looked past her toward the volleyball nets where four games had begun.

"Do you like your work?"

He kept his gaze trained on the games as he shrugged. "Sure. It's the family business."

"The store is too. *Mei aenti* and *onkel* have run it for years. My younger *bruder* works there too."

Jerry continued watching the game.

"What are you working on now?"

"Huh?" Jerry glanced over at her.

"What are you building? Where are you working?"

"Oh. We're working at a new housing complex."

"That sounds interesting. How do you—"

"Want to play volleyball?" he asked, interrupting her.

"Not really."

"Oh. Well, I'll see you later." Jerry took off toward the volleyball games. He joined Keith's team and started to play, leaving Savannah standing at the sidelines.

She hugged her arms to her waist and glanced around as humiliation heated her face. She wondered how many of her friends had seen Jerry walk away and leave her there alone, but when she scanned the area, it seemed no one had been paying attention.

Jerry never looked back at Savannah as he laughed with Keith. The two cousins leapt and sent the ball traveling over the net as their team took the lead.

Savannah leaned against a tree. Sadness rained down on her despite the bright April sun. She longed just to go home and escape this disastrous day. Frowning, she looked toward the road and wondered how long it would take her to walk home.

When her eyes wandered to the next volleyball net, she spotted Korey leaping into the air to hit the ball over to the opposing

AMY CLIPSTON

team, which included Macy, Keith, and Jerry. Korey's eyes were shielded by his mirrored sunglasses, and he seemed larger than life. He was so tall, so agile, and so graceful. When the opposing team missed the ball, Korey high-fived Jayden, Levi, and Dean, and they all grinned.

Savannah contemplated how nice Korey was to her brother, and she smiled. She pondered the rumors she'd heard about him—that he had been cruel to Michelle, that he had mistreated her, and that he had been disrespectful to her, which was why she left him for Tyler. She snorted. That couldn't possibly have been true.

A man who went out of his way to talk to her brother and invite him to youth group couldn't be callous. Korey had to possess a kind and thoughtful heart, no matter what anyone said about him. She would have to thank him for encouraging Toby to become active with their youth group.

For some strange reason, Savannah's heart gave a funny little kick at the thought of talking to Korey. What was wrong with her?

"So . . . what do you think of Jerry?" Willa's question yanked Savannah back to the present as Willa appeared beside Savannah with Jodie and Gail in tow.

"I don't really know him." Savannah frowned.

Jodie clucked her tongue. "Oh, come on, Savannah. Can't you be positive about anything?"

Savannah glared at Jodie. She was so tired of her snarky comments!

"He's cute, isn't he?" Gail asked.

Savannah looked out to where Jerry hit the ball and shrugged. "*Ya.* I guess so."

"I'm sure he'll give you a ride home," Jodie insisted.

Savannah folded her arms over her middle. "I guess we'll see."

"You're always so negative, Savannah," Gail frowned. "That's why none of the guys have asked you out."

Savannah glowered. "Excuse me? I just met him and I tried to get to know him. However, he decided to play volleyball instead of talking to me." She made a sweeping gesture toward the volleyball game. "I don't think he's avoiding me because I have a bad attitude. It's obvious he came here to play volleyball with his cousin instead of getting to know me." She pointed to the snack table. "Now, I think I'll go get a drink."

Without waiting for her friends to reply, Savannah marched toward the snack table.

As she picked up a cup of lemonade, Savannah wondered why she had come to the youth gathering today when she never had any intention of dating Jerry. And then she found herself pondering if her friends were truly her friends at all.

CHAPTER 8

SAVANNAH APPROACHED JERRY LATER THAT AFTERNOON AND held out a plate of her peanut butter brownies. Laughter and conversations drifted through the air while members of their youth group ate dessert and played volleyball. The games would continue until the sun went down, and then the youth group members would retreat to the barn to sing hymns.

Savannah pasted a smile on her face and was determined to give Jerry another chance. She had decided that she and Jerry had gotten off on the wrong foot earlier. Maybe she had expected too much from their first meeting. Perhaps Jerry had been excited to see his cousin and was thrilled to play volleyball with Keith. Now that a few hours had gone by, he might take the time to get to know Savannah.

While watching Jerry play volleyball, she had pondered their first meeting. She was aware of how quick-tempered she was, and she had decided that perhaps she had misjudged Jerry. Everyone deserved a second chance, and she had just met him. Maybe her friends were right and she needed to make an effort to get to know a man.

And, besides, her friends would blame her if it didn't work out between them; therefore, she was going to do her best to be friendly.

"Jerry," she said, holding out the plate of brownies. "Do you like peanut butter brownies?"

He rubbed his flat abdomen and smiled. "Oh *ya*. I do." He reached for one. "Where did you get these?"

"I made them."

He took a bite and nodded. "So *gut*."

"I'm glad you like them." She continued to hold the plate while he chewed. She glanced up at the blue sky as dusk began to roll in. A light breeze blew the ties on her prayer covering, and they flittered over her shoulders. "We've enjoyed such nice weather today."

He nodded.

"The sun is shining, and it's finally starting to warm up."

Jerry chewed while looking at her.

Savannah cleared her throat. "Do you have any siblings?"

"*Ya*, I have a *bruder*." Jerry bit into the brownie again.

"Older or younger?"

"Younger."

Savannah smiled. They had something in common! Perhaps there was still a chance that they could form a friendship. "*Mei bruder* is younger too. His name is Toby."

Jerry took another bite of the brownie. When he remained silent, she searched for something to keep the conversation going between them.

"He's nineteen," she said, hoping to prod him into sharing more information with her.

Jerry finished the brownie.

"How old is your *bruder*, and what is his—"

"We'll talk more later, okay?" Jerry tapped her arm. "*Danki* for the brownie." Then he trotted off to where Keith stood with

Dean and Levi. "We're running out of daylight. Are we going to start another game?"

Savannah's lips twisted as she continued to stand there holding the plate of brownies. She felt like a moron, a dope. She had hoped to convince Jerry to talk to her and make an effort to get to know her, but he just wanted to play volleyball.

When she turned toward the nets, her eyes immediately found Korey, and he seemed to be studying her. Her knees felt weak, and her breath caught, but then she silently chastised herself. With his mirrored sunglasses on, Savannah couldn't be certain if Korey was watching her or looking at someone else. But when he nodded, she knew for sure that he was in fact focused on her.

Savannah nodded in return, and then a dreadful thought hit her. If Korey had been watching her, then he might have caught her painfully awkward interaction with Jerry. She hoped he hadn't witnessed it. In fact, she hoped no one had seen it.

She groaned as she looked over to where her friends stood watching their boyfriends play volleyball. She was certain that her friends would blame her for how terribly her introduction had gone with Jerry. No matter what she said, they would insist it was her "bad attitude" that had doomed her from the start.

Savannah longed to just forget this day had ever happened. And she also yearned for a way to stop her friends from hounding her to date, but that seemed impossible.

<hr />

The air was cool and crisp, and the stars twinkled in the night sky while Savannah followed her friends out of the Kanagy family's barn later that evening. She and her youth group had sung hymns late into the evening, and now it was time to clean up and then head home.

Macy sidled up to Savannah. "How did it go with Jerry?"

"You really hadn't noticed?" Savannah snorted.

"No." Macy's brow creased. "I guess not well?"

"I tried to talk to him multiple times, but he was more interested in talking to his cousin, which is fine."

Macy frowned. "I'm sorry."

"It's not your fault." Savannah glanced behind them and spotted Jerry talking with Keith, Dean, and Ike.

While she'd managed to have a brief conversation with Jerry before they started singing hymns, she was still convinced that his motivation for coming to the youth group today was to see Keith and not her. And during the singing, she had glanced over at Jerry in the men's section and found him studying his hymnal without once looking up at her. She had just accepted that it wasn't meant to be between Jerry and her, but now she had another problem—she needed to find a ride home.

Savannah swiveled back to her best friend and opened her mouth to ask for a lift home, but then an idea filled her mind. Perhaps she could just ask Jerry for a ride. Then she could try to convince Toby to come next week. After all, surviving an awkward ride home from Jerry was better than being a burden on her friends.

Macy's light eyebrows lifted. "You okay?"

"*Ya.*" Savannah smiled. "I'll meet you in the kitchen." Then she pointed her flashlight toward the young men and hurried over to them.

She approached Jerry, who was laughing with Keith and Ike. "Jerry?"

"*Ya?*" He chuckled as he turned to Savannah.

"I was wondering if—" she began.

"Jerry!" another young man called from the barn. "Come here!"

Holding up his hand toward the other young man, Jerry called, "One second!" Then he looked at Savannah. "What did you need?"

"Could you possibly give me—" she tried again.

Another young man called Jerry's name.

Jerry waved them off before looking at Savannah again. "What was that?"

"Would you please give me a—?" she attempted to ask again, but she was interrupted by the two young men calling Jerry's name again, their voices sounding over her question.

"Hold on. Let me see what they want." Jerry sighed. "I'll come and talk to you in a minute, okay?"

Before she could respond, he started for the barn, where a group of men had gathered, their faces illuminated by their Coleman lanterns.

Savannah harrumphed. "Are you truly going to come and talk to me this time or are you going to ignore me yet again?"

He spun to face her, walking backward. "Where will you be?"

"In the kitchen, helping to clean up." She pointed toward the house.

He nodded and then turned toward his friends.

"Jerry," she called, "I just need a ride home!"

He kept walking with his back toward her, but he held up a hand.

She watched him for a moment, considering racing after him, but then she shook her head. She hoped that he'd heard her.

A line of horses and buggies moved down the rock driveway that led to the main road as the youth group members began their journeys home.

Savannah headed into the kitchen, where Macy was busy placing leftover desserts into containers and then setting them on a counter. "What can I do to help?" she asked her best friend.

"Would you please sweep up?" Maria Kanagy asked as she glided past, before setting utensils in a drawer. "The utility closet is over there." She pointed to the far end of the large kitchen.

"Of course." Savannah found the dustpan and broom, then set to work. She moved around the young women who were picking up their leftovers while chatting about how fun the evening had been.

Macy handed the last container of leftovers to a young Amish woman with bright red hair before turning to Savannah. "Do you need a ride home?"

"No, *danki*. Jerry said he would give me a ride." At least she hoped he had heard her ask him for a ride. She emptied the dustpan into the trash can and pulled out the full trash bag and tied it.

Macy grinned. "Oh *gut*! I'm glad to hear it. You'll have to let me know how it goes." She cupped her hand to her mouth to cover a yawn. "I'm going to head out." Then she gave Savannah a hug.

"I'll talk to you soon," Savannah told her.

While Macy and the rest of the young women filed out of the kitchen, Savannah slipped a new trash bag into the can and then began wiping down the counters while Maria continued washing and stowing dishes.

Savannah replaced the soiled tablecloth with a fresh one before dropping the dirty tablecloth into a laundry basket in the utility room.

Soon Savannah and Maria were the only two women left in the kitchen.

"*Danki*, Savannah, for staying late to help me clean up," Maria said once the kitchen was clean.

Savannah placed a stack of serving trays in the cabinet. "I'm happy to help."

"You should get going," Maria said. "It's late." She peered out the window and then turned to Savannah. "It looks like everyone is gone."

"Really?" Dread pooled in Savannah's belly. But she recalled how Jerry had waved to her after she'd asked him for a ride. Had he forgotten her?

"Let me know if you need a ride, and I'll ask Ben to take you home."

"I have a ride, but *danki*." Savannah picked up her empty container from her brownies and started for the door.

Maria looked unconvinced. "I don't see any buggies out there, so you'd better check. Let me know if I need to have Ben take you home."

"I will. *Gut nacht*." Flipping on her flashlight, Savannah zipped out to the porch and down the steps. She pointed the beam of her flashlight toward the field, and although earlier it had been peppered with buggies, now only one buggy sat near the barn. The sky above her was dark and clogged with gray clouds.

Fury and humiliation coursed through Savannah. It seemed as if Jerry had left her behind.

He had forgotten her.

No, he had *ignored her* once again!

Angry tears stung her eyes as she stalked down the rock driveway toward the road. Too embarrassed to admit that she'd been abandoned, Savannah decided to walk home instead of asking Ben Kanagy to give her a ride. It wasn't too far—only a few miles. She just hoped her aunt and uncle wouldn't worry about her.

CHAPTER 9

KOREY HOPPED INTO HIS BUGGY AND GUIDED HIS HORSE toward the road. He was surprised to find the pasture empty and all the buggies gone.

After saying good night to his friends and telling Jayden he'd see him at home, Korey had padded into the stable to retrieve his horse. Once in there, he ran into Ben Kanagy, and they soon were engrossed in a conversation about work. Before he knew it, everyone else had left.

When he merged onto the main road, he thought he saw a person trudging down the shoulder. As his horse approached, Korey realized it was an Amish woman walking alone. He pulled up beside her, and his heart picked up speed when he realized it was Savannah.

He called her name, and she looked up at him. "Are you okay?"

She snorted. "I'm just great." She lifted her chin and focused on the road ahead.

"Where's Jerry?"

She frowned, and he noticed that her eyes were red and puffy as if she'd been crying. "He left."

"He *left* you?" Korey asked as frustration filled him, but then guilt smacked him in the face. He had done something similar to Michelle when they were dating. He had abandoned her at a youth gathering on a day with a bad rainstorm. And Tyler had rightfully given Korey a piece of his mind after bringing Michelle home.

Korey frowned. He had made many mistakes in his past, but he was determined not to be that thoughtless person anymore.

He turned his focus to Savannah as she continued plodding forward on the side of the road.

"I'll give you a ride," Korey told her.

"I'm just fine. The walk will help me clear my head."

He sighed. "Get in the buggy."

"No."

"Please get in the buggy, Savannah." His words were measured.

When she continued stalking down the road, he shook his head. Boy, was she stubborn!

"Savannah," he began, trying to be patient. "It's dark out and you're wearing a gray dress, a black sweater, and a black apron. Those are dark clothes, which means you could get hit by a car. So stop being so stubborn and get in the buggy now."

She glared at him. "You're not *mei dat* or my boss."

"You're right," he said, resigned. "I'm not, but I'm your *freind*."

She stopped walking and stared at him, looking more shocked than angry.

"Please get in, Savannah. Let me take you safely home."

"Fine." She hurried around the buggy and climbed in the passenger side, which was the closest to the passing traffic.

They rode in silence for a few moments, and he waited for her to say something. Finally, he gave her a sideways glance and found her staring out the window toward the cars rumbling past them.

"What happened with Jerry?" he asked.

She kept her eyes on the traffic. "I had asked him to give me a ride home, but he seemed distracted. I guess he didn't hear me, or he forgot about me."

"He forgot you?" Korey asked. "How could he forget about you?"

She shrugged as if it weren't a big deal. "I don't know. He said he'd come to talk to me, and I told him I was going to be in the house. I stayed to help Maria clean up the kitchen. Dean planned to take Patience home, and Levi always takes Iris. I'm sure all of *mei freinden* rode with their boyfriends. Macy had offered me a ride, but I told her that I had one."

She held the container in her hands. "And no one thought of me."

"I would have given you a ride."

Savannah remained silent.

"I'm sorry it didn't work out with Jerry."

She snorted and crossed her arms over her black sweater. "I'm not."

"I saw you talking with him."

"What did you see?"

"It seemed like you were doing the talking, and he was very ... distracted."

"*Ya*, that about sums it up. I tried to get him to talk to me, but all he wanted to do was play volleyball and hang out with Keith and Keith's *freinden*." She looked down at the container in her hands. "I can't really blame him."

Korey frowned. "He seemed rude to me."

She finally looked him in the eye. "Do you think I'm negative?"

"Why?" He blanched. "Who said that?"

"Never mind," she muttered. "I knew that it wouldn't work out with Jerry, but *mei freinden* won't stop bugging me about dating someone. It's getting old."

Silence stretched between them, and he considered what she'd said.

"I can relate."

She faced him again. "What do you mean?"

"Everyone is nagging me about dating too."

"Who nags you?"

"*Mei dat, mei bruders,* Dwight." Korey could hear the edge in his voice. "They all think that I'll be so much happier if I settle down. But I'm not interested, especially after . . ." He let his words trail off. He couldn't bring himself to admit how much Michelle and Tyler had hurt him.

Once again, the buggy fell silent, except for the sound of the passing traffic. He longed to ask her why she didn't want to date, but it was none of his business. Still, he wanted to know. That question had haunted him ever since Toby had said Savannah wasn't interested in finding a boyfriend.

"Why are you so nice to *mei bruder*?"

Korey couldn't stop his wry laugh. "Does everyone really believe I'm awful?"

"Why would I think you're awful? I hardly know you." Her eyes seemed to assess him, and he suddenly felt itchy in his own skin.

Korey silently admired how pretty she looked in the warm yellow glow of the lantern at her feet. Her blue eyes were the perfect contrast to her dark hair. With her long neck and pink lips, she was a natural beauty.

He swallowed against his dry throat. "I like talking to Toby. He's a nice kid. I tried to convince him to come today, but he said he didn't feel comfortable. I told him that he could hang out with Jay and me."

"He told me you said that."

"Does that upset you?"

She shook her head. "I thought it was nice."

"See? I'm not so bad." He smiled, but she just stared at him. He longed to read her thoughts. "What's on your mind, Savannah?"

"What if I had a solution that would get our *freinden* to stop nagging us about dating?"

"I'm listening."

"What if we pretended to date?"

"Pretended to date whom?"

She motioned between them. "Each other."

Stunned by her words, he halted the horse at the side of the road so that he could find out exactly what she meant.

She looked anxious, her bright blue eyes wide with panic. "Why did you stop the horse? What are you doing?"

"Stopping so we can talk about this without the distractions of the passing traffic." He faced her. "Go on. Tell me what you mean about pretending to date."

"I was thinking that we can pretend to date so that everyone stops harassing us about finding a boyfriend or girlfriend. If we are already dating someone, then they'll leave us alone, right?"

He nodded. "*Ya,* that's true."

"We can just go through the motions, and everyone will believe we're actually in a relationship with each other. We can ride to and from youth group together and just act as if we like each other."

"So romantic." He chuckled.

She laughed too, and he enjoyed her gorgeous smile. "So, is that a yes?"

"You're asking me out?"

"Well, I guess I am." She actually blushed and looked adorable. "Is that too forward?"

He hesitated as confusion poured through him. This proposal was so unexpected. "You want to date me?"

"I want to *pretend* to date you." She lifted an eyebrow. "As long as you promise that you won't leave me stranded at a youth group event."

"Never." He paused, thinking this through. "I still don't understand why you'd want to pretend to date *me*. Out of all of the men in our youth group, why me?"

"Let's think about this. You're *freinden* with my *freinden*'s boyfriends, right?" she asked.

"*Ya*, and your cousins too."

"Then it will work. It makes sense, and everyone will believe that we connected and like each other. After all, we run in the same circles. That means it's only natural for us to date each other, right?"

"I guess so." He guided the horse back to the road as the plan settled over him. "So, it's set then."

"Not yet. You have to talk to *mei onkel* and ask permission to date me."

"Oh. Right." He shook his head. "I forgot. It's been a while."

"You didn't date anyone when you were away?"

"No."

"Ohio, right?"

He nodded, keeping his eyes trained on the road.

"Why did you go there?"

He peeked over at her. "Don't you know? I'm sure the rumors have been rampant."

"I've heard many things, and most of it I don't believe. So I'd rather hear the truth from you."

He paused while gathering his response. "It was difficult watching *mei bruder* and my ex-girlfriend fall in love. I thought it would be best for everyone if I went away for a while."

"Did it help?"

He gave her another sideways glance. "You don't mince words, do you?"

"What's the point? If you say what you mean, then you won't waste anyone's time."

He smiled and nodded. "That's very true."

"So, did getting away from your family help you deal with everything?"

"Somewhat."

"What do you mean by 'somewhat'?"

Korey sighed. "I'm trying to forgive Tyler and mend our relationship, but I can't get past the feeling that he betrayed me." He was surprised by how easy it was to tell her how he felt.

"But he's your *bruder*."

"It's not that simple."

"But it should be. I can't imagine losing *mei bruder*. He's all I have left of my immediate family."

Korey longed to know more about what she was thinking, but he kept his questions to himself. Maybe someday she would tell him about how she felt after losing her parents, but tonight he felt he should tread softly with her.

Still, he couldn't deny how intriguing he found Savannah, and he looked forward to getting to know her better.

Korey led his horse past Savannah's aunt and uncle's store and then halted it at the back of the house. He looked up at the two-story white house with the wraparound porch. Lanterns glowed on the first floor, and he pondered what it was like for her to grow up there with her brother but without her parents.

They climbed out of the buggy and walked up the back porch steps together.

"*Mei aenti* and *onkel* usually wait up for Dean and me to get home on Sunday nights," she said.

"*Mei dat* does too."

Korey followed her through the mudroom and into the kitchen, where he found her uncle sitting at the table with her aunt. Suddenly Korey's hands started to tremble at the thought of asking permission to date Savannah. What was his problem? After all, this wasn't a real relationship!

"*Onkel* Eddie," Savannah began, "Korey would like to talk to you for a minute."

Eddie's bushy gray eyebrows rose as he removed his reading glasses. "Is that so?" He stood. "Let's go out to the porch."

Korey noticed Dorothy give Savannah an excited expression before he followed the short middle-aged man outside.

"It's a nice night," Eddie commented.

"*Ya*, it is." Korey cleared his throat. "Savannah and I are getting to know each other, and I'd like to date her. Would you please give me your permission to ask her to be my girlfriend?"

"*Ya*, I'd be glad to. You have my blessing, Korey." Eddie shook Korey's hand. "This is wonderful news. It's about time she started dating. I'm trusting you to be respectful to her."

"Of course I will." Korey found it strange that she had never dated before. Surely a *maedel* as pretty as she was had caught the eye of another young man in their community. Why hadn't anyone else asked her out?

Korey followed Eddie back into the kitchen, where Dorothy immediately stopped speaking and smiled at him.

Savannah gave Korey a questioning looked, and he nodded. She smiled and then placed her hand on his forearm. "I'm going to walk Korey out," she told her aunt and uncle.

Korey allowed her to steer him back to his buggy.

Then she rubbed her hands together. "This is going to be perfect. We'll have everyone convinced, and I won't have to listen to *mei freinden* tell me that there's something wrong with me because I don't have a boyfriend."

"They say there's something wrong with you?" he asked, perplexed.

She waved off the question. "Never mind. It's not a big deal. Besides, it's all solved now. *Danki* for agreeing to do this for me. It doesn't need to be a permanent situation. We'll just pretend for a while. At least until *mei freinden* focus on something other than me. Maybe just a few months?"

"That sounds fine." He hesitated. "I guess I'll see you next Sunday. Or should I visit you during the week?" He shrugged and blew out a puff of air. "I don't know how to have a fake relationship."

"We'll play it by ear, but let's promise never to tell anyone the truth. We'll keep this between us and only us. Okay?"

"Okay." He held out his hand to her, and she gave it a firm shake. "Have a *gut* week."

"You too. And thank you for the ride home."

Savannah smiled as Korey's horse and buggy moved down the driveway, the flashers glowing in the dark. Relief filtered through her and she gave a little laugh. She now had a fake boyfriend, which would keep her friends off her back. No more nagging or comments that she was too negative to attract a man.

And an added bonus was that Korey was so good looking with those milk-chocolate-colored eyes, angular jaw, and smile that seemed to light up the room. Aside from the fact that he was athletic with broad shoulders, a trim waist, and that tall height. Plus, he was easy to talk to and was always nice to her brother, which she admired and appreciated.

Savannah hummed to herself as she hopped up the back steps and into the kitchen, where her aunt and uncle sat at the table.

Aenti Dorothy beamed. "What a nice surprise, Savannah! I thought Keith's cousin would be the one bringing you home, not Korey Bontrager."

"*Ya*, it was a surprise," Savannah agreed. "Jerry and I didn't seem to click, and I was grateful Korey gave me a ride home." She decided not to share how Jerry had not only ignored her but left her stranded. "Korey and I have been talking, and it just made sense that we would date."

Onkel Eddie nodded. "He's a nice young man."

"I think so too. It's getting late, so I'm going to head to bed. I'll see you in the morning. *Gut nacht.*" Savannah jogged up the stairs and knocked on Toby's door. When he told her to come in, she burst into his room. "I have news."

Toby sat up, his eyes sparkling with curiosity. "That Korey gave you a ride home?"

She pointed to the window beside Toby's bed. "Were you spying on us?"

"No, not spying. I heard the horse and buggy, and I looked out there." He seemed befuddled. "What happened with Keith's cousin?"

"How did you know about Jerry?"

"Keith was talking about it at church."

Savannah considered telling her brother what happened with Jerry, but she decided to keep that catastrophe private. "Jerry and I didn't click, but Korey gave me a ride home." She hesitated. "And he asked me to be his girlfriend."

Toby's smile was wide. "I approve. He's nice."

"I think so too." Guilt swamped her, and she considered telling him the truth. But she recalled the promise that she and Korey had made. *"Gut nacht."*

"See you in the morning," Toby said.

Savannah hurried off to her room, and while she readied for bed, she considered how to tell her friends her news.

CHAPTER 10

Korey's shoes crunched up the rock path as he walked from the barn to the house later that evening. When he looked up toward the porch, he was surprised to see two lanterns there. He stopped at the bottom of the steps and peered up at *Dat* and Jayden, both sitting on rocking chairs.

"Did you two wait up for me?" Korey asked as he climbed the stairs.

Jayden grinned. "We were wondering if you got lost. I almost headed back to the Kanagy farm to see if your buggy had broken down somewhere."

"I'm sorry I worried you. I didn't get lost." Korey stood in front of them and leaned back against the porch railing. "I took Savannah home."

"Savannah Zook?" *Dat* asked.

Korey nodded. "*Ya.*"

"Why did you have to take her home?" Jayden's brow pinched.

Korey explained that he had stayed late to talk to Ben, and when he started on his journey home, he found her walking along the shoulder stranded without a ride.

Dat looked aghast. "She was stranded?"

"*Ya.*" Korey frowned, shaking his head. "The person who

was supposed to give her a ride left her there." His anger flared, but when he recalled again how he'd done something similar to Michelle when they were dating, embarrassment mixed with his annoyance. He'd never forget how Tyler had given him a furious lecture when he'd rescued Michelle in the rain. Of course Tyler had been right, and now Korey held the same anger for Jerry, who had left Savannah stranded without a ride.

Jayden held up his hand. "Wait a minute. Didn't I hear Keith say something about planning to introduce Savannah to his cousin today?"

"*Ya*, he did. His cousin's name is Jerry, and from what Savannah told me, he was more interested in playing volleyball with Keith than in getting to know her. So I gave her a ride home when I found her walking along the road in the dark."

Korey rubbed at a spot on the back of his neck. "While I was at her *haus*, I talked to her *onkel* and asked if I could date her."

"You asked her out?" Jayden sat forward in the chair. "I didn't even know you liked her."

Dat clapped his hands. "That's great! I'm so *froh* to hear that. Having a girlfriend will help you feel connected to the community and also help you move on after—"

"I'm really tired," Korey interrupted him. "I'm going to go to bed. I'll see you in the morning." He sauntered into the house, leaving his straw hat and shoes in the mudroom before climbing the steep stairs to his bedroom.

Jayden trailed behind him. "Hold on, Kore. I have questions. Before today, I've never seen you even talk to her."

"I have been talking to her."

"I thought we told each other everything. I mean, I was the first person you told that you were going to move to Ohio."

Korey stopped in front of Jayden's bedroom door and faced his younger brother. "That's true."

"Then why didn't you tell me that you liked her?"

Korey folded his arms over his chest and looked up at the ceiling. He wanted to tell his brother the truth so badly that he could taste it, but he'd made a promise to Savannah—a promise he was determined not to break. That meant he had to tell Jayden only part of the story.

"Look, I know you're surprised, and I'm sorry that I didn't tell you anything about Savannah before tonight. We've just been talking on and off since I got home," Korey explained, and it wasn't a lie. "Asking her out was just a spur of the moment thing. We talked about how we run in the same circles at youth group. I'm friends with her cousins, and her friends' boyfriends. And, honestly, I like talking to Savannah. She's different from the other *maed* I know. Anyway, I just decided to take a chance."

"I think it's great." Jayden patted Korey's shoulder.

Korey blinked. "You do?"

"*Ya*, I do." Jay chuckled. "I was praying you'd find a way to be *froh* here, and Savannah could help you do that."

Korey's mouth dropped open. He hadn't expected his brother to be supportive of his decision to date Savannah. This was a shock.

"*Gut nacht!*" Jayden maneuvered past him. "I get the shower first!"

Korey stared after his younger brother, stunned by his words.

The following evening, Savannah rushed around the kitchen, preparing for a visit from her friends. Macy had called her at the store earlier in the day and asked if she, Willa, Jodie, and Gail could bring dessert over and hear the latest about her and Jerry. Savannah's hands trembled with a mixture of excitement and worry. She had mentally practiced nearly all afternoon how she would tell her friends the news about her and Korey.

After starting the percolator, she set the table with dishes and then added mugs for the coffee. She was grateful that Dean had gone to visit Patience, her aunt and uncle were in the family room reading, and Toby was upstairs, which meant she and her friends could speak freely.

A few moments later, knocks sounded on the back door. Savannah touched her prayer covering and then smoothed her hands down her apron and red dress before opening the door.

"Hi!" Macy said, her smile wide.

Savannah beckoned them. "Come in."

Her four friends joined her in the kitchen, and the smell of coffee wafted over them.

"We brought *kichlin* and *kuche*," Jodie said.

"*Danki*," Savannah said. "Have a seat, and we'll enjoy our desserts."

Soon they were sitting at the table eating oatmeal raisin cookies, sugar cookies, and pieces of carrot cake while sipping coffee.

"So," Macy began, "tell us everything about Jerry."

Savannah eyed her best friend. "What did Keith tell you?"

"Nothing." Macy gave her a palms-up. "As far as I know, he hasn't spoken to him since the youth gathering last night."

Jodie clapped. "Did Jerry ask you out?"

"No." Savannah snorted while cupping her hands around her

warm mug. "I had a brief conversation with him after we sang hymns. Well, I tried to have a conversation with him, but we kept getting interrupted by some of his friends. He promised me that he would talk to me later on, but he never came to find me."

Gail set her coffee cup down and leaned forward. "What do you mean?"

"He didn't take you home?" Willa waved a sugar cookie in the air.

"No, he didn't. In fact, I was stranded. I had asked him if he would give me a ride, and he waved at me in response. I thought that meant he would come and find me and give me a ride, but everyone was gone when I walked outside after helping Maria clean up the kitchen."

Macy raised her hand. "When I asked you if you needed a ride, you told me Jerry was going to take you home."

"That's right," Savannah said. "I thought he was going to give me a ride, but when I went outside, he was gone, along with almost everyone else."

Macy cupped her hand over her mouth. "What did you do?"

"Jerry left you?" Willa asked as she set a piece of carrot cake on her plate.

Jodie frowned. "What a creep."

"I was walking along the road, and Korey stopped and picked me up." Savannah sat up taller, lifting her chin. "We had a very nice long talk, and when he brought me home, he talked to *mei onkel*. So, now we're dating."

Savannah's four friends gasped in unison and then started shooting questions at her all at once.

Willa looked as if she smelled something foul. "You're dating Korey? Korey Bontrager?"

"What about what he did to Michelle?" Jodie demanded.

Gail shook her head. "Why would you want to date *him*?"

"What if he goes back to Ohio?" Willa asked. "Would you go with him?"

Macy tapped the table. "I'm confused. You just said you didn't want to date anyone, and now you're dating Korey Bontrager? This doesn't make any sense at all."

"Hold on." Savannah held up her hands. "Shhh!"

Her four friends fell silent.

"I don't know the details of his relationship with Michelle, and frankly, it's none of my business. And even if he did tell me, I wouldn't share it. Gossip is a sin."

All four of her friends looked embarrassed.

"Korey and I have been talking," Savannah continued. "We get along, and *ya*, I like him." And that was the truth. She *did* like him—as a friend—but she also *liked* him.

Willa looked around the table. "Well, he is handsome. All three of the Bontrager *sohns* are."

"That's true," Jodie agreed with a shrug. "He's very good-looking, and he seems nice."

Macy squinted as she stared at Savannah in disbelief. Savannah could almost hear her best friend's suspicious thoughts and questions.

Savannah needed to change the subject—*fast*! "How are your boyfriends?"

Willa began talking about Tommy, and soon Jodie chimed in discussing Peter.

Savannah picked up a cookie and took a bite while the conversation continued around her.

After a while, they all helped clean up the table and wash the dishes. Once the kitchen was clean, Savannah walked her friends out to the porch to meet their ride.

Willa, Jodie, and Gail descended the steps and climbed into the waiting van, but Macy lingered behind on the porch, a frown clouding her pretty face.

Savannah pasted a smile on her lips despite her growing anxiety. She was certain her best friend was about to grill her about her new boyfriend.

"Why do you suddenly like Korey?"

"We've been talking, and we get along. It just made sense for us to start dating." Savannah tilted her head. "Why all of the questions?"

Macy gave her a look of disbelief. "Because you've never mentioned him. If you like him so much, then why didn't you tell me?"

A van window opened, and Willa stuck out her head. "We need to go, Macy."

Macy spun to face them. "One moment." Then she pivoted toward Savannah again. "We'll talk later, Savannah."

"Okay." Savannah hugged her. "I'll see you Sunday."

Savannah leaned forward on the porch railing and waved as the van motored down the driveway. Once the van was out of view, she bowed her head and let a loud sigh escape. She finally had a boyfriend, but her friends were still interrogating her. Would they ever be satisfied with her life choices?

She strolled back into the house and shook her head. She hoped her friends would accept Korey soon. But no matter what, she would keep her arrangement with Korey a secret. No one needed to know the truth.

Korey walked into the kitchen Thursday evening just as Michelle placed a casserole dish on his father's kitchen table.

"Hi, Korey." Tyler smiled at Korey while standing at the kitchen counter. "Michelle made Italian meatball sandwich casserole for everyone. You're going to love it."

Korey nodded. *"Danki."*

Dat crossed over to the counter and began scrubbing his hands. "It smells fantastic. I appreciate it, Michelle."

"We've been talking about getting together for another meal, and Michelle suggested we do it tonight." Crystal placed a pitcher of water on the table. "I think we're all ready now."

Dat kissed Crystal's cheek before he took his usual spot at the head of the table.

After Korey and Jayden scrubbed their hands, they sat beside each other, across from Tyler and Michelle. After bowing their heads in silent prayer, they all began filling their plates with casserole and a roll.

"So, Korey." Tyler grinned at him across the table. "I heard that you have a new girlfriend."

Korey stopped buttering his roll. "Who told you?"

Tyler and Michelle shared a grin.

"Jay did, of course," Tyler exclaimed. "Who else would tell me?"

Crystal's smile was warm. "I'm *froh* to hear it, Korey. Savannah is such a nice *maedel*. You two will make a fantastic couple."

"Danki." Korey finished buttering his roll before taking a bite.

"Were you and Savannah *freinden* in school?" his stepmother asked.

Korey shook his head and swallowed. "Not really. She was a year behind me, so we didn't talk much."

"Well, the Lord works in mysterious ways," Crystal said. "He chose the time for you two to come together, and his timing is always perfect."

Korey smiled. "I guess so." He worked to maintain eye contact with his stepmother and not behave the way he had before he'd left, which had been rude and dismissive.

When Korey looked over at his father, he found *Dat* watching him with a pleased expression. Korey regretted how he had treated his stepmother in the past, and it was time for him to grow up. He took another bite of the roll.

"I'm so glad you're dating again," Michelle said, smiling over at him.

Korey stopped chewing and studied Michelle. Their breakup wound up being mutual when they both agreed they felt as if they were only friends. Yet he still remembered the pain and betrayal he felt when he realized she had fallen in love with Tyler.

Michelle's smile faded and her cheeks flushed before she looked down at her plate.

"The casserole is *appeditlich*, Michelle," Jayden announced, and everyone agreed.

Crystal nodded. "I'm so glad you decided to share it with us, Michelle."

"Happy to!" She smiled. "You're all my family."

Korey took a bite of the casserole and gazed across the table, where Tyler whispered something to his wife, and Michelle smiled, gazing at her husband with love. The intimacy between them made Korey uncomfortable, but he held his breath, working to keep his temper in check.

Dat, Jayden, and Tyler began talking about work, and the discussion continued while they finished the casserole. Korey chimed in too, and he noticed that *Dat* smiled every time he participated. Perhaps Korey was making some headway in feeling a part of the family again, but he still struggled with forgiving his older brother.

After they drank coffee and ate pieces of Crystal's coffee cake, Korey carried his plate and mug to the counter.

"I'm going to go take care of the animals," Korey said before walking toward the back door.

"Do you need help?" Jayden called after him.

"No thanks." Korey slipped on his shoes and set his hat on his head before pushing open the back door. As he flipped on his flashlight, he breathed in the warm late-April evening and took in the stars sparkling in the sky above.

He was grateful for a moment alone with his thoughts. His shoes crunched on hay, and he inhaled the scent of animals as he walked into the barn.

"Kore, wait!"

Korey bit back a groan at the sound of his older brother's voice. He wasn't in the mood for him tonight. Couldn't Tyler take a hint?

"Please!"

Korey stopped and spun around as Tyler approached him. "What do you want, Ty?"

"I'm so glad you're dating. I want you to be *froh.*"

"Thanks." Korey paused for a moment. "Is that it?"

Tyler held up his hands as if surrendering. "I truly mean it. I want you to find happiness, just like . . ."

"Like you've found with Michelle," Korey deadpanned.

Tyler's shoulders drooped.

Korey turned and walked toward the horses.

"I'm trying, Kore. I really am."

Korey stopped and closed his eyes for a moment, working to

calm his breathing. Then he turned and faced his older brother. "I'm trying too, but I told you that I need time."

Tyler gave him a solemn nod.

Korey continued toward the horses, grateful that Tyler hadn't followed him. When he reached the horse stalls, he closed his eyes.

Lord, help me forgive my brother. Help us repair our relationship.

CHAPTER 11

Korey climbed Savannah's porch steps Sunday after-noon. The sun was bright, and the sky was dotted with fluffy white clouds. Birds sang in nearby trees, and a couple of chipmunks chased each other down the rock driveway. When Korey reached the top step, the back door opened, and Dean stepped out.

"Hey, Dean," Korey said as he shook his hand.

Dean grinned. "I guess you're here for Savannah, huh?"

"I am."

"I'm on my way to pick up Patience. I'll see you at the youth gathering."

"Bye." Korey waved as Dean continued down the porch steps on his way to the barn. When Korey knocked on the back door, Dorothy opened it.

"Hello, Korey. Come on in. Savannah will be right down."

Korey smiled. "Thank you."

"I can hear those *froh* birds singing outside. It sounds as if they're thanking God for this glorious day we have. It's *schee* out there, huh?" Dorothy asked.

"It is, and May will be here this week."

"I know."

Toby burst into the kitchen. "Korey!"

"Hey, Toby." Korey shook his hand.

"I approve of you dating *mei schweschder.*"

Korey chuckled. "I'm so relieved to hear that. Are you going to join us at the youth gathering today?"

"No." Toby's smile faded.

Korey gave him a hopeful expression. "Would you please go?"

Toby hesitated and bit his lower lip.

"If you go, you can be on my volleyball team. I'm sure that Jayden will play with us too." Then he leaned forward and lowered his voice. "I'll also try to get Savannah to play since I haven't seen her join in a game yet. All she does is sit on the grass and watch. I want to see if she actually knows how to hit a ball."

Toby's face lit up with a smile. "I'd like to see her try to play too. Hang on a minute, and I'll go change. Wait for me." Then he hurried out of the kitchen.

"Korey!" Dorothy exclaimed. "Savannah has been begging him to go, but he just wouldn't. How did you do that?"

"I honestly don't know. I figured I'd just ask him again since I've asked him before."

Savannah hurried into the kitchen. "I'm so sorry for making you wait. I'm really not that kind of *maedel.*"

"It's no problem at all." Korey couldn't take his eyes off of her. She looked lovely in a sky-blue dress that complemented her pretty eyes.

He mentally shook himself. *She's just your friend! She's not really your girlfriend!*

"I'm ready." She turned toward her aunt. "I'll be home at the regular time."

Korey held up his hand. "We can't leave yet."

"Why?"

"Because we have to wait for Toby." Korey smiled. "He's going to follow us."

Savannah's eyes widened. "He's coming with us?"

"*Ya*, he is. Korey convinced your *bruder* to go with you two to the youth gathering," Dorothy said.

Savannah took Korey's hand in hers, and heat skittered up his arm. "Korey, how did you do that?"

"I just asked, and I sort of made him a promise."

Her forehead crinkled as her eyes searched his. "What promise?"

"Well . . ." He leaned forward and lowered his voice. "I promised the three of us would play volleyball together. *Mei bruder* will be part of our team too."

She shook her head, and the ribbons from her prayer covering bounced off her slight shoulders. "Oh no. No, no, no. I'm not playing volleyball."

He threaded his fingers with hers, and his skin quivered at the feel of her touch. "Yes, you will."

"No, I won't." Her eyes danced as if she enjoyed their playful banter.

"You will, Savannah, because I promised your *bruder* you would."

"Fine." She sighed and released his hand before retrieving a cake pan from the counter. "Do you like chocolate *kuche*?"

"Who doesn't?" he teased, and she laughed.

Toby reappeared in the kitchen dressed in dark trousers, a blue shirt, and suspenders. "Are you ready to go?"

Savannah smiled and looked at Korey. "Yes, we are."

Korey's heart did a little dance. He couldn't wait to enjoy the afternoon with his new friends.

"How was your week?" Korey asked Savannah as they rode in his buggy toward the youth gathering with Toby following in his buggy.

She balanced her cake saver on her lap and looked over at him. "It was *gut* but very busy at the store. I hardly had time to get all of my chores done at home because I couldn't get away from the store long enough to do them. How about your week?"

"Exhausting but *gut*. We finished a big job over in Paradise. We worked on a bed and breakfast over there."

"Really?"

He nodded. "I love the work, so I like the big jobs."

"You like it more than the work you did in Ohio?"

"A lot more."

"Why?"

He considered his response. "I like being outside. Working in a factory felt so stuffy." He peeked over at her and found her watching him. "And I like working with *mei dat*."

"It's *gut* that you're back then." She paused for a moment. "Did you tell your family that we're . . . dating?"

"I did."

"And they believed you?"

"*Ya*, and they were very supportive."

"I'm glad to hear it." She smiled. "*Mei freinden* were shocked."

His brows drew together. "What do you mean by shocked?"

She explained that her friends had brought over dessert Monday night to ask for the details about her and Jerry, and she told them that Korey had brought her home and then asked her to be his girlfriend. "They started firing off questions about you."

"What did they ask?"

"They wanted to know the details about what happened between you and Michelle, and they wanted to know why I would date you."

He cringed. It sounded like he had earned himself a bad reputation when he and Michelle had broken up and then he'd fled to Ohio. "What did you tell them?"

"I told them that I didn't know the details about what happened between you and Michelle, and if I did, I wouldn't tell them because gossip is a sin."

He grinned, grateful for her outspokenness. But more than that, he appreciated how she defended him, and she wasn't even his real girlfriend. *"Danki."*

"It's the truth." She sat up taller. "They all seemed to accept that we're dating, but Macy is suspicious because I never talked to her about you before."

"How are you going to handle that?"

"I'm not worried about it. You and I are dating, and that's it. She'll have to accept it."

He smiled again and turned his attention toward the road. He'd never known a *maedel* who was so blunt and sure of herself. He found her endearing.

"Why are you smiling like that?"

"No reason." He gave her a sideways glance. "So, why are you so determined to sit out of the volleyball games? For as confident as you are, I assumed you'd play like a champ and win every game."

"You think I'm confident?"

He scoffed. "Very. So, tell me why you're afraid of volleyball."

"I'm not afraid." She ran her hands over the cake saver. "I'm just not very *gut*. Now you, on the other hand, look like an athlete out there."

He guffawed. "An athlete? Hardly!"

"You do. You leap and smack the ball as if you've done it professionally. It's really something to watch."

"You watch me play?" His heart did a little dance.

Her eyes widened, and then she looked out the side window as a truck rumbled by the buggy. "Well, I mean, sometimes I just happened to notice . . ." Her voice trailed off.

Was she embarrassed? How curious. "As your pretend boyfriend, I'm insisting that you play at least one game with Jay, Toby, and me."

"So my pretend boyfriend gets to boss me around?" Her blue eyes sparkled.

"*Ya*, and my pretend girlfriend gets to boss me too."

"Huh." Savannah rested her finger on her chin. "I could use this to my advantage."

Korey laughed. He was going to enjoy this fake relationship for sure.

Later that afternoon, Savannah sat on the grass near the volleyball games and worked to catch her breath. She had played three games of volleyball with Korey, Toby, and Jayden, and she had never laughed so much in her life.

She had been impressed with how well Korey and Jayden played, and she was grateful when Korey took the time to show her how to serve the ball. He was so patient with her, and she enjoyed the sound of his warm laugh.

But the best part had been witnessing her brother's delight while he played on their team. Toby was a good player, bumping the ball to his teammates and also spiking it over the net. He had also joked with Korey and Jayden, and he seemed to feel a part of their youth group and their community. Her heart lifted. Her brother was finally making friends, and she owed it all to Korey.

Savannah placed her elbow on her bent knee and watched Toby, Korey, and Jayden plan another game. Korey said something to Toby, and her brother laughed in response. Savannah smiled as a happy sigh escaped her lips.

Just then, Macy sank down beside her. "You looked like you were having fun playing volleyball earlier."

"I was." Savannah grinned at her best friend. "I didn't realize how much I liked the game."

Macy seemed to study her. Then she leaned forward and lowered her voice. "Tell me the truth, Savannah. Why Korey?"

"Look at how he is with Toby." She pointed toward where her brother played volleyball. "Why wouldn't I want to date someone who is nice to *mei bruder*? Korey has gone out of his way to talk to Toby ever since he got back from Ohio. He was the one who convinced him to come to youth group today. I've been trying for months, and he refused to come. Why wouldn't I want to spend time with someone like him?"

Macy gazed out toward the volleyball game and then back at Savannah. "But what about how he treated Michelle? Aren't you afraid he'll break your heart too?"

"What makes you think he was the one who did the heart breaking?"

"He told you that she broke up with him?"

"If Michelle isn't the one God had chosen for him, then

the relationship never would have worked. She married Tyler, didn't she?"

"You think you're the one God has chosen for Korey? And Korey's the one he's chosen for you?"

Savannah's heart rate jumped as she peered toward the volleyball game once again. While she watched, Korey rested his hands on Toby's shoulder and cheered. Could Korey be her future husband, the man with whom she would spend the rest of her life?

Then she did a mental head shake. *This relationship isn't real. Don't allow yourself to get attached to Korey.*

Besides, her focus was on Toby, not her own future. She needed to watch out for her brother instead of worrying about finding a husband.

"I didn't say that," Savannah finally told her best friend. "We're just enjoying getting to know each other. We haven't talked about the future. Have you and Keith discussed getting married?"

"No, we haven't, but that's beside the point. I just don't understand why you didn't tell me that you like Korey." Macy's pretty face darkened with a frown. "Did I do something to make you not trust me anymore?"

Guilt hit Savannah in the chest, hard and fast, stealing her words for a moment. "No, no, it's not that." She paused for a beat. "Honestly, this came out of the blue. He gave me a ride home, and we started talking and decided it would make sense if we dated. He's a really *gut freind* to Toby and me."

"I suppose that makes *gut* sense." When the stubborn line of her mouth tipped up into a smile, Savannah felt the knots in her stomach begin to unwind.

"How's Keith?"

Macy grinned. "He's great."

Savannah smiled as Macy shared stories about her time with Keith. She was grateful that her friend believed her and also forgave her. As much as she longed to tell her best friend the truth, Savannah couldn't bring herself to break her promise to Korey.

Savannah relaxed in the passenger seat beside Korey during their journey home later that evening. The stars in the dark sky above sparkled, and the air filling the buggy smelled like moist earth and animals.

Glancing in the mirror, she spotted Toby's horse and buggy following them, and she gave a happy sigh. It had been the perfect day, watching Toby play volleyball and laugh with Korey and their friends, eating supper together, and later singing hymns with their youth group until it was time to go home. She hadn't ever imagined she would convince Toby to join her at a youth gathering, and yet he had not only joined her, but he also had a wonderful time—because of Korey.

She smiled over at Korey, grateful for the glow of the lantern on the buggy floor that illuminated his face. "I had fun today."

"I did too." He gave a little laugh. "Your *bruder* is a hoot. Jayden enjoyed him too."

"*Danki* for being so nice to him."

"You can stop thanking me."

She didn't think she could ever stop thanking him.

"And I don't see why you were so opposed to playing volleyball," he said. "You're a *gut* player."

"Not really."

"You just need a little coaching."

She took in his profile, with his angular jaw and milk-chocolate-brown eyes, along with those broad shoulders, muscular arms, and trim waist. Korey was handsome—*really handsome*—and for a moment, he took her breath away.

"Does Toby still struggle with reading and math?"

"*Ya.*" She peered down at her apron to force herself to stop staring at him. "He believes he'll never amount to anything because of it. He constantly calls himself stupid and compares himself to Levi and Dean. It drives me crazy. I tell him all the time that we all have our gifts, and his are different than our cousins', but it doesn't make him less than they are."

Korey frowned. "I'm so sorry to hear that. I remember how cruel the other *kinner* were to him in school."

"Oh, they made me so angry I could taste it," Savannah groaned.

"I remember how you defended him. I always admired you for that."

"You did?" She stared at him. "Really?"

"Oh *ya*. I would have done the same for *mei bruders*, and I think they would have defended me too."

"I was always in trouble, though."

He snickered. "I'm sorry to laugh. I just admire how you always speak your mind."

She fought the blush that tried to rise in her cheeks.

"I'll try to think of a way to help Toby."

"I appreciate that. The other day I tried to tell him that he could find another job, but he said he would struggle to even complete an application. I understand what he's saying, but there has to be something he can do other than work in a store. I believe that we each have a calling, and if we find it, it will make us happy. If it's possible, we should enjoy our work."

She picked at a piece of lint on her apron. "But, I've decided that no matter what, I'm going to always be there for him. I'll support him emotionally and financially if he needs me to. That's why I don't have time to date. It's my job to take care of him since *Mamm* died delivering him and then *Dat* took off."

"I understand."

"But I have my pretend boyfriend."

He laughed, and she enjoyed the warm sound. "That's what pretend boyfriends are for." He winked at her, and she chuckled.

When they arrived at her aunt and uncle's house, Korey halted his horse by the porch. Then he turned toward her. "We're here."

"We are." She was surprised to feel disappointment thread through her. If only they could talk all night long. But he wasn't her real boyfriend.

Toby walked over to Korey's buggy as they climbed out. "I guess I'll see you next week," he told Korey.

"I look forward to it." Korey gave Toby a high five.

Toby grinned as he began unhitching his horse by the light of his Coleman lantern.

Korey turned toward Savannah. "May I escort you up the stairs?"

She nodded, and her heart gave a little bump.

They walked up to the back door with their flashlights guiding their way.

When they reached the porch, he held out his hand to her. "Have a *gut* week."

"You too." She shook his hand.

Savannah leaned on the porch railing as he jogged back down to his buggy, returned to the driver's seat, and guided the horse toward the road. She remained on the porch and inhaled the cool spring air and studied the stars while waiting for her brother to return from the barn after taking care of his horse and buggy.

Soon Toby's tall and lean silhouette, illuminated by his lantern, loped toward the porch, and he came over to stand by her.

"I like Korey," he said.

Savannah smiled. "I do too."

CHAPTER 12

"IT'S A *SCHEE* DAY!" TOBY ANNOUNCED AS SAVANNAH FLIPPED the Closed sign to Open the following morning.

Savannah looked up at her brother and grinned. "You're in an awfully *gut* mood."

"Why not? The sun is shining and the birds are singing. 'This is the day that the Lord has made.'"

"'Let us rejoice and be glad in it,'" she finished the Scripture verse.

Toby started toward the back of the store. "I'll be in the stockroom. Call me if you need me."

"Okay." Savannah gave a little laugh as she moved to the register, where her aunt was busy opening it for the day.

Aenti Dorothy looked up at her. "Your *bruder* is in a *gut* mood today."

"I know. I think it's because he had fun yesterday." She thought of Korey, and her smile widened. "I did too."

Aenti Dorothy gave Savannah's shoulder a rub. "That's *gut*, *mei liewe*. I'm always grateful when *mei kinner* are *froh*. That's what every *mamm* prays for her *kinner*."

Savannah's heart warmed for her aunt. She couldn't imagine her life without her precious aunt and uncle.

133

The bell above the door chimed, announcing the first customers of the day, a young *Englisher* couple, and Savannah turned and waved. "Good morning. Welcome to Blanks' Bulk Foods."

Later that morning, Savannah finished ringing up the last customer in line, and she slipped down the aisle to where her aunt straightened boxes of cereal. "Toby hasn't been out front all morning. Have you seen him?"

"*Ya*, he's been busy working on a project in the stockroom."

"A project?"

Aenti gave a knowing smile. "I'll watch the front. Go see for yourself what your *bruder* has been doing."

Curiosity niggled at Savannah as she weaved past the customers in the aisles and pushed open the door to the stockroom. She found her brother hammering boards into place, creating a tall shelving unit in the far corner.

"Toby!" she exclaimed when he stopped hammering. "That's fantastic!"

He spun toward her and grinned. "*Danki*. Last night I was thinking about how we have this empty corner, and I thought I could build shelves here to keep the cat and dog food until we have room in the store. That way we don't have to trip over the pallets. I asked *Onkel* Eddie what he thought, and he said it was a *gut* idea."

"It's a marvelous idea!"

Toby stood a little taller. "*Onkel* Eddie said I did a great job."

"You did." Savannah's heart took on wings at the pride in her younger brother's eyes. She couldn't remember the last time he'd ever looked so pleased with himself.

Then his forehead puckered. "Oh no. I didn't even think to ask you if you needed anything before I started on this project. I'm so sorry. Did you need my help?" He set the hammer on the shelf.

"No, no, no!" She held up her hand. "I just wanted to see what you were doing. Everything is fine out front."

"Okay." His expression relaxed.

She moved to the door. "You keep doing what you're doing. I'll call you if I need you."

He waved before picking up his hammer.

Savannah double-timed it to the front of the store, where her uncle ran the register and *Aenti* Dorothy arranged a display of sprinkles. "*Aenti*, have you seen the shelves Toby is building?"

"*Ya*, your *onkel* is delighted."

"I am too," Savannah said. "This is all because of Korey."

Aenti Dorothy angled her body toward Savannah. "What do you mean?"

"I've never seen Toby so *froh* and confident, and I owe it all to Korey."

"You think so?"

"Absolutely," Savannah said. "Korey convinced Toby that he's worthy of friendship, and he proved to Toby that he can be a part of the community." She leaned on the shelf beside her. "I want to do something nice for Korey."

"Like what?"

"I don't know . . ." Savannah tapped her chin.

"What if you brought him a special meal or dessert?"

Savannah frowned. "Would you let me take off early one day and have our driver take me to his *haus*?"

"Of course I would, Savannah." *Aenti* Dorothy touched her hand. "Korey is a special man. I'm so glad you found each other."

Savannah smiled, but deep down she wondered if Korey could ever think of her as more than a friend, and her heartbeat tripped over itself.

Then she reminded herself that she needed to focus on her brother, not her pretend relationship with Korey. All that mattered was that Toby was happy, and she would make sure he had what he needed, no matter what it would cost her.

Savannah balanced her casserole dish and cupcake carrier in her arms and knocked on Korey's back door Thursday afternoon.

Footfalls sounded from somewhere in the house, and then the door opened, revealing Crystal, Korey's stepmom, smiling in the doorway. With her red hair and pretty green eyes, Savannah had always thought Crystal was beautiful.

"Savannah!" Crystal reached out and took the cupcake carrier from on top of the casserole dish. "Let me help you with that."

"Danki."

"Come inside." Crystal held the door open with her free hand and beckoned Savannah to enter the house. "I was so excited when you called me on Monday and offered to bring a meal. I know Korey is going to be very surprised."

Savannah walked through the mudroom and into the kitchen. "I'm so grateful to be able to do something nice for him."

"Well, Duane and I are just thrilled that you and Korey are dating. We both had been praying fervently that God would lead him back home, and I'm certain that dating you will help him feel a part of the community again."

Savannah set the casserole dish on the counter and tried to

ignore the guilt that swarmed in her chest. She would hate for Korey's parents to find out that their relationship wasn't real, but she was grateful that they were happy to have Korey back in their lives. Savannah certainly was grateful to have Korey in her life as well.

"The casserole smells delicious. What did you make?" Crystal put the cupcake carrier on the table and then joined Savannah at the counter.

Savannah lifted the lid on the dish. "Hamburger pie casserole." Then she pointed to the table. "And chocolate cupcakes for dessert." She grimaced. "I hope he likes them."

"Are you kidding? He'll love them!"

"Oh *gut*. I wanted to do something special for him since he's been so kind to *mei bruder*. Korey has really made a difference in Toby's life."

Crystal looked curious. "Is that right?"

"*Ya*, Toby always had a hard time in school and also struggled socially." Savannah explained how Toby was bullied due to struggling with reading and math. "Many of the other *kinner* were cruel to him, and that affected his self-esteem."

"*Ach!* That is just *bedauerlich*. I'm so sorry to hear that."

"*Danki*. He doesn't feel like he's *gut* enough to do anything other than work in the store, and he constantly compares himself to our cousins who both work in construction. He also refused to go to youth group because he doesn't have any *freinden*. I've been begging him to go for a long time."

"Oh no." Crystal touched Savannah's shoulder. "I had no idea he was struggling so much."

"*Danki*, but Korey has truly changed *mei bruder*'s life. Korey started talking to Toby at our store one day. Then he struck up a conversation with him at church and started sitting with him during the service and lunch too." Savannah's smile was wide. "Korey convinced Toby to go to youth group with us on Sunday, and he had a blast. And Toby hasn't stopped smiling since then. He even built a new shelving unit in the stockroom."

Crystal beamed. "That is fantastic!"

"I agree. That's why I'm here. I wanted to thank Korey for making such a difference."

"I'm so *froh* to hear that, but honestly, I have always believed that all three of my stepsons have *gut* hearts like their *dat*."

Savannah pointed to the oven. "Is it okay if I turn on the oven so that we can warm up the casserole?"

Crystal chuckled. "Of course it is, Savannah. Please help yourself."

Savannah flipped on the oven and set it to the correct temperature.

"We have some time before we need to set the table." Crystal pointed to the table. "Would you like to have some tea and talk while we wait for the oven to preheat and the casserole to warm up?"

Savannah smiled. "I would like that very much."

Crystal filled the kettle and set it on the stove while Savannah gathered two mugs and tea bags. Once the kettle boiled, they sat together at the table.

"Do Duane and Jayden know that I'm bringing supper over tonight?" Savannah asked as she added milk to her cup of tea.

Crystal shook her head. "No, I was afraid they might spoil the surprise."

"This will be fun." Savannah lifted her cup of tea and took a sip.

"It's just so *gut* to have Korey back home again. Our family felt so incomplete without him. We all missed him, but Duane really took it hard when he left. I know he wants to keep his *sohns* close since he lost their *mamm*. Of course he expects them all to grow up and have lives of their own, but it's his prayer that they stay in our community."

Savannah nodded as she trailed her finger over her mug. "Korey hasn't told me much about why he left." She held up her hand. "I'm sorry, Crystal. I didn't mean to sound like I was prying into family business. I was just saying that we really haven't talked about it much."

"It's okay. Korey has had a tough few years. He had a difficult time when Duane and I started dating, and he was very upset when Duane married me. He feels that it was too soon after his *mamm* passed away." Crystal fiddled with her spoon.

"I understand how he feels, but Duane and I fell in love, and we felt God leading us to each other." She stirred milk and sugar into her mug. "Korey has struggled with accepting me, and I have told Duane to just let him be. I keep praying for God to soften Korey's heart toward me, and he seems to have matured since he's come back home. I think he did some growing up while he was in Ohio, and I'm grateful for that."

Savannah nodded slowly, pondering Crystal's words. She hoped Korey would open up to her soon and share his feelings about his father's remarriage and his relationship with Crystal, who seemed like such a kind and loving stepmother. "I remember when Korey's *mamm* passed away. It was a terrible time for them."

Crystal's expression became thoughtful. "I know that you've experienced loss too, and my heart goes out to you and Toby." She reached over and touched Savannah's hand. "I lost my parents as well. I was much older than you, but I know how much it hurts."

"*Danki*. I'm sorry for your loss as well."

They both sipped their tea, and the oven buzzed, indicating that it had finished preheating.

Savannah hopped up from her chair and placed the casserole into the oven before setting the timer. Then she returned to her seat. "So, Crystal, what do you normally like to make for supper?"

As Crystal began discussing recipes, Savannah smiled. She was going to enjoy her evening with Korey and his family.

Her heart gave a little kick as she imagined Korey's surprise when he got home. She couldn't wait to see him.

Later that evening, Korey hauled himself toward the back porch. He felt as if his horse had dragged him the length of his father's field after his long day of roofing.

It seemed that everything he touched today had gone wrong. He'd hammered his thumb at least three times, and a colorful bruise had already spread across it, spilling toward his palm. He had also managed to drop a box of nails from a roof down to the grass below and had spent precious time retrieving them.

He was grateful to finally be home and couldn't wait to kick off his boots and relax. He prayed the Lord would bless him with a better day tomorrow.

After removing his hat and boots in the mudroom, he stilled when he heard two female voices talking in the kitchen. He recognized one as his stepmother, and when he realized the second one was Savannah, his foul mood dissolved.

He moved to the doorway and leaned against it as Savannah swept around the kitchen, setting the table for five. She was effortlessly beautiful in a green dress and black apron. The delicious smell of beef, tomato soup, and cheese filled his senses.

When she turned toward him, she gasped, pressing her hand to her chest. "Korey! I didn't see you standing there. How was your day?"

"It's better now." Korey grinned, and he was almost certain her cheeks flushed. "What a nice surprise."

His father sidled up to him and peered over his shoulder. "What surprise? Oh, Savannah! *Wie geht's?*"

Savannah made a sweeping gesture toward the counter, where a large casserole dish sat. "I wanted to do something nice for Korey, so I brought over a casserole for supper and cupcakes for dessert." She turned toward his stepmother. "I called Crystal on Monday and asked if it would be okay."

"And I told her of course it was," Crystal added.

Savannah looked sheepish. "I hope you like hamburger pie casserole and chocolate cupcakes."

"Wow." Korey's heart swelled with admiration for this sweet *maedel*. "I-I don't know what to say."

Jayden walked into the kitchen from the family room, rubbing his hands together. "I say, let's eat!"

"I agree," *Dat* said, and everyone chuckled.

After washing his hands at the sink, Korey sat beside Savannah at the table. They bowed their heads in silent prayer before *Dat* pushed the casserole dish toward Korey.

"Since this is your special meal, you should take the first piece, Korey," *Dat* said.

Korey glanced at Savannah. "How about I serve your piece since you made this scrumptious casserole for us?"

"Okay." Savannah nodded.

Korey cut a piece and set it on her plate. Out of the corner of his eye, he spotted his stepmother giving him a warm smile. For a moment, he felt terrible for allowing his family to believe that he and Savannah were truly a couple, but at the same time, he was grateful to see the joy on his stepmother's face.

After cutting himself a piece, Korey pushed the dish toward Crystal.

Soon they were all eating the delicious casserole.

"This is fantastic," Korey told Savannah. "*Danki* for making it."

"I'm glad you like it. You never answered my question earlier, Korey. How was your day?" she asked.

Dat chuckled. "I believe we all had a better day than Korey did."

"What happened?" Crystal asked.

Jayden snickered. "This ought to be *gut*."

Korey explained the pitfalls that happened during his day, and everyone gasped.

"Oh no!" Savannah reached for his hand. "How's your poor thumb?"

Korey held out his hand to her, and she clucked her tongue as she ran her fingers gently over the bruise. His mouth dried, and he enjoyed the feeling of her warm skin caressing his. For a moment, his words were trapped in his throat. "It's fine," he managed to say. "Just a little bruised."

"I'm so sorry." Savannah returned to eating her casserole.

Korey met Jayden's gaze, and his younger brother grinned. *Oh no.* He would be teased later for sure!

"How are your *aenti* and *onkel*, Savannah?" *Dat* asked.

"Just fine," she said. "The store has been busy, and they like to stay busy."

Crystal picked up her glass of water. "How long have they owned the store?"

"I think they opened it about twenty-five years ago. *Onkel* Eddie took over the store when the couple who first owned it retired. He bought it from them."

"It's definitely a staple in our community," *Dat* said.

Savannah looked at Jayden. "How was your day?"

"Definitely better than Kore's," Jayden joked, and everyone laughed.

Korey glanced around the table, and he was struck by how Savannah seemed to fit in with his family. It was as if she belonged there as she laughed and joked with his father, stepmother, and brother.

Then he did a mental headshake. He was kidding himself to think that Savannah might be a part of his future. Their relationship wasn't real.

Besides, he wasn't interested in dating anytime soon after the way Michelle had hurt him. How could he possibly allow his heart to trust a *maedel* after the way Michelle initiated their breakup and then married his older brother?

After they all finished their casserole, Savannah served the chocolate cupcakes while Crystal brewed coffee.

Korey took a bite of the cupcake and swallowed. "How did you know chocolate was my favorite, Savannah?"

"I just guessed." She shrugged. "I'm glad I guessed correctly."

Korey bumped his shoulder against hers. "You certainly did. *Danki.*"

"You are spoiling us," Jayden said after swallowing a bite of his cupcake.

Dat lifted his mug of coffee. "I was thinking the same thing. You're welcome to bring us supper and dessert anytime."

"I agree. These cupcakes are so moist." Crystal smiled at Savannah. "You are a *gut* cook."

Savannah looked down at her mug of coffee as if embarrassed. "I'm so glad you like them." Then she looked up at Crystal. "Do you have a big family?"

"She only has one *bruder,* but she has quite a few *bruderskinner,*" Korey said. "Right, Crystal?"

His stepmother wiped her mouth with a paper napkin. "Oh *ya.*"

"Tell me about all of your nieces and nephews," Savannah said.

"Well, I have five nieces and three nephews," Crystal explained.

Savannah grinned. "I'm sure they are a lot of fun to be around."

"It's definitely chaotic at her *bruder's haus,*" Jayden agreed.

While they all finished their dessert, Savannah peppered Crystal with questions about her brother's children.

Once they were done eating, *Dat* and Jayden went out to take care of the animals while Crystal and Savannah handled the dishes, and Korey wiped up the table and swept the floor.

Crystal studied Korey after the dishes were done. "You didn't need to help us, Korey."

"I wanted to help." He returned the dustpan and broom to the utility room. "I have an ulterior motive."

"And what is that?" Crystal gave a little laugh.

He touched Savannah's hand. "I was hoping to sit on the porch with Savannah until she has to leave."

"I can sit with you as long as you'd like since I planned to ask you to take me home." Savannah's smile was coy.

He grinned. "Is that right?"

"You two go out there now," Crystal said. "I'll finish up the dishes."

Savannah pointed to the stack of dishes that needed to be put in the cabinet. "Oh no. I'll put all of these away first."

"Enjoy this lovely evening." Crystal winked at Korey. "Go on now before it gets too late."

Savannah set her dish towel on the counter. "May I use the restroom before we head outside?"

"Of course." Korey pointed to the doorway, and Savannah passed through. Once she was gone, he turned to Crystal. And he suddenly realized just how important Crystal was to their family. "Thank you."

"For what?"

He took a deep breath, recalling how rude he'd been to his stepmother since his father had started dating her nearly four years ago. He felt a prick of remorse as well as the need to tell her how much she meant to him and the rest of his family at that very moment.

"*Danki* for everything you do. For being part of our family." Korey's voice shook. "For taking care of all of us. For making *mei dat* so *froh*." He opened his mouth to apologize to her for his past rude and inexcusable behavior toward her, but his throat felt thick, and his words dissolved.

Her green eyes sparkled with tears. "You're...you're welcome."

The back door opened and clicked shut and then *Dat* and Jayden walked into the kitchen.

Dat divided a look between them as his mouth formed a hard line and a frown darkened his features. "Is everything okay in here?"

"*Ya.*" Crystal sniffed and took *Dat*'s hand in hers. "Everything is perfect."

Jayden looked suspicious, and Korey shook his head, trying to communicate to him that everything was okay.

When Savannah stepped into the kitchen, Korey threaded her fingers with his.

"We're going to visit on the porch for a while," Korey told his family.

Then he steered her out through the mudroom to the porch.

CHAPTER 13

THE SUN BEGAN TO SET, SENDING VIBRANT COLORS ACROSS THE sky as Korey sat beside Savannah on the porch swing. He gave the swing a gentle push, and they began rocking back and forth. The warm early-May air held the hint of honeysuckle. A lantern at their feet cast a happy yellow glow over the porch.

"It's such a *schee* night," Savannah said with a sigh. "You looked so surprised to see me when you got home."

He angled his body toward her. "I was very surprised and delighted to see you after a tough day." He checked the back door, making sure none of his family members were spying on them through the storm door. Then he lowered his voice. "It's always a nice treat to see my fake girlfriend."

She laughed, and he enjoyed her sweet lilt.

"You said you wanted to do something nice for me. What's the occasion?" Korey asked.

"I wanted to thank you for being so wonderful to Toby. He has been in such a *gut* mood at work all week. He even built a shelving unit for one of our empty corners in the stockroom. He did such a *gut* job, and for once he believed us when we told him that he has skill."

Korey considered her words. "He doesn't believe you when you tell him that he did a *gut* job?"

"No." She frowned. "He has the lowest self-esteem of anyone I know. He has no confidence in himself at all, and I blame all of the *kinner* who bullied him at school. It makes me so angry when I think about what they put him through."

Korey rested his arm on the back of the swing, stretching it out behind her shoulders. "So, he likes to build things?"

"That's right."

"Who taught him how?"

Savannah shrugged. "I think he taught himself. He always used to play with wood when he was little. It just came naturally to him. It's a gift."

"Dean works in construction, and Levi builds kitchen cabinets, right?"

Savannah nodded.

"Why doesn't Toby work with them?"

"He thinks he's not *gut* enough, and he says he would struggle with the math and measurements."

Korey shook his head. "But he could still try. I'm sure there's someone out there who would take him under his wing and let him work as an apprentice."

"It's not that simple. He would struggle with the job application too."

"You or I could help him with that." Korey scoffed. "There has to be a way he could do what he loves."

She took his hand in hers, and he felt a spark of heat burning up his arm. Then it occurred to him that he never recalled feeling such an attraction to any other woman before—even Michelle—and it baffled him.

But this relationship wasn't real. Savannah was his good friend and nothing more. He was just playing the part of her boyfriend. Perhaps he was imagining the attraction. But it felt as real as her warm touch against his skin.

"I can't tell you how much it means to me that you care about *mei bruder*. You have truly changed his life. *Danki*, Korey."

"That's what fake boyfriends are for, right?" He gave a little laugh, but her expression was serious and intense, making his pulse gallop. "Honestly, I'll do what I can to help him. If I hear of a job in construction that he can do, I'll let you know."

"*Danki*." Her lips tipped up in a smile. "How are things going here at home?"

Korey looked out toward his father's barn. "Better. At least with Crystal."

"What do you mean?"

"I had trouble accepting her when *mei dat* started dating her. I felt as if it was too soon after losing *mei mamm*, and I accused *mei dat* of trying to replace her with Crystal." He glided his fingers over the wooden armrest and kept his eyes focused on the barn to avoid facing Savannah's disapproval. "Being away for more than a year has given me time to think about it all, and I've realized how important Crystal is to my family and *mei dat*."

"Have you told her that?"

"*Ya*. I did earlier when you stepped out of the kitchen."

"Tonight?"

He nodded and faced her, surprised to see approval and not disgust on her face.

"Family is so important, Korey. Family is a gift from God."

"I know. Someone told me something similar in Ohio."

"What about Tyler? Have things gotten better with him too?"

Korey sat up straighter and turned toward his brother's house. "My issues with Tyler are much more complicated."

"But he's your *bruder*."

"I know. I remember what you said about how you couldn't imagine being estranged from Toby, but it's different between Ty and me. We've never really been close. I've always been closer to Jay."

"But wouldn't you like to be close to Tyler too?"

Korey let that idea settle over him, but then he shook it off. "That's not possible."

"Why not?"

"Because we've always been at odds."

Her blue eyes squinted and then recovered. "At odds? I don't understand what you mean."

"Ty and I have always been in competition. I think it's because we're so close in age. He's only fourteen months older than I am. He hid toys from me when we were *kinner* because he didn't want to share. As we got older, he was always trying to outdo me. He even convinced *Dat* to give him his own roofing crew before I could get one."

Savannah blinked, and he could feel disapproval coming off her in waves.

"You think I'm *gegisch*. Go ahead and say that I'm an immature *dummkopp*."

"No," she began slowly, "it's not that, but I think maybe you should look at your relationship with your *bruder* with a more mature perspective."

He snorted. "So, you *do* think I'm immature."

"Not exactly." She hesitated. "You need to have faith and ask God to help you heal your heart and warm it toward Tyler.

It sounds like there's a lot of hurt there, but God can get you through it."

He nodded. "All right."

"Oh, I meant to tell you that Toby's birthday is coming up soon, and as my fake boyfriend, you should probably come to his party."

"I'd love to."

"He'll be so *froh* that you're coming to celebrate with us. It's next Friday." She covered her mouth to shield a yawn.

"I have a feeling it's time to take you home."

She frowned. "So soon?"

"I feel the same way, but we both need to work tomorrow." He stood and flipped on his flashlight. "I'll get my horse and buggy ready, and we'll head out."

Disappointment weighed heavily on Savannah's shoulders as she and Korey climbed the back porch steps at her house later that evening. The ride home had gone by too quickly while they reminisced about their days in school and old friends. She longed for the evening to go on for a few more hours so they could continue their conversation, talking about anything and everything as the night wore on.

Joy swirled in her chest as she considered how attentive he'd been as they'd discussed her brother while they sat on his father's back porch. And her pulse picked up speed as she recalled how his hand had brushed her shoulders, sending sparks cascading down her back. She'd never felt so close to a man, so attracted to one.

But he'd made a point of mentioning twice tonight that their relationship wasn't real, calling her his "fake girlfriend" and referring to himself as her "fake boyfriend," which meant he only saw her as a friend. She was wasting her emotions on him, but at the same time, she couldn't ignore them. Her body's reaction to his nearness was intense and exciting but also a little frightening.

How would she cope when it was time to end this pretend relationship?

But then she reminded herself that she didn't need a real boyfriend since her goal was to make sure Toby was set for life. Her mother would want her to look out for Toby and not worry about finding a boyfriend and then a husband.

"I guess I'll see you Sunday," Korey said, yanking her from her thoughts.

She was almost certain she'd found disappointment in his gorgeous milk-chocolate-colored eyes. "*Ya.*"

He held out his hand to her, and for a moment, she felt the urge to set her serving dishes on the rocking chair and then pull him in for a hug and thank him for being such a good friend to Toby and her. But she balanced her serving dishes with one hand and shook his hand instead.

Korey held her hand for a moment longer, and she relished the feeling of their skin touching. "*Gut nacht.*"

"See you Sunday," she told him.

She waited on the porch as he jogged down the steps and climbed into the buggy. She waved as the flashing lights on the back of his buggy disappeared into the darkness. Then she slipped into the house and found her aunt sitting at the kitchen table, flipping through a cookbook.

"How did it go?" *Aenti* Dorothy asked.

Savannah placed the serving dishes on the counter and then

leaned back against it. "It went well. Korey and his family enjoyed supper, and then Korey and I sat on the porch and talked. It was really nice. *Danki* for letting me take the time off from work to make the meal and then go over to the Bontragers'."

"Everyone deserves a night off. You need to enjoy being young while you can, *mei liewe*. Someday you'll be married and have your own *haus* to care for."

Savannah shook her head as she placed the empty cupcake carrier and the casserole dish in the cabinet.

"Why are you shaking your head?"

Savannah twisted to face her aunt. "Because I doubt I'll be married anytime soon."

"I wouldn't say that." *Aenti* Dorothy gave her a knowing look. "I have a strong feeling about you and Korey. You may be married sooner than you think."

If only I could tell Aenti *the truth . . .*

"Well, we'd better get to bed. I'll see you in the morning." Savannah switched on her flashlight and made her way up the stairs. As she padded into her bedroom, she wondered what it would be like to truly be Korey's girlfriend. She imagined stealing kisses on the porch swing and dreaming of a future with him.

But the truth took hold of her as she changed into her nightgown. Surely Korey had better prospects than her. Plus, her focus was on her brother. She'd made a vow when her father left that she would always be there for Toby, and nothing would ever change that—not even Korey Bontrager.

<hr />

Korey's steps felt light as he traipsed from the barn to the house later that evening. He slowed his gait when he saw his father sitting on the porch, a lantern glowing at his feet. His stomach tightened as his mind clicked through all of the arguments Korey and Tyler had had on that porch and all of the times *Dat* had to break them up.

He closed his eyes for a moment and rubbed his hand over his mouth, preparing himself for an emotional discussion.

"*Dat*," Korey said, climbing the stairs. "Is something wrong?"

His father smiled. "Why would something be wrong?"

The muscles in Korey's shoulders relaxed.

"I just wanted to talk to you."

Korey leaned back on the railing. "What's up?"

"I wanted to tell you how delighted I am for you."

"Delighted? Why?"

"Because you found Savannah." *Dat's* smile widened. "You two seem so *froh* together and so in tune with each other. I'm grateful to see you so connected to the community already, and you haven't been here very long. It's my prayer to see all of *mei sohns* settled and in happy relationships. I'm grateful that the Lord is blessing you."

Korey nodded as shame bubbled up in his gut. He wanted to tell his father the truth about his relationship with Savannah, but he couldn't break his father's heart. Korey had hurt his father enough in the past. He would allow his father this illusion for a little while longer.

"And I wanted to discuss something else with you."

"What is it?" Korey set his lantern on the railing and then leaned back.

"I want to thank you for being so respectful and kind to Crystal. She told me what you said to her earlier. I've also been praying for you to accept Crystal as a part of our family, and I'm grateful that you're finally seeing how important she is to me and to the rest of us."

More remorse poured through Korey. "I know."

"When you left for Ohio, I feared I would never see you again." *Dat*'s words sounded throaty. "I thought that I'd lost you like I lost your *mamm.*"

Tears burned Korey's eyes. "*Dat*, I'm sorry, but I—"

"No, no." *Dat* interrupted him and held up his hand. "I'm not saying this to make you feel bad. Please let me finish."

Korey sniffed and wiped his eyes with the back of his hand.

"But I see now that God needed you to leave us in order to give you a new perspective on life and help you understand why I felt the need to marry Crystal."

Korey nodded, unable to speak.

"I'm proud of you, *sohn.*"

Those words were too much for Korey to bear. He fought to stop the lump swelling in his dry throat.

"I just hope you can find a way to forgive your *bruder* too. He loves you and has missed you since the day you left. When I'm gone, you'll only have your *bruders*. Since I'm an only child, I never knew the blessing of siblings. I hope someday you'll see what a gift both of your *bruders* are."

Korey sniffed.

"Well, it's late. That's enough of a lecture for one night." *Dat* stood and patted Korey's shoulder. "We have an early day tomorrow."

As Korey walked into the house, he worked to calm his emotions while he contemplated his father's words.

If only he could find a way to trust Tyler again, but he could only do it with the Lord's help.

God, help me to forgive my brother.

CHAPTER 14

"Toby," Korey began Sunday afternoon while they ate lunch after the church service, "what do you like to do for fun?"

Korey had sat between Toby and Jayden during the service, and he'd had a difficult time concentrating on the minister's holy words. Instead, his eyes kept defying him and focusing on how pretty Savannah looked in her yellow dress.

She'd seemed somehow even more attractive than usual. She had blessed him with a beautiful smile each time she'd caught him looking at her. He'd tried in vain to stop staring at her, but it had seemed impossible since she'd taken permanent residency in the back of his mind. No matter how hard he'd tried to convince himself that he didn't care for her, he felt his heart longing for her.

After the service, Korey, Jayden, and Toby worked together to help convert the benches into tables for lunch, and then they'd found a spot where they could sit beside each other. Dwight took a seat across from them.

"What do I do for fun?" Toby repeated Korey's question as if it were the most difficult subject. "I guess I like to build things."

Korey made a mental note to pick up some tools for Toby for his birthday. "What do you like to build?"

"Oh, I don't know. I've been working on fixing shelving units in the stockroom at *mei onkel*'s store. He hasn't had the time to work on them, and since I'm not comfortable running the register, I normally stock the shelves. I'm trying to organize the stockroom better to make it easier to find what we need. So I fixed a few shelves and then built a new unit for the pet supplies."

Korey smiled. "That's fantastic."

Toby shrugged.

"What else do you like to build?" Jayden asked.

Toby smothered a piece of bread with peanut butter spread. "I've built a few birdhouses and fixed *mei onkel*'s fence, but I'm not much of a carpenter. Working with wood is more of a hobby or a stress reliever. It helps calm me when I've had a bad day."

"That's great. We all need a *gut* hobby." Korey popped a pretzel into his mouth and then looked over at Dwight. "How's Kendra feeling?"

"Anxious. We're both excited. The baby will be here soon." Dwight's face lit with excitement.

"Kaffi?"

Korey peered over his shoulder to where Savannah held a carafe. *"Ya, danki."* He took in her beautiful smile, and his heart turned cartwheels in his chest. He couldn't wait to ride to the youth gathering with her.

She filled his cup and then Jayden's, Toby's, and Dwight's before moving down the table.

"I would imagine that you and Savannah will be married this fall," Dwight quipped before taking a sip of his coffee.

"What?" Korey asked, stunned.

Dwight chuckled. "Don't act so surprised. It's so obvious you two care about each other."

"Why do you think that?"

"Please, Korey." Dwight snorted. "The way you two look at each other makes it clear that you truly care. You'll be counting down the days until you're no longer a bachelor."

I doubt that. Korey turned toward his brother, desperate to change the subject. "How's work?"

Jayden looked confused for a moment, and then he picked up his coffee cup and understanding lit on his face. "*Gut.* We're starting a new job over in Gordonville tomorrow."

Korey felt his body relax as his brother talked on about work. He peeked down the table, where Savannah smiled and filled another man's cup.

While he admitted to himself that he cared for Savannah, he had convinced himself that they'd only ever be friends. He wasn't ready to trust another woman, no matter how important she'd become to him.

<hr />

Later that afternoon, Korey and Jayden stood by their horses and buggies while waiting to leave for the youth gathering. Korey looked toward the Flaud family's house, hoping to see Savannah exit through the back door after helping the women clean up after lunch.

"So, what's really going on between you and Savannah?" Jayden asked.

Korey placed his mirrored sunglasses onto his face, then turned toward his younger brother. "What do you mean?"

"Please, Kore. You looked like you were going to panic when Dwight mentioned that you and Savannah might get married this fall." Jayden seemed to study him. "Is everything all right between you two?"

"*Ya*. I'm just not ready to think about marriage." Korey shrugged, hoping to convince his younger brother that nothing was amiss.

Jayden nodded slowly, and Korey fought a grimace. His younger brother was so intuitive that it shocked him. Sometimes Korey found himself wondering if Jayden could read his thoughts.

"Do you love Savannah?" Jayden asked.

"Love her?" Korey scoffed. "We haven't been dating that long. Why would you ask me that?"

"You're just different with Savannah than you were with Michelle."

"Different how?"

"Happier. It's like you two are more suited for each other."

Dat's words from Thursday echoed through his mind: *"You two seem so* froh *together and so in tune with each other."*

"Well, you know, sometimes you just click with someone."

"Exactly." Jayden opened his mouth to say something and then stilled, smiling at something over Korey's shoulder.

"Is everything okay here?" Savannah appeared behind Korey and looked between the two brothers.

"*Ya*, of course." Korey pinned a pleasant expression on his face. "You ready to head out?"

She smiled. "*Ya*, I need to stop at *mei haus* to get my dessert and change my dress."

"Sounds *gut*." Korey turned to his brother. "We'll see you at the youth gathering."

Korey, Jayden, and Toby traded high fives after winning another volleyball game later that afternoon.

"We make a *gut* team," Jayden exclaimed.

Toby beamed.

"I agree." Korey looked toward the snack table, where Savannah, Macy, and Willa arranged bowls and trays of food. He had hoped to convince her to play volleyball, but she insisted she had to help her friends.

Jayden rubbed his hands together. "Let's play another game and show the other teams how it's done."

"I think I'll take a break." Toby's smile faded as he took a step away from them. "I'm going to check on *mei schweschder.*"

"Was iss letz?" Korey asked.

"Nothing, I just—"

"Toby!" Mahlon Stoltzfoos, a former schoolmate, sauntered over to them. "What a surprise to see you here."

When Toby's expression clouded with a glower, Korey took a step forward toward Mahlon. He remembered Mahlon teasing Toby and other students at their school. He would not allow Mahlon to harass Toby or anyone else at this youth gathering— not now, not ever.

"What do you want, Mahlon?" Korey snapped, pushing his sunglasses up on top of his head.

The other man shook his head. "Nothing. I was just wondering if Toby ever figured out what two plus two equals." He cackled.

"Leave him alone." Korey's hands balled into fists as fury churned through him.

Jayden glowered. "Get out of here if you're just going to be a bully."

"Where's your *schweschder,* Toby? Doesn't she normally fight your battles for you?" Mahlon glanced around. "I guess you need the Bontragers to defend you when she's not here, huh?" He gave a derisive snort.

Korey took another step forward. "I'm warning you to get out of here."

"Or what?" Mahlon's toned challenged him, but Korey was at least two inches taller than he was.

Jayden lifted his chin. "Or we'll escort you off of the Wengerds' farm. Won't we, Kore?"

"We certainly will."

Mahlon's smirk faded.

<hr>

Savannah's eyes lifted from arranging a couple of bowls of chips and froze when she spotted Mahlon Stoltzfoos sneering while talking to her brother, Korey, and Jayden.

Her heart began to thunder in her ears as she recalled all of the times he'd bullied her brother in school, reducing poor Toby to tears in front of the entire student body. She set her jaw as anger flooded her. She would not allow that man to hurt Toby ever again!

"Savannah?" Macy asked beside her. "Are you okay?"

"No, I'm not!" Savannah stalked toward where the group of men stood together.

By the time she reached them, Mahlon had scurried toward the far volleyball game, leaving Toby, Korey, and Jayden behind.

Korey spun to face Savannah as she approached. He took her arm and led her away from the group of people near them. "I handled him," he said once they were out of earshot of the young folks standing nearby. "Mahlon won't bother your *bruder* again."

"He won't?"

"No." Korey scowled. "Jayden and I warned him to either stay away from Toby or leave. Jayden told him that if he didn't leave Toby alone, we'd escort him off the farm." He grinned. "I would have enjoyed that very much. I remember how he tortured your *bruder* and others at school."

"Danki." Savannah breathed the word.

"There's no need to thank me. You know I think the world of Toby."

And I think the world of you, Korey.

"Kore!" Jayden called. "Let's play another game."

Toby grinned. "Let's show the other teams how it's done."

Korey waved to Jayden and Toby and then turned his milk-chocolate eyes back toward her. "You okay?"

"I'm just fine now." Savannah touched his arm and then glanced behind him and found their brothers along with other members of the youth group watching them. "Everyone is watching us, so hold my hand, okay?"

He quirked an eyebrow and then took her hand in his, and she relished the feeling of his warm skin against hers. "Is that better?"

"Ya, much better."

His dark eyebrows lifted. "Will you join us for a game of volleyball?"

"Later, okay?"

"Promise?"

She laughed at his eager expression. *"Ya,* I promise." She released his hand and immediately missed the comfort of his touch.

Her heart lifted as Korey positioned his sunglasses on his face and joined her brother and Jayden on a volleyball court before inviting Dean to join their team.

Savannah turned just as Macy, Jodie, Gail, and Willa gathered around her.

"You ran off so quickly. What happened?" Gail asked.

"Mahlon Stoltzfoos started picking on *mei bruder*, but Korey and Jayden handled it. They defended Toby and convinced Mahlon to leave."

Jodie clucked her tongue. *"Ach*. I remember how cruel Mahlon was to him in school."

"He's just mean." Gail frowned. "He was the ringleader of all of the bullies."

Willa nodded. "I'm so glad Korey defended him."

"I am too." Savannah pivoted toward the volleyball game just as Korey jumped up and hit the ball over the net. "He's a blessing."

"Would you help me finish setting up the snacks?" Willa asked.

Macy placed her hand on Savannah's arm, holding her back while Jodie and Gail followed Willa to the snack table.

"I'm sorry I doubted Korey," Macy said softy. "I see why you like him so much. He's a really great guy."

Savannah smiled. *"Ya*, he is."

Savannah settled in the passenger seat of Korey's buggy later that evening and blew out a delighted sigh. She had enjoyed her day with Toby, Korey, and her friends, playing volleyball, eating supper, and then singing hymns late into the night. She was so grateful that God had allowed her path to cross with Korey's. She couldn't remember a time when she'd been so happy.

She glanced in the side mirror and spotted Toby's horse and buggy following close behind them.

"What was that happy sigh for?" A smile played on Korey's lips.

"It was a *gut* day."

"*Ya*, I agree."

A comfortable silence filled the buggy, and she looked out the window, watching a few cars motor past them. She recalled her aunt's comments about marriage, and she turned back toward Korey.

"What do you see in your future?"

"My future?" His brow pinched.

She nodded. "*Ya*. Your future." She held her breath, awaiting his response.

"Well, I'd like my own *haus* and a stable job—possibly my own roofing crew with *mei dat*'s company."

She waited for him to elaborate, but he kept his eyes on the road ahead. "Do you want a family?"

He shrugged.

Her eyes widened as shock rocked her. "You don't want a family?"

"It's not that I don't want one . . ."

"What is it then? Why wouldn't you like a family? Isn't that what all Amish pray for?"

He gave her a sideways glance. "You're not shy, are you?"

"That's true. I'm not shy. Now, tell me why you don't want a family."

He licked his lips and kept his eyes trained on the road ahead. "I'm not sure if I can trust yet."

"What do you mean?"

He frowned. "Even though my breakup with Michelle was mutual, I'm not ready to face that heartache again anytime soon."

Savannah nodded slowly.

"I know you have an opinion about what I said. So, go ahead, Savannah. Tell me what you're thinking."

"I understand being afraid of heartache, but you can't let that fear hold you back from living the life God has given you. He has the perfect plan for all of us."

He smiled.

As Savannah took in his handsome profile, she found herself imagining a future with Korey. Somewhere deep in her heart, she wondered if she and Korey could make it work between them, but she was certain his fear of rejection would hold him back from truly giving her a chance.

Yet at the same time, she knew her obligation to her brother would also prevent her from planning a future with Korey.

And for some reason, that truth sent sadness wrapping around her heart like tendrils on a vine.

"*Danki* again for defending Toby," Savannah told Korey as they stood on her porch. "If you and Jayden hadn't been there, I think Toby would have gone home to get away from Mahlon."

"*Gern gschehne*, but Jay and I only did what was right. Bullies have no business in our community or at youth gatherings."

She touched his hand. "I look forward to seeing you Friday at Toby's party."

"I do too." He glanced behind them to where Toby led his horse to the barn. "I have a great idea for a gift for him."

"What is it?"

"You'll be just as surprised as he will be." He grinned and touched her cheek. "See you Friday, Savannah."

"*Gut nacht*," she called as he took the steps two at a time on his way back to his horse and buggy.

Happiness poured through her as she watched Korey drive away. Friday couldn't come fast enough.

CHAPTER 15

KOREY SAT BESIDE SAVANNAH AT HER AUNT'S KITCHEN TABLE
Friday night. He grinned as Dorothy put a chocolate cake in front
of Toby.

Dean and Patience sat together across from them along with
Levi and Iris. Eddie was at one end of the table while Toby had
squeezed in beside Savannah. The delicious aroma of coffee overtook the kitchen while the percolator hissed to life.

Dorothy stood behind Toby. "Okay. Let's sing!"

When they finished serenading Toby, they all clapped as
Dorothy cut the cake and began distributing pieces. Savannah
popped up from her chair and started filling mugs with coffee.

Korey joined her at the counter and began delivering the mugs
to her family members.

"*Danki*," she said, giving him a sweet smile as she handed him
two more mugs.

Once they all had coffee, they began to dig into the scrumptious cake.

"This *kuche* is perfect, *Aenti* Dorothy," Toby said.

Patience held up her fork. "*Ya*, it's so moist."

"It is," Iris agreed.

Dorothy smiled. *"Danki.* I just followed the directions on the box."

They all laughed.

Korey pushed back his chair and retrieved the gift he had left in the mudroom. Then he carried it over to Toby. "I have something for you." He handed Toby the box. "Happy Birthday, buddy."

Toby's face filled with surprise. *"Danki."* He opened the box and pulled out the tool set. Toby grinned as he moved his fingers over the hammer, screwdrivers, measuring tape, sockets, and wrenches. Then he met Korey's gaze. "This is perfect."

"I'm so glad you like it." Korey returned to his seat beside Savannah.

Eddie wiped his graying dark-brown beard with a paper napkin. "That's a really nice tool set."

"I might have to borrow it," Dean said.

Toby shook his head and chuckled. "No one is borrowing this. It's mine."

"I don't blame you," Levi chimed in. "I would keep that locked in my room when you're not using it."

"We share a room, so I'll find it," Dean teased.

Everyone laughed.

Savannah rested her hand on Korey's and leaned in so close that he could breathe in the scent of her flowery shampoo, which made his senses spin with delight. "That is the most thoughtful gift. You are truly a wonderful and thoughtful *freind."*

"I told you I had the perfect gift," he whispered before giving her hand a gentle squeeze.

Later, after finishing their cake and coffee, the women cleaned up the kitchen before Dean left to take Patience home, and Levi and Iris headed out for the night.

Korey lingered in the doorway to the mudroom, not ready to say good night to Savannah. "Do you want me to leave?" he asked after her aunt and uncle had retired to the family room and Toby took his gifts upstairs.

"No." Her cheeks glowed bright pink, and she looked adorable. "Do you want to go?"

"Of course not. How about we visit on the porch for a while?"

"Perfect."

They sat together on the glider, and the mid-May evening was warm.

"Pretty soon the lightning bugs and the cicadas will be back, and the summer heat will be here," he said as he pushed the glider into motion. "*Danki* for inviting me tonight. I had a lot of fun with your family."

She nodded, but she seemed to be deep in thought as she stared out toward her aunt and uncle's store.

"You okay?"

"*Ya.*" She examined her hands resting on her black apron.

Korey stopped the glider and turned toward her as worry moved through him. "Savannah, please talk to me."

When she met his gaze, her blue eyes glittered in the light of the lantern at their feet. His stomach tied itself into a worried knot.

"Whenever it's Toby's birthday or mine, I can't help but think about what my parents are missing. They'll never get to see him turn twenty." Her voice was soft, reminding him of a child. "It makes me *bedauerlich*."

He took her hand in his. "I'm so sorry. I can't even imagine how

169

much you miss them both." He paused. "What do you remember about them?"

"I remember a lot." She sniffed and looked out toward the store once again. "*Mei mamm* was so *schee*. She had light-brown hair and gorgeous blue eyes."

"Eyes like yours," he whispered.

Her gaze snapped to his. She blinked and then continued. "She had the most beautiful voice. She loved to read to me, and she loved to laugh." Her smile was hesitant. "She used to tickle me to make me laugh too. I remember laughing until my belly ached, and then she would tickle me some more. It was our special game."

"What a sweet memory, Savannah." He gave her hand a gentle squeeze.

"And she adored *mei dat*. I would walk into the kitchen and find them stealing kisses or giving each other a quick hug. They used to tease each other and laugh. I don't remember ever hearing them argue or get upset with each other. They were *froh* together from what I remember."

"That's a wonderful memory."

"I miss her so much that my heart hurts, Korey." Her voice was so thin it sounded as if it might break. "There's so much I want to tell her and ask her." When she started to sob, she covered her face with her hands. "I'm sorry." Her voice was a ragged whisper. "I shouldn't cry in front of you."

"Hey. It's okay." Korey looped his arm around her shoulder and pulled her to him. She curled against him as if she were a fragile kitten, and he cherished the feeling of having her in his arms. It felt so good—as if she belonged there.

Savannah pulled a tissue from her pocket and wiped her eyes

and nose, and then she leaned against him, resting her head on his chest. "Sometimes it feels like yesterday when I lost her."

He nodded. He knew that feeling all too well.

"I miss *mei dat* too. When he first left, I was only five. I used to sit on the porch every day, waiting for him to come back for me and Toby. I was convinced he had just gone on a trip and was going to come back soon and take us home. I wanted him to come back so I could tell him that I needed his help taking care of the *boppli*. I felt like Toby was *mei boppli* since *mei mamm* was gone. I was so lost and confused."

Korey clucked his tongue and shook his head. "I'm sorry, Savannah."

He'd never understand why her father left her. Her pain and grief nearly broke his heart.

"*Mei aenti* would let me sit out here. When I was older, I asked her why she didn't tell me he wasn't coming back, and she said she couldn't stand the thought of breaking my heart." She brushed her hands down her apron, smoothing it out. "I finally realized that he wasn't coming back, and for a long time I thought I'd done something to make him leave. I believed that maybe if I'd been more helpful with Toby or if I'd done a better job of picking up my toys, maybe he would have stayed."

"Savannah . . . you were five years old. Tell me you didn't believe that it was your fault he left."

"I did." She nodded. "I told *mei aenti*, and she insisted that I hadn't done anything wrong at all. She said that *mei dat* just couldn't handle losing *mei mamm* and raising two *kinner* alone." Her lip began to tremble. "But Toby and I lost her too. So why couldn't we all grieve together? Isn't that what families are supposed to do?" More tears poured down her cheeks.

Korey reached over and wiped her tears away with the tip of his finger. Heat zipped up his hand to his arm at the contact, and his heart turned over in his chest. If only he could take away her pain. "I'm so sorry he hurt you, Savannah."

"I still believe he'll come back one day."

"And what would you say to him if he did?"

She sat up straighter in the glider and squared her shoulders as if confidence had just exploded through her. "I would demand that he explain to me why he left. I'd want to know where he's been and why he thought it was okay to leave his *kinner*."

Then her courage seemed to fizzle out of her, and she slouched back on the glider. "And I'd want to know why Toby and I weren't *gut* enough for him. What did we do wrong to send him away from us?"

Savannah leaned forward, and he rubbed her back, drawing invisible circles on the soft fabric of her dress.

"You didn't do anything wrong, Savannah, and you didn't send him away. Your *dat* is the one who was wrong to leave you. He abandoned you and Toby. Stop thinking like the five-year-old you once were, okay? Stop punishing yourself for your *daed*'s mistakes."

Savannah peered up at him over her shoulder, and their eyes locked. The air around them felt electrified as if a summer storm was on the verge of erupting in the sky.

He reached up and touched her face, and the urge to kiss her overwhelmed him. He looked down at her lips as he heard her suck in a breath. He leaned down toward her and then froze.

What was he doing? They weren't even really dating!

Savannah blinked and then shifted away from his touch. "What about your *mamm*?"

Korey tensed and a muscle jumped in his jaw.

"I'm sorry. I shouldn't have brought that up. That was thoughtless of me."

He swallowed. "It's okay." His voice was rough. "She was *schee*. She had dark-brown hair and hazel eyes. *Mei bruders* got her eyes, and I wound up with *dat's*."

He shifted on the glider and looked out toward the store to avoid her sympathetic stare. "She was quiet, almost shy around other people sometimes, but she loved to laugh like your *mamm*. She rarely raised her voice. She was kind and thoughtful and loving. She gave the best hugs. And when she spoke, people listened to her since she always had something profound to say."

"She was *krank*, right? Cancer?" Savannah's words were quiet again, almost reverent.

"*Ya*," he managed to say, rubbing his temple. "It was torture watching her suffer. And then when we lost her . . ." His voice trailed off, and he sniffed. "When *mei dat* admitted that he cared for Crystal, it really hurt. Like I told you, I was afraid he was trying to replace *Mamm*. I told him so, and he insisted he wasn't. At first I didn't believe him. And then he said he was going to get married."

"That had to be difficult."

Korey released a deep breath he hadn't realized he'd been holding. "It hurt so much. I cried at their wedding." He shook his head, humiliated that he admitted that secret aloud. But it seemed natural to bare his soul to Savannah, and he'd never felt like that with anyone else—not even Jayden.

"I'm so sorry," she told him softly. "If it's any consolation, I can tell that Crystal cares about you all."

He frowned as embarrassment and culpability nipped at him. "I know. I've been a real jerk to her, but I'm trying to do better."

Then he looked down at her sweet and supportive expression. "It helps to talk about it with you."

"I'll listen anytime, Korey." Reaching up, she cupped her hand to his cheek.

He leaned into her touch and closed his eyes, relishing both her closeness and the encouragement in her warm skin.

When he heard a horse and buggy moving up the rock driveway, Korey angled his body away from her, and her hand fell to her side.

Savannah peered toward where the horse and buggy moved toward the barn. "I guess Dean is back already. It seems like he just left."

"I should probably get going." Korey stood. "*Danki* again for inviting me tonight."

Savannah shook his hand. "*Gut nacht*, Korey."

"I'll see you soon." Korey pulled his flashlight from his pocket and hurried toward the barn to gather his horse and buggy.

Korey's thoughts raced as he guided his horse toward home. He'd never felt as close to a woman as he did with Savannah. He'd never felt so comfortable sharing his deepest feelings and his most precious memories with anyone else, and he found it confusing, mind-boggling.

The only woman he'd ever dated was Michelle, and he had never felt compelled to tell her his deepest feelings or express his sorrows about losing his mother, even though Michelle had been a lifelong friend and had grown up knowing his mother since their mothers were close childhood friends.

With Savannah, however, Korey not only felt led to tell her his secrets, but he longed to tell her *everything*. If only the night had been younger, they could have talked longer, and he would have spilled more of his secrets.

Korey halted the horse at a red light and contemplated his time spent on the glider with Savannah. He had enjoyed holding her close and rubbing her back. And more than once he'd longed to kiss her until she was breathless.

He closed his eyes as the truth hit him hard and fast—he was falling in love with Savannah. It was a feeling he'd never experienced before. But here he was falling in love with his *pretend* girlfriend—the young woman who wanted to call him her boyfriend to keep her friends from nagging her about enjoying remaining single.

When a car horn tooted behind him, Korey guided the horse through the intersection while pondering his predicament. Savannah Zook had carved out a piece of his heart, and now he had no idea how to handle it. She had made it clear that she only wanted to be friends, and Korey wasn't ready for a serious relationship. But there Savannah was, rooted deep in his heart and his mind.

All he could do was turn to God for the answers.

"Lord," he whispered, "please guide my confused heart."

After saying good night to her aunt and uncle, Savannah knocked on Toby's door.

"Come in," Toby called.

Savannah leaned on the doorframe. "Did you have a nice birthday?"

"*Ya.*" Her younger brother pointed to the tool set sitting on his desk. "I can't wait to use my new tools."

"That was your favorite gift, huh?"

"Oh *ya.*" Toby grinned. "Did you and Korey have a *gut* talk on the porch?"

She dispelled a horrified gasp. "Were you spying on us?"

"No." He chuckled and pointed toward his window. "I can't see the porch from here, but I saw him leave. I had a feeling he would stay and visit with you. He really likes you."

"You think so?"

Toby rolled his eyes. "Please. The way he looks at you makes it so obvious, Vannah. You two are smitten with each other."

Smitten. Her heart danced at the sound of the word. "Well, *gut nacht.*" She backed out of his doorway.

"See you tomorrow," he called after her.

Savannah entered her room and flopped down on her bed while she contemplated Korey. She relished their time together on the porch and longed to spend more time with him. She'd been surprised by how easily she opened her heart to him and shared her most private thoughts and memories of her parents. She felt comfortable with him and safe, especially when he held her close.

She sighed. She cared for him—deeply. She bit her lower lip and recalled how she'd almost been certain that he was going to kiss her. She hugged her arms to middle as she recalled how his eyes had lingered on her lips. A sudden wave of dizziness passed over her at the thought of kissing him. As she had longed for it and had even imagined how his lips might have felt and tasted, something warm and fuzzy fluttered in her stomach.

But Korey was her friend—and suddenly her *best* friend. She felt closer to him than she'd ever felt even to Macy.

Savannah groaned and covered her face with her hands. She had to quash her silly fantasies about Korey Bontrager. He would never be more than just a friend, and she had to find a way to accept that even though her heart craved so much more.

But she didn't need a boyfriend! She had to keep her goal in focus, and that was taking care of Toby. She couldn't allow Korey to take her attention when Toby clearly needed her. Her brother had to come first, no matter the cost.

CHAPTER 16

KOREY CLIMBED DOWN THE LADDER FROM THE ROOF OF THE hotel in Bird-in-Hand on a Thursday morning two weeks later. He lifted his sunglasses and wiped his forearm over his sweaty brow, then poured a cup of water from the large water cooler they kept on a picnic table. He was grateful for the beautiful blue sky, but the sun was hot beating down on him while he hammered shingles onto the new roof.

After tossing the cup into the nearby trash can, Korey picked up a box of nails and started toward the ladder again.

"Korey," *Dat* called as he came around the corner of the building. "You're just the man I wanted to see. Could we talk for a moment?"

Uh-oh. Korey set the box of nails and hammer down on a toolbox. He couldn't imagine what he'd done wrong, but *Dat's* serious expression made him anxious. "Sure, *Dat*. What's up?"

"I've been doing a lot of thinking, Korey, and I have been so impressed by how mature you've been with Crystal."

"*Danki.* I appreciate it, but you've mentioned that already."

"There's more. I've noticed how much you've grown since you came home, and I'm proud of you. You're doing such a great job on this crew, and you've become a leader. The other guys come to you with questions, and you always patiently help them. You're also professional with the customers. You keep your emotions in check, even when the customers aren't *froh*."

Korey snorted. "You're talking about that apartment manager who thought that job should have taken one day instead of three."

"Exactly." *Dat* held up a finger. "I was impressed by how you patiently explained how long it takes to reroof an enormous apartment complex. You never lost your cool, even when the manager started to get belligerent."

Korey shook his head. "Some people."

"That's very true. You meet all kinds of people when you work with the public like we do." *Dat* smiled. "You've come a long way from the time when you and your *bruder* would argue on the job about every little thing. You've matured quite a bit, and that's why I want to ask you a question." He clasped his hands together. "Would you consider running your own crew?"

Korey blinked. "Are you serious?"

"*Ya*, very serious. You've shown me that you're ready, and I know that you have the professionalism and maturity to do it."

"*Dat*, I'd love to! I was just telling Savannah that running my own crew is one of my goals."

"I'm so relieved to hear it, because I want you to keep working for me. I trust you and I believe in you."

Pride and happiness swelled in Korey's chest. "*Danki, Dat*." Then a checklist began clicking off in his mind. "I'll have to get a cell phone to use for the business, and I'll have to find a driver to take the equipment. Then I need to find a crew." An idea filled his mind, and a smile overtook his lips. "I know someone I want to hire first."

"Who?"

"Toby Zook. I think he'd excel at it." He explained how Toby struggled with math and reading but loved to work with wood. He told his father about the shelving units that Toby had built at work and how he purchased a tool set for him for his birthday.

"I think working on a roofing crew would not only help his self-esteem but also make him happy. Savannah is worried that Toby will never be happy, and I want to help them."

Dat patted Korey's shoulder. "Korey, you never cease to amaze me. I'm so proud of you for thinking of someone other than yourself. You have such a big heart. Your mother would be so proud of you too."

"*Danki, Dat.*" Korey smiled as tears filled his eyes.

"You just need to check with Eddie and Dorothy to make sure they will allow him to work somewhere else. But if Toby is unhappy, I have a feeling they will appreciate your offer."

"I will. And I'll find a driver and a couple of other guys to work with me." Korey rubbed his hands together. He couldn't wait to start running his own crew.

The following morning, Korey pushed open the door at Blanks' Bulk Foods, and the bell above the door chimed, announcing his arrival. He scanned the store and spotted customers rambling around the aisles, filling their shopping carts with groceries.

He was disappointed when he didn't see Savannah but instead found her aunt running the cash register.

"*Gude mariye,*" Dorothy said as he approached the counter. "Savannah is in the *haus* doing a little cleaning. You're more than welcome to go see her."

"*Danki.* I was hoping to talk to Toby first."

Dorothy pointed toward the back of the store. "He's in the stockroom."

Korey nodded and then weaved through the aisles past the customers, waving to Eddie while he stocked a shelf of coffee.

When he reached the stockroom, Korey pushed open the door and found Toby breaking down boxes and stacking them in the corner.

Toby's expression brightened. "Korey! *Wie geht's?*" He shook Korey's hand. "Savannah's doing chores in the *haus.*"

"Your *aenti* told me. I wanted to talk to you before I went to see her."

"Oh." Toby's brow knitted. "Why?"

Korey leaned against a nearby shelf containing cleaning supplies. "I have a question for you. If you could pick any job, what would it be?"

"I already told you that I like to work with wood." He pointed to a large shelving unit in the corner of the room. "I built that." Then he pointed across the room. "And I fixed that one as well as the one over there."

Korey ran his fingers over the shelving unit Toby had built. "You do *gut* work."

"You're just being nice."

Korey spun to face Toby's frown. "I'm not just being nice. I'm telling the truth." He paused. "*Mei dat* has given me permission to run my own roofing crew, which is something I have always wanted to do. Would you consider working as a roofer on my crew?"

Toby stilled and stared at Korey, his blue eyes wide. "I-I . . ." He stopped and then scowled. "I can't fill out an application without help."

"That right there is your application." Korey pointed to the shelving unit. "You can use a hammer, which means you can do that job."

Toby lifted an eyebrow. "Are you teasing me?"

"No." Korey shook his head. "I would never tease you, Toby. You should know me better than that by now."

"You really mean it, Korey?" Toby continued to look suspicious.

"*Ya*, I mean it. When *mei dat* asked me yesterday if I wanted to run my own roofing crew, you were the first person I wanted to ask to join me. Savannah had told me that you didn't really like your job here, and then you shared that you enjoyed working with wood. I'm certain that you'll do a fantastic job as a roofer if you give yourself a chance. So, what do you say?"

A smile broke out on Toby's face. "I'd love to work for you."

"Great! We just need to ask your *onkel* if it's okay."

"Let's go," Toby said, heading toward the doorway that led out to the store.

Korey and Toby found Eddie stocking shelves with boxes of assorted teas.

"*Onkel* Eddie," Toby began, "Korey has asked if I'd like to work on his roofing crew."

Eddie set another box of tea on the shelf and then faced them. "Is that what you'd like to do?"

Toby nodded. "*Ya*, I would. I'm grateful for this job, but I've always wanted to work in construction." He swung his gaze to Korey. "I'm so thankful that Korey is willing to give me a chance." Then he turned his attention back to his uncle. "Would it be okay if I took the job?"

"Of course it would be. Dorothy and I have always agreed

that we'll support our *kinner* in whatever they feel they are called to do. If that's what your heart desires, then we both are *froh* for you, *sohn*."

Toby grinned as he shook Korey's hand. "I can't wait to work for you."

"I'm so glad. I'll let you know when I have everything ready to start my crew."

Savannah stepped out onto the back porch and did a double take when she spotted Korey standing in the driveway talking to Toby. Her heartbeat notched up as she descended the stairs and rushed over to them.

"I'll keep you posted. Have a *gut* day," Korey told Toby as he shook his hand.

"You too." Toby grinned at Savannah. "Korey just offered me a job, and I accepted it."

Confused, Savannah looked at each of them. "What job?"

"Could we talk for a minute before I have *mei dat*'s driver take me back to work?" Korey pointed to where a pickup truck sat in the driveway waiting for him.

"*Ya*, of course."

Toby said goodbye to Korey and then reentered the store through the back door.

"What's going on?" Savannah asked Korey as he took her arm and steered her toward the barn, away from the nosy customers standing in the parking lot, watching them.

A smile overtook Korey's handsome face. "One of my goals for my future came true yesterday. *Mei dat* asked if I wanted to run my own crew. He *asked* me, Savannah. I didn't even have to beg for it. He told me that he's proud of me, trusts me, and wants me to keep working for him." The joy on his face was palpable.

"Korey, that's wonderful. I'm proud of you too."

"*Danki.* I'm going to have to put a crew together, and the first person I thought of was Toby. So, I came here today and asked him to work for me." His smile dimmed. "I guess I should have asked you first. Are you okay with it?"

"Are you kidding me? I'm thrilled!" Then without thinking, she launched herself into his arms, breathing in his familiar scent—soap mixed with sandalwood and something that was uniquely Korey.

He stilled, and then he wrapped his arms around her, holding her tight.

When Savannah realized what she'd done, she stepped back, and he released her. "I'm so sorry. I didn't mean to be so forward." She was certain her cheeks might spontaneously combust.

"It's okay." He touched her hand. "I'm so glad you approve."

"Korey, you're a blessing to Toby and to me. I'm so honored that you want to give him a chance to work for you."

He smiled. "I'm just grateful that I could help Toby in some way. When you said that he was miserable in the store, I told you that I was determined to help him find a job he would like." Then he gave a little laugh. "And now I'll pray that he likes the job and likes working for me."

"He will, Korey. I know in my heart that he will."

"*Gut.*" Korey glanced over at the waiting pickup truck. "I'd better get to work."

"Have a *gut* day," she told him before he made for the truck.

As she watched the truck drive away, Savannah sent a silent prayer up to God:

Thank you, Lord, for bringing Korey into my life and Toby's life.

Korey's pulse ratcheted up speed as he stood at the worksite—*his* worksite—on Monday, two weeks later. His goal had finally come to life. He now had his own crew, and they were ready to reroof a small medical office in Smoketown. And Korey was in charge. He was so excited that he thought he might burst.

"So." Toby came to stand beside Korey and cleared his throat. "I . . . um . . . I'm not sure what I'm supposed to do." He rubbed the back of his neck as he frowned. "You know, I think I should just go back to the store. You really should have hired someone else."

Korey shook his head as he took in the fear and worry on his friend's face. "That's not true. I hired you because I wanted you to work for me, and I know you can do the job."

"I don't know about that, Korey. Gary and Herschel have experience and will do a much better job than I will." Toby pointed toward the pickup truck, where the other two crew members, young Amish men from neighboring communities, unloaded the tools and supplies. "You don't even have to pay me for today. Just have your driver take me back to the store, and I'll pay your driver for his time and mileage."

Korey rested his hands on his waist while considering his words. "Toby, do you remember the first time you built a birdhouse?"

"*Ya*, vaguely. Why?" Toby's eyes crinkled around the edges.

"Were you *naerfich*?"

Toby turned his attention to the toes of his work boots and then met Korey's gaze and nodded. "A little."

"Who taught you how to build birdhouses?"

Toby looked incredulous. "No one did."

"Really?" Korey was impressed. "Then how did you learn how to build them?"

"I took one apart and then put it back together. What's your point, Korey?"

"My point is that you can do anything you set your mind to." Korey nodded toward the roof of the medical office. "If you want to fix this roof, then you can. All you need to do is decide that you're capable of the work."

Toby's expression softened. "You really think so?"

"*Ya*, Toby, I do, which is why you were the first person I wanted to join my crew. If I hired people who couldn't do the job, it would be bad for *mei dat*'s business."

Toby studied Korey again. "You sound like *mei schweschder*."

"I'm going to take that as a compliment." Korey chuckled. "But what exactly do you mean?"

"Savannah always tells me that I can do anything I set my mind to."

"She's right." Korey patted Toby's shoulder. "Now I want you to start believing that."

"Korey!" Herschel hollered from the truck. "Are we ready to get started?"

Korey nodded at him. "*Ya.*" Then he turned his attention back to Toby. "I promised this customer that we'd finish this job by Tuesday evening, so we'd better get going. You ready?"

"*Ya*, I am." Toby smiled. "*Danki*, Korey."

"*Gern gschehne.* Now, let's get to work."

"How do you like running your own crew so far, Korey?" *Dat* asked while they ate breakfast the following Sunday morning.

Since it was an off-Sunday without a service, Korey and Jayden planned to eat breakfast and then meet their friends for the youth gathering.

"It's been *gut*." Korey held his cup of coffee. "It's a lot of responsibility, but I love it."

Jayden added syrup to his waffles. "How's your crew doing?"

"I'm so proud of Toby. He's the hardest worker of the three of them."

"Really?" Crystal asked.

Korey nodded as he picked up a piece of bacon. "He works circles around Gary and Herschel, and he's meticulous."

"You had *gut* intuition about him." *Dat* pointed his fork at Korey. "You were right to hire him."

"*Danki*. He was really nervous for the first couple of days, but he hit his stride quickly." Korey smiled as he considered the last week. Not only was Toby happy, but Savannah was also delighted that her brother had found a job he loved. When Korey visited her at the store during lunch on Thursday, it seemed she couldn't stop thanking him for hiring Toby.

Korey was grateful that God had given him the opportunity to help them both.

Crystal took a bite of bacon and then scowled. "Does this bacon taste okay to you?" she asked, peering around the table.

Korey nodded, as did his father and brother.

"It tastes fine to me, *mei liewe*," *Dat* said.

Crystal shook her head. "Huh. I guess it must just be me this morning." She pushed the bacon away from her waffles. "It just doesn't appeal to me for some reason."

The back door opened and clicked shut before Michelle and Tyler stepped into the kitchen.

"Gude mariye!" Crystal announced as she popped up from her chair. "Join us for breakfast. I have plenty of waffles and bacon."

Michelle ambled slowly to the table, holding her abdomen. Her fingers moved over her belly as if she were smoothing her dress.

Korey stilled, and a chill slithered through him as he watched her gingerly sit down across from him. She looked different—as if her skin had a glow.

When Tyler sat down beside his wife, he murmured something to her and then tenderly rubbed her shoulder.

Crystal fluttered over, delivering two plates and two sets of utensils. Then she brought a platter of bacon and waffles to the table. Finally, she left mugs of coffee in front of Tyler and Michelle.

"Danki," Michelle said. "It smells *appeditlich.*"

Tyler studied his wife. "The smell isn't getting to you, is it?"

Michelle shook her head and added cream and sugar to her coffee.

"What's the news around here?" Tyler asked.

Jayden swallowed a bite of waffle and pointed to Korey. "We were just hearing about how Kore's new crew is going. He says Toby Zook is his best worker."

"That's great. How do you like running your own crew?" Tyler asked while covering a waffle with butter.

Korey took a deep breath, working to keep his emotions in check. "I like it."

Tyler picked up the syrup and then stilled, studying Korey. "Are you okay, Korey?"

"*Ya.*" Korey turned his attention to Michelle. "How are you?"

Michelle rubbed her abdomen again and smiled. "I'm doing better. *Danki.*"

"Better?" Korey's gaze darted to Tyler and then back at Michelle. "I feel left out. Am I missing something here?"

Michelle blushed and looked down.

Korey held his breath, silently preparing himself for whatever news Michelle and Tyler were about to share with him.

Tyler cleared his throat. "We're . . . Uh . . . well. We're expecting. Michelle is due in September."

"Oh." Korey nodded slowly as Tyler's words soaked through his mind. "That's great." Then he hesitated. "Am I the only one who didn't know?"

Everyone exchanged anxious expressions around the table.

"Huh." Korey forced a smile. "Well, congratulations." Then he pushed back his chair and carried his dishes to the sink while his hands shook. "*Danki* for breakfast, Crystal."

When he turned to his older brother, Tyler looked stricken. "Kore, I'm sorry. I wanted to tell you. I really did. There were so many times when the words were on the tip of my tongue, but I was too *naerfich*. I thought it would upset you, and I was trying to figure out how to tell you. You know how badly I'm trying to win your trust, and the last thing I wanted to do was hurt you again. You have to believe that I'm telling you the truth. Please don't be upset. I'm begging you."

"It's fine. I'm actually not surprised, Ty." Korey glanced at his *dat* and Crystal and then Jayden. "I'll see you later." He trudged toward the mudroom.

"Kore, wait!" Tyler called.

"Let him go," Korey heard his father say.

Korey stepped out onto the porch and breathed in the early June morning air. Then closing his eyes, he whispered, "Please calm me, Lord."

And when he opened his eyes, he knew what he needed at that moment.

Korey needed Savannah.

CHAPTER 17

Savannah pulled the back door open, and when she took in the anguish etched on Korey's face, she gasped. "Korey! *Was iss letz?*"

"I know I'm early." His tone was raspy. "Can we go somewhere and talk?"

The pain in his eyes nearly cut her in two. "*Ya*, of course. I just need to let *mei aenti* and *onkel* know where I'm going."

She placed her hand on his arm and steered him inside, where her aunt, uncle, cousin, and brother sat at the kitchen table. The smell of eggs, bacon, and freshly baked bread filled the kitchen. They all looked surprised as they greeted him.

"*Gude mariye.*" Korey plastered a smile on his face and lifted his hand in a wave.

Savannah threaded her warm fingers with his. "Korey and I are going to go for a walk. We'll be close by."

Her aunt and uncle nodded, and then she towed him outside, down the porch steps, and across the pasture to a bench at the back of her aunt and uncle's property, overlooking the rolling patchwork of fields that made up nearby farms.

"It's *schee* here," he whispered as his brown eyes focused out toward the farms.

She nodded. "I like to come here when I just need some time alone to think. Seeing the beautiful pastures and barns calms me when I've had a tough day."

Silence stretched between them, and she took in the sadness lining his handsome face. She couldn't stand his reticence anymore. Seeing him so distraught was tearing her in two. She had to know what was bothering him.

"Korey, I can't sit here and watch you suffer any longer. Please tell me why you're so upset."

He huffed out a breath. "I feel like a complete *dummkopp*."

"What do you mean?"

"I just figured out this morning that Michelle is expecting. She's due in September."

Savannah's stomach constricted and her hands began to tremble. "Do you still love Michelle?"

"No, no, no." Korey scoffed. "I was never truly in love with Michelle. That's not what upset me."

"Then what is it?"

"I'm hurt because no one told me. I feel left out and forgotten. I've been trying my best to fit in with my family, but I'm still the last one anyone thinks about. I'm the last one to know. I still feel like a stranger in my own home."

He pushed his hand through his thick brown hair and sniffed. "I already told you that I always felt like Ty was trying to outdo me. It was as if we were in competition. I was convinced he was trying to take over the company and leave me in the dust, which was why I was upset when *Dat* gave him his own crew to run before he gave me one. I thought he wanted to take the company out from under me when I wasn't looking. Then when I found out he had feelings for Michelle, I thought he was trying to take her away from me like he was going to take the company. I assumed he was trying to steal everything I cared about in order to hurt me and prove he was better than I am."

Savannah scrunched her nose and waved her hands in the air. "Hold on. I'm confused, Korey. You just told me that you didn't really love her, and then you said that you thought Tyler was trying to take Michelle away from you to hurt you."

"I loved her the way you love a *freind*, and I was hurt that *mei bruder* had feelings for her when I was still dating her. This was all because I felt like he wanted to prove he was the better *sohn*, the most important one."

She nodded, trying to understand his complicated relationship with his older brother.

"I left because I couldn't stand the idea of seeing them together. When they started dating, I felt as if Tyler was rubbing it in my face that I couldn't make it work with Michelle, but he was going to show me how to do it right." He paused and picked at a loose piece of wood on the bench.

"I came back home because I became *freinden* with an elderly man who lived next door to *mei mamm's* cousin who let me move in with him in Sugarcreek. The older man's name was Sherman. We struck up a friendship, and we used to spend evenings drinking lemonade and talking about life. One night he asked me why I came to Ohio, and I told him that I had a falling out with *mei bruder*. And I'll never forget what he said to me." Korey paused and licked his lips.

"What did he say?"

"Sherman told me to repent and work things out with my family. He said he regretted never working things out with his own *bruder* before he passed away." He sniffed. "He said, 'You're hiding from your problems here. Family is God's gift to us. Don't forsake your family.'"

"That makes a lot of sense, Korey. You don't want to run out of time to work things out with Tyler. He's your *bruder*."

"I know, but I can't bring myself to forgive him, even though I know it's our way to forgive, no matter what. I keep praying for God to put forgiveness in my heart, but I can't get there, and I don't know how." He covered his face with his hands.

"Oh, Korey." She rubbed his back while his shoulders shook. "It's going to be okay. Just keep praying, and God will help heal your heart. I've struggled with forgiveness myself. I've had to ask God to help me forgive *mei daed* after he left us. I've also struggled forgiving the bullies that tormented Toby at school."

Savannah pulled a tissue from the pocket of her apron and placed it in Korey's hand. He wiped his eyes and nose.

"You must think I'm ridiculous."

"No, I don't." She leaned her head on his muscular shoulder. "I actually respect you for being so honest with me. It takes a lot of courage to admit the secrets that burden your heart."

"How did you manage to forgive your *daed* and the bullies?"

She grimaced. "Some days are easier than others."

He chuckled, and relief flittered through her.

"It's so *gut* to see you smile again." She sat up straight.

"*Danki* for being *mei freind*."

She smiled, but her heart sank. Deep down, she longed for Korey to cup his hands to her cheeks and kiss her. She yearned to hear him say that he cared about her—possibly even loved her—and he wanted to be her true boyfriend.

But Korey only wanted her friendship, which was best for both of them. Neither of them was ready for a serious relationship, and staying friends meant he would never break her heart. Besides, Korey had made it clear that he wasn't ready to trust again, and Savannah had Toby's future to consider.

If only she could convince her stubborn heart to accept that friendship was the best solution.

"I'm not in the mood to hang out and play volleyball today," he said. "Would it be all right if we skipped the youth gathering?"

"*Ya*, of course we can skip it. We could spend the day here with my family if you'd like."

He took her hand in his. "That sounds perfect."

Later that evening, Korey and Savannah walked out to her uncle's barn. He had enjoyed the day visiting with her aunt, uncle, and brother, but he still felt hollowed out and hurt. He longed to have the close relationship with Tyler that he had with Jayden, but he didn't know how to make it happen.

Help me, Lord.

Savannah held a lantern while Korey hitched up his horse and buggy.

"Do you feel any better?" she asked as they led his horse toward the driveway.

Korey nodded. "*Ya*, I do. I had a nice time with your family."

"I'm glad you came to see me." She touched his cheek, and he leaned into the warmth of her hand. "Don't give up on your family, Korey."

"I won't. I'll see you next Sunday."

She smiled. "I'll look forward to it."

When Korey arrived home, he was surprised to see a lantern glowing in the kitchen. He left his shoes and hat in the mudroom and then walked into the kitchen, where Crystal sat at the table.

"Crystal. Hi."

She smiled, but her green eyes didn't have their usual sparkle. Instead, they looked tired. She pointed to a chair across from her. "Would you please sit with me?"

He sat down and swallowed as a feeling of foreboding gripped him. "What do you want to talk about?"

"Tell me why you got so upset this morning when you found out Tyler's and Michelle's news."

Korey looked down at the tabletop and began drawing invisible circles on the wood with his fingers. "I felt as if I had been forgotten or ignored. I've been trying to fix things between Ty and me, but then he left me out when he shared his big news. It truly hurt to be the only one who didn't know that they're expecting."

When he looked up, he found Crystal's lips formed a straight line. "Do you know why they didn't tell you?" she asked.

Korey shook his head. "No, I don't."

"If I tell you, will you promise me that you'll stay calm and listen to what I have to say?"

He nodded.

"Okay." Crystal tapped the tabletop. "The truth is that Tyler and Michelle feel like they're always walking on eggshells around you. They both fear that if they say the wrong thing to you, your temper will go off like a bomb. They didn't want to tell you their news because they were afraid you'd get upset. Yet, by not telling you, you still were upset."

Korey covered his face with his hands. "I know I've been rude, thoughtless, quick-tempered, and arrogant. I want to fix it, but I don't know how. I feel like all I do is mess up."

"That's not true, Korey."

He peeked at her through his splayed fingers. "It's not?"

"No." She smiled. "You *are* fixing things. Your *dat* and I can tell that you're truly trying to change your ways, and we're grateful."

"Does that mean you don't hate me?"

She clucked her tongue. "Oh, Korey. I could never hate you. You're my stepson. You're part of my family." Then her expression became somber. "Do you dislike me, Korey?"

"No." He shook his head. "And I'm trying to make things right and fix my broken relationships."

"I know. I see a big difference in you since you've come home." She reached across the table and touched his hand. "And I believe you'll work things out with Tyler if you just make an effort. He's been trying with you. I know he's attempted to talk to you, but you keep pushing him away. If you truly want to fix things, then you have to do your part too. Your relationship with your *bruder* is a two-way street. He can't do all of the work alone."

Korey nodded. "I know that you're right."

Crystal cupped her hand to her mouth to cover a yawn. "Excuse me, but I need to get to bed."

"I do too." Korey stood and started for the doorway and then stopped and craned his neck over his shoulder. "*Danki*, Crystal, for being honest with me."

Her expression was warm. "Thank you for talking honestly with me too. See you in the morning."

Korey made his way up to the second floor, where Jayden stood in the hallway at the top of the stairs.

AMY CLIPSTON

"I missed you and Toby at the youth gathering."

"*Ya.*" Korey leaned against the wall. "I decided to stay and visit with Savannah's family instead of going to the youth gathering today."

"I'm glad you and Savannah are so close."

"I'm grateful for her." Korey fiddled with his suspenders. "Is Ty upset with me?"

"*Ya.*"

Korey blew out a puff of air as more anguish threatened to pull him under and drown him.

"You know, I actually have quite a few memories of the three of us having fun together."

"Like what?"

"We used to go fishing. Remember that time I fell into the pond, and you and Ty were so worried that *Mamm* was going to be angry when you brought me home soaking wet from head to toe?"

Korey guffawed. "*Ya,* and when we got home, she laughed."

"Exactly!" Jayden chuckled. "And another time we ice-skated on that pond, and when we got bored, we put on our boots, grabbed our sleds, and went sledding. Then we crashed the sleds and wound up having a snowball fight."

"And we came home soaking wet, and *Mamm* laughed again."

Jayden held up his finger. "There seems to be a theme here."

Korey snickered.

"I honestly can't remember her ever raising her voice at any of us."

Korey nodded. "That's true." He hugged his arms to his chest as more memories of his mother filled his mind—singing to Korey and his brothers at bedtime, laughing while they shared funny stories about their day, clapping for them during the Christmas program at school. He missed his mother so much that his chest squeezed.

"Tyler, you, and I had some *gut* times, Kore, and we can have that again if you give Ty a chance. We're *bruders*." Jayden gestured between them. "We're going to argue and disagree, but we still love each other. At the end of the day, we're related. We're family, and nothing is more important than family. You have to agree with me there."

Korey rubbed the bridge of his nose. "You've become quite the philosopher, huh, baby *bruder*?"

Jayden gave Korey's shoulder a gentle punch. "We'd better get to bed."

As Korey headed to his room, he once again recalled Sherman's wise words: *"You're hiding from your problems here. Family is God's gift to us. Don't forsake your family."*

"Help me fix my broken relationship with *mei bruder*, Lord," he whispered as he climbed into bed. "Give me the patience and understanding to forgive him and help me find the right words to ask for his forgiveness as well."

CHAPTER 18

THE FOLLOWING MORNING KOREY WALKED OVER TO WHERE Toby worked hammering shingles on a roof on a large home in New Holland. The blue sky was dotted with white puffy clouds, and the mid-June sun was bright and hot. Mosquitoes buzzed by while the hum of a lawn mower sounded in the distance.

Korey stood over Toby and smiled while he worked.

Toby tented his hand over his eyes and squinted up at him. "Did you need something, boss?"

"I told you not to call me boss." Korey snickered and crouched down beside him. "I just wanted to let you know that you're doing a great job."

"*Danki*, but you told me that already. In fact, you remind me just about every day."

"I do, don't I? Well, I mean it, Toby."

"Thanks." Toby seemed to study him. "Is everything all right?"

Korey pushed his mirrored sunglasses up higher on his nose. "*Ya*. Why?"

"You seemed upset yesterday."

"Hmm." Korey sat back on his heels and sighed. He'd been up

most of the night praying and trying to come up with a solution for how to start a new relationship with his older brother and let go of all of the hurt he had carried in his heart for years.

"Do you want to talk about it?" Toby's words were cautious.

"I do, actually."

"Okay." Toby set his hammer on the roof and sat down. "I'm listening."

"I had an argument with my older *bruder*. We've been arguing for years, which is why I had to leave for a while. He married my ex-girlfriend, and yesterday I found out that they're expecting. I was the last one to know, which hurt, but I understand now why they didn't tell me." Korey grimaced. "I haven't exactly made it easy for *mei bruder* to talk to me. I've been . . . difficult."

"Do you want to fix things with your *bruder*?"

"*Ya*, I do."

"Are you asking for my advice, Korey?"

"*Ya*, I am."

Toby picked up the hammer. "Sometimes Savannah and I argue because she seems to smother me. She acts like she's *mei mamm* instead of *mei schweschder*. She treats me like I'm five instead of twenty, and it really gets under my skin. But I always forgive her because I know she loves me and wants the best for me. I know in my heart that she's trying to compensate for what our *dat* did to us when he left."

"I understand." Korey nodded.

Then Toby looked over at Korey, his eyes serious. "Do you love your *bruder*?"

"*Ya*, I do."

"So tell him that." Toby shrugged. "Apologize and try harder to be the *bruder* you want him to be to you. Make an effort and don't always assume the worst when he does something to upset you. We all make mistakes because we all fall short of the glory of God."

Korey grinned. "You are really *schmaert*."

"Sometimes." Toby shrugged.

"Naw, you're always *schmaert*." Korey stood. *"Danki."* Then he pointed to the roof. "Now, get back to work."

"Ya, boss."

They both chuckled as Korey walked toward the far side of the roof to check on the other members of his crew. His mind spun with what he would say when he apologized to Tyler.

He would face Tyler tonight and try, once and for all, to bridge the giant chasm that had grown between them.

Korey just had to pray for the right words.

The aroma of tuna casserole filled Korey's senses as he kicked off his work boots and hung his straw hat on a peg on the wall. When he stepped through the doorway into the kitchen, he smiled at Crystal, who was setting the table.

"You're home a little early today," she said.

Korey crossed to the sink and began scrubbing his hands. He glanced over his shoulder at his stepmother and noticed that she looked a little pale, and there were dark circles under her eyes. "Are you feeling okay?"

"Ya. Why?" She peered up at him while setting a plate at Jayden's spot.

"You look tired."

"I haven't been sleeping well, but I'm fine. *Danki* for asking."

Korey dried his hands with a paper towel. "*Dat* and Jay aren't home yet?"

Crystal set the last plate by his father's seat and then began pulling utensils out of the drawer. "No, they're not." Then she returned to the table and began setting each place.

"*Gut,*" he said.

Her red eyebrows rose. "*Gut?*"

"I was hoping to talk to you alone." Korey made a sweeping gesture toward the table. "Could we have a moment before they get here?"

"*Ya.*" She finished distributing the utensils and then sat down in her usual spot.

Korey dropped onto the chair beside hers. "I'm going to talk to Tyler tonight."

"That's fantastic." She clapped her hands. "What are you going to say?"

He pinched the bridge of his nose. "I've been thinking about it all day, and I've been praying. But I still don't know what to say to him. He and I have always rubbed each other the wrong way. I know I get under his skin, but he upsets me too. How do I move past that?"

"Well . . ." Crystal picked up a spoon and examined it as if it held all of the answers. "If you know that your words upset him, then try to remember the importance of family before you speak. Keep reminding yourself that Tyler is the only older *bruder* you'll ever have, and your words will determine your relationship with him from now into the future."

Korey pursed his lips, pondering her advice.

"I know that you and Tyler get on each other's nerves, and that's because you're very different. Tyler will always be Tyler, and you'll always be you. You can find a way to compromise and get along without changing each other."

"That's true." He rested his elbow on the table and his chin on his palm.

"So maybe if you choose your words with care and don't accuse him of things, the conversation will go well." She hesitated. "Korey, did something happen today that inspired you to try again with Tyler?"

"*Ya*, I realized something."

"And what did you realize?"

Korey ran his fingers over the edge of the table. "I want to be a part of my niece's or nephew's life, and that means I need to fix things with *mei bruder* in order to make that happen."

Crystal smiled. "I'm so glad to hear you say that." She paused and something unreadable flickered over her face. "*Kinner* can bring people together."

"That's true."

The back door opened and clicked shut, and Crystal pushed herself up from the table. "They're home."

Korey popped up from his chair and grabbed two pot holders. "Would you like me to get the casserole out of the oven?"

"Oh, that sounds wonderful." Closing her eyes, Crystal leaned on the counter, and worry gripped Korey.

"Crystal, are you sure you're—" Korey began.

"We're home!" *Dat* announced before closing the distance between himself and his wife and kissing her cheek. "How are you feeling?"

She touched his cheek. "A little tired." She nodded at Korey as he pulled the casserole from the oven. "Korey came home early and is helping me with supper."

"Isn't that nice?" *Dat* touched Korey's shoulder.

Jayden stepped into the kitchen. "Supper smells *appeditlich.*"

Korey delivered the casserole to the table while his brother and father scrubbed their hands.

Soon they were sitting at the table and eating the delicious food. Korey did his best to try to participate in the discussion of work while they ate, but his mind was stuck on two issues—worrying about Crystal's health and fixing his relationship with his brother.

After supper Korey carried the dishes to the table while Jayden collected the glasses, and *Dat* carried the casserole dish to the counter.

Then Jayden started for the door. "I'm going to go take care of the animals," he announced before disappearing through the doorway.

"Would you like me to wash the dishes so you can rest?" Korey asked his stepmother.

Crystal shook her head. "No, *danki.*" She turned to the sink and began filling one side with soapy water.

"You should go sit down," Korey said. "You don't look well."

Dat placed his hand on Korey's shoulder. "*Danki* for offering, but I'll help her." He smiled at Korey. "Crystal is fine. She's just had some trouble sleeping the past few nights."

"Are you sure?"

"*Ya,* I'm positive." *Dat* and Crystal shared a smile. "You can go help your *bruder* in the stable, and I'll take care of things here."

"I'm actually going to talk to Tyler."

Dat's expression was hopeful. "To work things out?"

Korey nodded and held on to the edge of the counter as more anxiety filled him.

"I'm so *froh* to hear that. Go and take your time."

"I will." Korey took a deep breath and then headed for the door.

His boots crunched along the rock path that led to his brother's house. As he drew closer to the front door, his hands started to tremble, and his pulse spiked. His mind kept repeating Sherman's words and Crystal's advice.

Lord, help me choose the right words to mend the broken relationships between Tyler and me. Help me remember how important family is.

When Korey reached the front door, he lifted his hand and closed his eyes. Then he knocked. After a moment, heavy footsteps echoed from inside the house. Then the door opened, and his older brother peered out at him, surprise lighting his face.

Tyler pushed opened the storm door and smiled. "Kore. *Wie geht's?*"

"I was hoping we could talk."

"Come in." Tyler beckoned him. "We just finished supper, and I'm sure we can find something for dessert. Michelle has been on a *kichlin* kick lately. I'm getting spoiled with a different variety of *kichlin* every day. I'm certain my trousers are going to be too tight pretty soon."

Korey shook his head. "I was hoping we could talk in private." He pointed toward the two rocking chairs on the porch. "Maybe out here?"

"Oh. Of course." Tyler's smile faded, and he stepped out onto the porch.

"Tyler? Who's here?" Michelle called before appearing at the door. "Oh, Korey. Hi." Her expression was hesitant.

Korey couldn't help but notice how her abdomen was distended. How had he missed that before? Perhaps he never paid enough attention to others because he was too busy thinking of himself. More guilt pummeled him. "Hi, Michelle."

"We're going to talk out here for a little bit," Tyler said, and a look passed between him and his wife.

Michelle nodded. "It's muggy out today. Would you like some iced tea?"

"That sounds nice." Tyler looked at Korey, and he shrugged. Then Tyler reached for the doorknob. "I'll get it."

"Don't be *gegisch*. I'm happy to get it for you both. I'll be right back." Then Michelle disappeared into the house.

Korey sank down onto a rocking chair and looked out toward his father's house while working to gather his thoughts. He tried to remember the words he'd wanted to say, but his mind came up blank. Perhaps he should have grabbed a notepad and written down the points he'd hoped to make.

"How's work?" Tyler asked as he perched on the chair beside him.

"*Gut*. How about for you?"

Tyler absently touched his dark beard. "We're working at a car dealership. It's a big job. We should have it finished in a few days."

"That's *gut*."

"*Ya.*"

Silence fell between them, and Korey tried to work up the nerve to make amends with Tyler. Why was it easier to talk to strangers than his own brother?

The storm door squeaked open, and Michelle stepped out onto the porch carrying a tray containing two large glasses of iced tea and a plate of oatmeal raisin cookies.

"Didn't I tell you she was on a *kichlin* kick?" Tyler chuckled as he took the tray from her and placed it on the small table between the rocking chairs. "*Danki, mei liewe.*"

Korey picked up a cookie. "Thank you, Michelle."

She nodded before returning inside the house.

They each ate a cookie and took a sip of iced tea while staring out toward *Dat*'s house.

Then Korey felt a surge of courage as his words returned to him. It was time to share what he'd come here to say. "I'm sorry for the way I behaved when you and Michelle shared your *froh* news."

Tyler's dark eyebrows careened toward his hairline as he stared at Korey.

"I spoke to Crystal when I got home from Savannah's last night, and she explained why you and Michelle didn't tell me when you shared the news with everyone else."

"What did she say?" Tyler's question was soft and hesitant.

"She said that you and Michelle feel as if you have to walk on eggshells around me, and I don't blame you. I haven't made it easy for either of you since I came back." He snorted. "I didn't make it easy before I left either. I was downright rotten to many people, and you and Michelle took the brunt of my ire."

Tyler remained silent.

"I know I've been difficult, but it was because I was hurt." Korey paused. "I want to work things out with you, and I've been begging God to guide me to a solution to our problems. I just don't know where to begin."

"I'm glad to hear you say that. I meant it when I told you that I wanted you to stay. I never wanted you to go to Ohio. After losing *Mamm*, the last thing I want is to lose another member of my family."

"I know." Korey took another sip of tea.

"You didn't need to leave."

"I did need to leave." Korey set his glass down on the tray and chose another cookie. "It was better that way. I needed time to sort through all of my emotions and figure out how to move forward with my life."

"But now that you're back, we can start over."

Korey nodded. "*Ya*, but we need to clear the air between us."

"Okay." Tyler nodded and sat up straight. "Say what you need to say, Kore. I'm ready, and I'm listening."

Korey took a deep breath. "I know that you and Michelle are *froh*. It's obvious, but I can't escape the thought that you and Michelle fell in love while she was still dating me."

Tyler sighed.

"Kore," he began, "Michelle and I started out as *freinden*. We had an instant connection, and no matter how hard I tried, I couldn't get her out of my mind."

"What about Charity?"

"When I asked Charity to be my girlfriend, I had every intention of making it work, but we didn't connect." Tyler picked up his glass of tea and ran his fingers through the condensation. "In some ways, I think I dated Charity to try to get Michelle out of my mind, but that didn't work. All I wound up doing was hurting Charity. I never meant to hurt her, and I never meant to hurt you either. In fact, when I realized that I cared for Michelle, I stopped talking to her because I wanted to save my relationship with you. I put your feelings before my own because you're *mei bruder*."

Korey blinked.

"I kept trying to tell you that, but you were too focused on wanting to believe that I was out to ruin your life to listen to what I was saying to you. It was killing me to stay away from Michelle, but it was also killing me to think of losing you. No matter what I did, you kept accusing me of betraying you. I never betrayed you,

Kore. You just had it in your head that I was always out to get you. You invented this competition between us. I was never in competition with you. I just wanted to be as close to you as I am with Jay."

Korey tried to swallow as his throat thickened. He wanted that too, but it seemed impossible that he and Tyler would ever truly trust each other that way.

Tyler took a long drink of iced tea and then placed the glass on the tray. "The day Michelle and her younger *schweschder* were in the accident, I was going out of my mind." He looked out in the direction of Michelle's parents' house. "I couldn't imagine losing her. I was so grateful that you finally gave your blessing for me to date her. I didn't know how I could go on without her in my life, but I also didn't want to lose you."

Tyler turned toward Korey, and his hazel eyes were misted over. "Korey, I feel like I've lost you, but I'd do anything to have you in my life. I just need you to stop hating me."

"I don't hate you, Tyler." Korey's voice trembled. "I'm sorry for all of the pain I've caused you. I was so focused on blaming you for my own unhappiness that I didn't realize that you and I are just different. I also knew in my heart that I wasn't the right man for Michelle, but I didn't want to entertain the thought that you might be the right man for her. It took going away for more than a year for me to think about how selfish and immature I'd been. And I'm sorry, Ty. I truly am."

"Does that mean you want me in your life?"

Korey nodded. "I want to be a part of your *boppli*'s life too."

"Michelle and I would like that." Tyler smiled. "Truce?"

Korey nodded. "*Ya*, truce." And then he shook his brother's hand as a weight lifted off his shoulders.

CHAPTER 19

THE FOLLOWING AFTERNOON, SAVANNAH MOVED TOWARD THE
front of the store just as Korey walked in carrying a bag and a tray
of drinks. Excitement rocketed through her as her feet picked up
speed.

"Korey!" Savannah hurried over to him. "What a surprise!"

He looked sheepish. "Could you possibly take a lunch break?"

"*Ya.*" She turned toward her aunt, who was running the register. "*Aenti* Dorothy, could I have lunch with Korey?"

Her aunt waved at Korey. "*Ya,* of course. Go take your time
and enjoy."

"*Danki.*" Savannah took the drink tray from Korey and then
pushed the door open with her hip. "Let's go sit at the picnic table
and visit."

"Perfect."

They walked toward the picnic table that was located behind
the store.

"What brought you out this way?" she asked as she set the
drink carrier on the table.

"Supply run. I thought I'd pick up lunch while I was out here
and surprise you."

"The best surprise from the best fake boyfriend." She smiled up at him and then rested her arm on his muscular bicep.

They sat at the picnic table, and he pulled out two bacon, lettuce, and tomato sandwiches and two bags of chips. They bowed their heads in silent prayer and then began to eat their lunch.

"I have to tell you what happened last night." Korey's smile was wide, and his dark eyes sparkled.

Savannah lifted her cup of iced tea. "It sounds exciting. What happened?"

"Ty and I finally worked things out."

"Oh, praise God!"

"I know." Korey continued to beam. "Your *bruder* actually inspired me to apologize to Ty."

"No kidding. I need to hear that story too."

Korey explained how he had spoken to Crystal and Jayden before getting Toby's advice. "I arrived home early yesterday, so I had a chance to talk to Crystal again. Then, after supper, I went over to Tyler's *haus*, and we sat on the porch and hashed it all out."

"And everything is okay?"

"*Ya*. I apologized to him and told him that I want to be in his *boppli*'s life."

Savannah took a bite of her sandwich and studied Korey's handsome face as he talked on about working things out with his older brother. The joy in his face and the gleam in his eyes sent her heart into a fluttering frenzy.

At that moment, she realized just how much she cared for him. No, she *loved* him. She loved how he had agreed to pretend to date her in order to help her. She loved how he had taken her brother under his wing and changed his life. Toby now came home happy after work, and she had Korey to thank for that.

And she loved how Korey listened to her when she poured out her heart to him, how he held her hand, how he brought her lunch, how he touched her face, how he held her close, and how he made her laugh.

Savannah's head started to swim as reality brought her back to earth. She was in love with a man who could never love her back. He'd made it clear that he had trust issues, which was why they were better off as friends. Besides that, she also was determined not to become distracted by a romance when she had an obligation to her brother. Therefore, a relationship between her and Korey would never work.

But would friendship ever be enough to sustain Savannah?

"So, anyway," Korey continued. "I'm just so excited. I feel as if this giant weight has been lifted off my back and chest, and I needed to tell you as soon as possible, which is why I wanted to bring you lunch today."

Savannah swallowed another bite of sandwich.

Korey leaned forward and his brow pinched. "You okay?"

"Uh-huh."

He lifted an eyebrow. "You look upset."

"No, I'm fine." She waved off the comment. "I'm so *froh* for you, Korey. I knew that you would realize how important your family is and forgive Tyler. That's the best news. And I'm truly honored that I was the first person you wanted to tell."

"*Danki.*"

"How's work going?" she asked.

"Great." While they ate their sandwiches and chips, Korey talked on about his crew's current project, pointing out what a wonderful job her brother was doing.

After they finished their lunch, Savannah rushed into the

house for the homemade chocolate chip cookies she had baked yesterday so they could enjoy them for dessert. Then she walked Korey to the driveway.

"Where's your driver?" she asked.

Korey pointed toward the road. "He said he'd stay at the diner and have lunch while he waited for me. I'm going to walk over to meet him." He took her hand in his, and his smile sent a giddy rush through her. "*Danki* for being *mei freind*—my best *freind.*"

Her happiness suddenly evaporated. "*Gern gschehne,*" she managed to say, but his words were like shards of glass to her soul.

She could hardly stand being his friend when her heart craved so much more from him. If only he would kiss her cheek and tell her that he cared for her as more than a friend. But that felt like a fantasy as he held her hand.

Korey gave her hand a gentle squeeze. "I'll see you soon."

As he sauntered down the driveway toward the road, Savannah considered telling him that they should pretend to break up and end their fake relationship. But letting him go felt just as painful as only being his friend. She couldn't imagine her life without him in it when she cared for him so deeply.

⁓⁓☙❦❧⁓⁓

Later that afternoon, Korey loaded supplies into the back of his driver's pickup truck. "Great job today," he told Toby as he set a toolbox on the bed. "Do you like the work?"

"I do. I think I've found my calling."

"That's great." Korey gave his shoulder a pat. "I'm grateful that you came to work for me."

"*Danki,* but I'm not as *schmaert* as Dean and Levi."

"That's not true. You're *schmaert* in your own way. We're all different. I'm different from *mei bruders*, but God gives us all our own gifts." Korey held up his hands. "For example, you gave me excellent advice about how to handle my situation with *mei* older *bruder*, Tyler."

"So you talked to him?"

"I did, and we worked it out."

Toby grinned. "That's great."

"And it proves my point that we're all *schmaert* and have special gifts."

Toby shrugged. "I guess you're right."

"You know I am." Korey grinned as he pondered how much joy Toby and Savannah had brought to his life. If only he and Savannah could be more than friends. But was Korey truly ready to trust her with this heart?

Lord, help me find a way to keep Savannah and Toby in my life permanently.

<hr>

Korey walked out onto the porch later that evening to check on the animals just as Michelle climbed the back steps holding a book in her hands. "Hi," he said.

"Hi Korey." She lifted up the novel. "I was just going to give this to Crystal. She let me borrow it, and I finished it today."

He held out his hand. "Would you like me to give it to her?"

"Sure." Michelle handed him the book, and then they stared awkwardly at each other. "Well, *gut nacht.*" She gave him a wave before moving toward the steps. Then she stopped and spun to face him. "Actually, I wanted to say something to you."

"Okay . . ."

"Tyler told me that you had a nice talk with him last night and you worked everything out."

"That's true."

"I wanted to thank you for that." She jammed her thumb toward the house. "He's been heartbroken since you left, and I'm glad you're finally back in our lives. Today he was really *froh*. I knew he would never feel settled until you came home and you two worked out all your differences."

Not sure what to say, Korey nodded.

"You're part of our family, and we need you."

He just studied her.

"Okay. That's what I wanted to tell you." She turned toward the steps, and then stopped again and swiveled toward him. "Actually, I need to say something else." She ducked her head and studied her black apron for a moment, then focused on him once again. "I want you to know that when I suggested we break up, it wasn't so that I could go after your older *bruder*."

Still holding the book, Korey stuck his free hand in his pocket.

"It was never my intention to trade you in for Tyler, but I know you think that's what I did."

"I never said that."

"No, but you've implied it over and over again." Her brow puckered. "If you recall our conversation the day we mutually agreed to break up, it was because neither of us was truly in love with the other. You admitted that you held on to me because you believed your *mamm* would approve of our relationship. You said being with me was a way to hold on to your *mamm*'s memory."

She pointed to her chest. "I, on the other hand, was immature and completely obsessed with getting married, which was why I held on to you, even though I knew deep in my heart that I wasn't in love with you anymore. We outgrew each other."

Korey heaved out a breath. "That's true."

"Tyler and I seemed to just click. We started out as *freinden*, but then our friendship grew into so much more. When we were together, we never ran out of words, and we never argued. Everything with him was just easy and natural."

"I know."

"So then you must know that I never cheated on you." Her words trembled. "I was faithful to you, and I never wanted to hurt you. Your friendship always meant too much for me to even consider hurting you. In fact, it was killing me that I was falling for Tyler because I never wanted to cause you any pain or come between you and your *bruder*."

"I know that now, Michelle."

"*Gut.*" Her blue eyes glistened.

"And I never meant to hurt you either. I didn't treat you right, especially when I left you at that youth gathering in the rain. I made many mistakes, and I'm sorry for the hurtful things I did and the pain I caused you." Korey shook his head. "I know that we grew apart, and I'm sorry I never admitted that to you. I kept punishing you when I should have just faced the truth."

She sniffed and pulled a tissue from her pocket and wiped her eyes and nose. "*Danki.*"

"If you go home with red and puffy eyes, you know *mei bruder* will come over here and let me have it for making you cry." His lips twitched.

She laughed, and he smiled.

"Do you think there's any possible way we could be *freinden*?" she asked.

"*Ya*, of course." He held out his hand to her, and she shook it. "*Danki* for talking this out with me. You're my sister-in-law, and we need to get along."

"That's true. *Gut nacht.*"

"*Gut nacht*," he told her before she descended the steps and headed back toward her house. Korey smiled, grateful that he'd cleared the air with Michelle.

For the first time since he'd arrived back in Bird-in-Hand, he felt as if he was truly home.

"I'm so grateful that you all came over to help me clean," Macy said while she stood in the kitchen with Savannah, Gail, Jodie, and Willa. "It's been so long since I've hosted the youth gathering, and there's always so much to do to prepare."

Savannah smiled. "You know we'll always help you," she said, and their friends agreed.

It was Friday afternoon six weeks later, and the humid late-July breeze drifted in through the open windows. Savannah was grateful her aunt and uncle had allowed her to leave work early to join her friends in helping Macy clean the house and weed the garden in preparation for the youth gathering on Sunday.

"Now we can have a snack," Macy announced as she pulled out a container and opened it. "Lemon bars."

Willa clapped her hands. "I love your lemon bars."

"We all do," Gail agreed.

Savannah gathered five glasses. "I'll pour some lemonade." She brought the glasses and the pitcher of lemonade to the table, and they all sat down for their snack.

"I have some news," Jodie announced.

Gail lifted her glass of lemonade. "What is it?"

"Well..." Jodie's smile was wide. "I have a feeling that Peter is going to propose soon."

Savannah and her friends gasped in unison.

"Tell us more," Macy insisted.

Jodie absently folded her napkin into small squares and then unfolded it. "It's just a feeling I have. He's been talking about a future. He says he wants to build a *haus* on his *dat*'s farm, and he even mentioned *kinner* the other day."

"Oh my goodness!" Willa exclaimed. "That's so romantic."

Jodie nodded. "*Ya*, I know. I'd love to get married this fall."

"So soon?" Gail asked.

Macy waved her off. "We could help Jodie get ready, right? I think we could arrange a November wedding."

"What about the rest of you?" Jodie glanced around the table. "Do you think any of you will be engaged soon?"

Gail smiled. "I'd be so excited if Ike asked. I'd love to plan a future with him. I think we get along really well and would make each other *froh*."

"*Ya*, I feel the same way about Tommy," Willa agreed.

Savannah felt her posture wilt with the disappointment weighing down on her as she considered the past six weeks. Nothing had changed with Korey. He still talked about what a wonderful friend she was, and every time they parted ways, he shook her hand.

At night she dreamed of how his kisses might taste as she imagined hearing him telling her that he loved her. But every morning when she awoke, Savannah would bury her face in her pillow as reality rained down on her—Korey was only her friend and her pretend boyfriend, nothing more.

While Savannah was grateful that Korey was sweet and attentive at youth gatherings, she was tired of the façade. She wanted more out of the relationship; she wanted a *real* relationship with him. Still, it was growing more and more obvious that having Korey as her true boyfriend wasn't ever going to happen.

Korey had made it clear he wasn't ready to commit to a relationship, and Savannah couldn't make romance a bigger priority than taking care of her brother. And yet the truth grew more painful with each passing day—Savannah was wasting her time with Korey, but she didn't know how to let him go without crushing her own heart.

"What about you and Korey?" Jodie's brown eyes were focused on Savannah. "You two seem so *froh* together. Do you think he'll propose soon?"

"I-I doubt it," Savannah stammered.

Gail rolled her eyes. "Oh please, Savannah. Korey is so smitten with you. It's written all over his face every time he sees you."

"I agree," Willa chimed in. "He hangs on your every word. I've also watched him staring at you during church. I could definitely see you and Korey getting married, if not this season, definitely next season."

Savannah shook her head. "I don't think so."

"Why not?" Macy looked confused.

Savannah gnawed her lower lip. Oh, how she longed to tell her friends the truth! But if she did, then they all would be angry and hurt that she'd kept her secret this long.

And Macy would take the news the hardest since Savannah had to convince her that her relationship with Korey was real. The last she thing she wanted to do was lose Macy's trust. They'd been best friends since first grade, and she couldn't imagine losing her. She needed Macy in her life.

"Well," Savannah began, while moving her fingers over the hem of the blue tablecloth, "we've only been together three months. I'm sure he's not ready to start talking about the future just yet. It is a little soon, and I certainly don't want to bring it up and scare him away. You know how some men get when you mention the future."

Jodie blinked and looked over at Willa. "It's only been three months?"

"It seems like you and Korey have been together forever," Gail said with a chuckle.

Macy nodded. "That's true. They do fit together so well."

"How are you and Keith?" Savannah asked Macy, desperate to take the focus off of herself.

Macy smiled and her cheeks reddened. "We're doing really well."

"Oooh!" Willa sang. "Do tell."

Macy picked at her lemon bar. "Keith is very sweet and thoughtful, and we have a deep connection. When he comes to visit me, we sit on the porch and talk for hours. I feel like I can say anything to him and he understands."

"Oh, Macy, that's so exciting!" Gail said.

Willa clapped her hands. "I think you'll be engaged soon too."

"Maybe we'll all be planning weddings together," Jodie added.

"I would love that," Macy said. "Keith told me that he loved me last week, and I love him too. I've never been so *froh*."

Savannah sighed as her best friend talked on about her boyfriend. It sounded as if Macy were describing Savannah's relationship with Korey. But the major difference was that Macy and Keith were truly dating, and Savannah and Korey were only pretending.

And that was when Savannah realized the truth. She couldn't go on with the pretend relationship. Either she had to be honest with Korey about her feelings and risk scaring him away or she had to end their ruse for good.

Savannah would pray about it and see where God led her. She just hoped that somehow she and Korey could work it out and truly be together. But she doubted that was possible when he had already made it clear that he wasn't ready to have a true relationship.

CHAPTER 20

THE DELICIOUS SMELL OF APPLE AND CINNAMON OATMEAL filled Korey's nostrils as he jogged down the stairs Sunday morning on his way to the kitchen. When he stepped into the kitchen doorway, he froze, surprised to see *Dat* stirring the oatmeal in a pot instead of Crystal.

"*Gude mariye*," *Dat* said. His dark eyes were dull, and his face seemed to be lined with worry or exhaustion.

Korey walked over to him. "Where's Crystal?"

"She's not feeling well." *Dat* began scooping the oatmeal into bowls. "I told her to rest."

Anxiety gripped Korey. "*Dat*, is she okay?"

His father nodded.

"What's going on?" Jayden joined them in the kitchen.

Dat handed Korey a bowl of oatmeal. "Crystal isn't feeling well, so she's going to sleep in today. I'm going to stay home with her."

"Is she *krank*?" Jayden looked as concerned as Korey felt.

"I'm going to make an appointment with the doctor to make sure everything is okay, and then we'll let you know what's going on."

Korey and Jayden shared a confused expression as *Dat* brought two more bowls of oatmeal to the table.

Then a thought hit Korey—what if she was ill like *Mamm* had been? And what if *Dat* lost Crystal the same way? He would never recover, and neither would Korey and his siblings.

Oh no.

He closed his eyes and sent up a quick prayer to God:

Please, Lord, heal Crystal. Please don't let her have cancer or any other serious disease.

While they ate their breakfast, Korey and Jayden discussed work and upcoming jobs. *Dat* nodded along with their conversation, but he kept his eyes focused on his bowl of food. He seemed to be lost in thought.

Korey swallowed more oatmeal as anxiety continued to pound him.

Lord, please heal my stepmother and help us through whatever illness she may be facing.

Later that morning, Savannah climbed out of Toby's buggy and spotted her friends talking by the King family's barn. As she made her way toward them, she noticed that her friends were grinning while Jodie shared a story.

"What's going on?" Savannah asked as she approached them.

Jodie's dark eyes glistened. "Peter asked me to marry him last night!"

"Oh my goodness!" Savannah gushed. "Tell me everything."

"He came over to *mei haus*, and I noticed that my parents were sharing funny looks. It turns out, he had visited the farm during the day yesterday and asked *mei dat*'s permission. *Mei dat* said yes, so he proposed last night."

Macy grabbed Savannah's arm. "Isn't that fantastic?"

"*Ya*, that is the best news." Savannah smiled as happiness filled her for her friend. "Did you pick a date?"

"We're going to get married the third Thursday in October. I'm so *froh*! But I have so much to do."

"We'll all help you—if you'd like us to," Willa said, looking around the circle of friends. "Right, *maed*?"

"Absolutely," Gail said, and everyone nodded.

Jodie clasped her hands together. "*Danki*. I'm so grateful for all of you. And I'm sure you'll all be next."

"Did he talk about building a *haus*?" Macy asked.

Jodie smiled. "*Ya*. He said that he and his *dat* are going to start very soon. I can't wait! He says he wants at least two bedrooms and maybe more. Of course we both will pray for *kinner*."

Savannah glanced across the pasture just as Korey climbed out of his buggy, and her heart sank. She knew to the depth of her bones that she wanted all of those things with Korey—a home, a family, and a future—but he didn't see her as more than a special friend.

She had stayed up late both Friday night and last night praying about Korey and asking God to guide her heart toward the best decision.

And as she stood by her friends listening to Jodie discuss her future with Peter, Savannah realized the only logical decision was to tell Korey how she felt. She couldn't stand to live in this charade any longer.

Her hands began to shake as she imagined telling Korey that she loved him. She just had to find the courage to do it. She would pray until she found the perfect moment to share that she truly cared about him and hoped he felt the same way.

Give me strength, Lord.

"You've been quiet today," *Aenti* Dorothy said Thursday evening while she and Savannah cleaned up the kitchen after supper. She craned her neck over her shoulder to focus her eyes where Savannah swept the floor. "Is there something on your mind?"

Savannah stopped, blinked, and then she returned to sweeping. All week Savannah had prayed and contemplated how to handle the situation with Korey. They had enjoyed each other's company at the youth gathering on Sunday, and then he had held her hand during the ride home. He had also stopped by to bring her lunch on Tuesday. Still, she hadn't found the courage to tell him how she really felt about him.

"I'm fine," Savannah insisted while she swept her pile of crumbs into the dustpan.

"Savannah," *Aenti* Dorothy said. "Savannah, please look at me."

When she met her aunt's sympathetic gaze, her lower lip began to tremble.

"*Mei liewe,* I can tell when something is bothering you, and it breaks my heart when one of *mei kinner* is hurting. Please tell me what is going on."

Savannah leaned the broom against the wall and then sat down at the table. "It's a long story."

"Okay." *Aenti* Dorothy sat down across from her. "Take all the time you need."

"Korey and I haven't really been dating."

"What do you mean?"

"It's all been pretend." Then she explained how her friends had been nagging her to date and tried to set her up with Keith's cousin. She told her aunt how she and Jerry didn't click, and how she'd stayed late to help clean up after the youth gathering.

"When I went outside, everyone had left, so I started walking home. Korey came along and insisted on giving me a ride. I told him what happened, and he said that his family and *freinden* were pressuring him to date too. So that was when we hatched the plan. We decided to pretend to date, but we promised each other that we would never tell anyone the truth."

Her aunt snorted. "Well, you two had everyone fooled. You both act so in love."

"That's the problem. I fell in love with him." Savannah's voice quaked. "And now I don't know what to do because I don't think he loves me." Her voice broke, and she covered her face with her hands as tears flowed from her eyes.

"*Ach*, Savannah." Her aunt clucked her tongue.

While Savannah worked to get her emotions under control, she heard her aunt's chair scrape across the floor before the chair beside her moved. Then she felt her aunt's hand on her shoulder as she pushed a tissue into Savannah's hand.

Savannah sniffed and wiped her eyes and nose with the tissue before she looked over at her aunt. "Korey is everything to me, *Aenti*. He's my best *freind*. He's done so much for Toby by giving him a job that he loves. Korey is my greatest confidant, and I've told him things that I've never told anyone. And now Jodie is engaged, and I'm so *froh* for her. But her engagement made me realize that I love a man who will never want to give me those

227

things—a future, a family, a life together. I'm just his fake girl-friend that he's using to keep his family and *freinden* from nagging him to find a real one."

"Oh, Savannah." Her aunt shook her head. "I don't believe that for a minute."

"I'm telling you the truth. He may have asked *Onkel* Eddie permission to date me, but it wasn't to truly date me. It was all a ruse."

"I believe you, but I don't think you're the only one who fell in love."

"Why would you say that?"

"Because I see the way he looks at you in church. He watches you with love in his eyes."

Savannah snorted. "Please."

"I mean it. Remember that day he came to see you and you stayed here instead of going to youth group?"

Savannah nodded.

"Why did he come to see you that day?"

"I'm sorry, but I can't tell you that." Savannah grimaced. "It was a private family matter."

Aenti gave her a knowing look. "He was upset about some-thing, right?" she asked, and Savannah nodded. "Who did he come to when he was upset?"

Savannah shrugged.

"He came to *you*, Savannah." Her aunt rubbed her shoulder. "When he needed someone to talk to, he came here. Doesn't that prove he loves you?"

"No, it doesn't. He tells me all the time that I'm his best *freind*. He's never once kissed my cheek or told me that he wants to make our relationship real."

"Have you told him how you feel?"

Savannah shook her head and cast her eyes down toward the gray tablecloth. "No."

"Why not?"

She lifted one shoulder in a half shrug while still studying the tablecloth. "What's the point? If he cared, he would have told me by now."

"Maybe he's afraid to tell you how he feels because he's afraid you'll reject him. Or maybe he's convinced that you don't feel the same way, so he'd rather keep you as a *freind* than risk losing you altogether."

Savannah rested her elbows on the table and her chin on her palm. "That doesn't make sense. It's always the man who asks the *maedel* to date. Why would he assume that I would initiate the conversation?"

"Didn't his ex-girlfriend marry his *bruder*?"

"*Ya*. Why?"

"Did it hurt him when his *bruder* started dating her?"

Savannah nodded.

"Perhaps he's afraid of getting hurt, so he's taking his time and waiting to see how you feel before he risks his heart on you."

"He did say he has trouble trusting after what happened with Michelle." Savannah sniffed. "And that's probably why he'll never date me. He'll never trust me enough."

Her aunt's expression brightened. "Or you've already helped him trust again, and he's just waiting for the right time to tell you how he feels and ask you to be his girlfriend for real."

"I don't think so. He would have asked me by now if that were true."

"Have you prayed about it?"

Savannah nodded. "I've prayed so much that God is probably tired of hearing about Korey."

Her aunt chuckled, and Savannah smiled despite her heartbreak. "And what do you believe God is telling you to do?"

"To tell Korey how I feel about him." Savannah gulped.

Her aunt smiled. "And are you going to do that?"

"I've been trying to find the courage to tell him. I almost told him when he brought me lunch on Tuesday, but I couldn't find the words."

Aenti Dorothy covered Savannah's hand with hers. "Sweetheart, you have always been the bravest *maedel* I've known. I can't think of one time when you haven't spoken your mind." Then she grinned. "I still clearly remember all of those times you had to stay late to help clean up the schoolhouse after defending Toby from those bullies."

"*Ya*, I know." Savannah sighed.

"Well, if you were brave enough to stand up to those bullies, then surely you can find the courage to tell Korey Bontrager how you feel about him."

Savannah nodded as a spark of hope took root in her heart. "So you're saying that if God is guiding me toward Korey, then I need to find the courage to tell him that I love him?"

"That's exactly what I'm saying."

Excitement coursed through Savannah's veins. "You're right! If God is telling me to share my feelings with Korey, then I need to do it. I'll tell him on Sunday when he picks me up for youth group." Her hands trembled as she imagined sharing her heart with Korey. Maybe then he'd finally kiss her! Her stomach swooped at the thought.

"When I met your *onkel*, I felt God guiding me toward him. I truly believe that God put Korey in your life so that you two could plan a future together. Trust God."

"I will. I mean, I always trust God." Then Savannah grimaced. "Now I have to find the right words to tell Korey how I feel."

Her aunt snorted. "You are someone who is never short on words. I'm certain you will find the perfect way not only to tell Korey how you feel but to help him find the courage to tell you how he feels as well."

Savannah smiled as hope blossomed in her soul. "*Danki, Aenti.* I always appreciate our talks."

"I do as well." *Aenti* Dorothy gave Savannah's hand one last pat and then stood. "Let's get this kitchen cleaned up, and then we can sit on the porch and enjoy this *schee* August evening and drink some tea."

As Savannah returned to sweeping, her mind began ticking through a mental list of what she would tell Korey on Sunday. She couldn't wait to see him, and she hoped he would tell her he felt the same way and they could start planning a future—a real future—as *true* girlfriend and boyfriend. She smiled as she once again tried to imagine how it would feel when he finally kissed her.

CHAPTER 21

CRYSTAL PLACED A PLATTER OF TOAST AND A BOWL OF SCRAM-
bled eggs on the table the following morning. With the dark circles
under her dull green eyes and her pale complexion, she looked as
if she felt terrible.

"Are you okay?" Korey asked, worry threading through him.

His stepmother looked like she was trying to smile, but
instead, she appeared as if she might be sick. She turned to *Dat*.
"Duane, I need to lie down."

"Go get some rest. I'll wake you when it's time to leave for the
doctor's office." *Dat* touched her arm. "We'll all clean up before we
go to work. Right, Korey and Jayden?"

"Of course," Jayden said, and Korey nodded.

Crystal hurried out of the kitchen and toward her downstairs
bedroom.

"I'm really worried about her," Jayden said.

Korey chose a piece of toast. "I am too, *Dat*. Please let us know
what the doctor says."

"You know I will." *Dat* stood and grabbed the carafe from the
stove before filling their mugs.

Jayden ate a forkful of eggs and then turned to Korey. "Have
you spoken to Savannah?"

"Not since I brought her lunch on Tuesday." Korey shook his head. "But the week is going by quickly. I was going to go see her last night, but I've just been exhausted this week. I can barely keep my eyes open when I get home from work. I was afraid that if I went to see her I might fall asleep on the way home. Working in this August heat is taking a toll on me."

Dat nodded. "That is a true statement. The summers are brutal when you're working on a roof all day."

"I feel like I can't catch my breath when I get home, and then I just fall into bed and sleep instantly," Korey said.

Jayden buttered his toast. "*Ya*, I feel that way too." Then he scooped some more scrambled eggs onto his plate. "Are you going to work after Crystal's appointment, *Dat*?"

"*Ya*," *Dat* said. "I've left one of the other guys in charge. They shouldn't have any problems. The job is really straightforward."

"We'll be praying for Crystal," Korey said.

His father gave them a warm smile. "I have a feeling that everything is going to turn out just fine."

Korey swallowed a bite of toast. He hoped his father was right about Crystal. He couldn't imagine losing his wonderful stepmother.

Later that morning, Savannah rang up a customer and then glanced toward the front window of the store. She took in the gray clouds clogging the sky and pondered how they were the opposite of her happy mood. She had hummed to herself while she worked in the store all morning and thought about seeing Korey on Sunday. She couldn't wait to tell Korey how she felt about him, and she was almost certain she had the perfect speech prepared. Now Sunday couldn't come soon enough.

Aenti Dorothy sidled up to her and touched her arm. "How are you doing today?"

"I feel fantastic. *Danki* so much for talking to me about Korey," Savannah said as her lips turned up in a smile. "I prayed about it again last night, and I know for sure now that God is leading me to tell Korey the truth. I've been mentally preparing what I'm going to say to him, and I plan to find my courage and share everything that's in my heart. I think you were right when you said that if I'm brave enough to tell him how I feel, then he'll also feel safe enough to tell me how he feels. And maybe Sunday night I'll officially be his real girlfriend instead of his fake girlfriend."

Aenti Dorothy grinned. "That's the spirit! I'm certain that you'll find the perfect words. After all, you've always been courageous enough to speak your mind. Once you get started, the words will just tumble out of you. I imagine he'll be relieved that you were brave enough to share the truth, and then he will be too."

"*Danki, Aenti.* I'm so grateful for you." Savannah's heart swelled with appreciation for her sweet aunt.

"Excuse me," an Amish woman with pale-blond hair under her prayer covering and thick glasses called. "Would you please help me find the brown sugar?"

Savannah came out from behind the counter. "I'll help her," she told her aunt. Then she hurried off to assist the customer.

Rain beat a loud and angry cadence on the skylights and the roof of the store while Savannah finished ringing up an elderly Amish woman's groceries later that afternoon. A bright flash of lightning lit up the store and was followed by a loud rumble of thunder. Out of the corner of her eye, she noticed an Amish man saunter into the store, but she kept her attention on the cash register instead of focusing on him.

"*Danki* for coming in today. Be careful in the rain," Savannah told the woman as she handed her the receipt and her change.

The woman smiled. "You too, sweetie." Then she hobbled toward the door where a young Amish man waited for her, holding an umbrella in his hand.

When Savannah felt someone watching her, she looked up. She took in the middle-aged man's familiar gray eyes, and her heart began to pound in her ears.

"Savannah?" he asked in that familiar voice.

Her stomach dropped. "Yes?"

"I'm . . . I'm Lee. Your *dat*."

Her eyes welled up, and she felt as if the ground dropped out below her feet. She grabbed onto the counter to stop herself from falling to the floor.

"You're so *schee*, Savannah," he continued in that same sweet voice she recalled reading her bedtime stories when she was little. "You look just like her. I mean, you look just like your *mamm*." His voice was gravelly.

She opened her mouth to respond, but a sob broke free as her body started to tremble. She hugged her arms to her chest and closed her eyes while fighting to get her emotions under control.

"Savannah!" *Aenti* Dorothy swooped over and pulled her into her arms. "Calm down. Calm down." She placed a tissue into Savannah's palm. "It's all right."

Savannah sniffed and mopped up her tears before wiping her nose.

"What are you doing here, Lee?" *Aenti* Dorothy asked, her voice strained.

Savannah took a deep breath in through her nose and found her confidence once again. She squared her shoulders. "Where have you been all this time? It's been nineteen years now. You've been gone for *nineteen years!*"

Her aunt touched her shoulder as if to calm her.

Lee rubbed his dark-brown beard that was threaded with gray, as his expression became sheepish. "I'd like to talk to you and explain everything—if you'll give me a chance."

Savannah turned toward her aunt, who looked suspicious. "Would it be all right if we talked in the back room?"

"Do you want me to come with you?" her aunt offered.

"No, I'll be fine." She faced her father as her anger swelled, crowding her rib cage. "Come with me to the back room, and you can explain why you abandoned Toby and me."

CHAPTER 22

"I WAITED MY WHOLE LIFE FOR YOU TO COME BACK TO ME."
Savannah wiped her cheeks with a tissue as she sat on a folding
chair and stared at the man who had once been her father—her
daddy—but was now a stranger. "I sat on the porch and waited for
you every night after you left. I cried for you and prayed for you.
Where were you?"

Outside the rain continued to pound the roof and skylights
while thunder rumbled in the distance.

Lee rubbed his hands down his face, and his gray eyes pooled
with tears. "I couldn't handle losing your *mamm*. It was too much
for me to bear. I was broken, and every day was a challenge. I had
days when I couldn't get out of bed."

He looked toward the shelf that Toby had built, which was
stacked with pet supplies. "I tried to handle it all, and although I
even hired a young woman to help me, it was just too much. Since
I was such a mess, I assumed you and Tobias were better off without me."

"Better off without you?" Savannah exclaimed. "You were our
only parent left. We needed you."

Lee shook his head. "I'm sorry, Savannah. I'm so, so sorry."

"Where have you been this whole time?"

"I traveled around for a bit. I visited different Amish communities. I was in Florida, Kentucky, and Delaware for a while. Then I came back to Pennsylvania ten years ago, and I decided to settle in New Wilmington. I have a farm there, and I—"

Savannah jumped up with such force that her chair collapsed behind her with a loud clatter. "You've been in Pennsylvania for *ten years*, but this is the first time you've come to Bird-in-Hand?" She nearly yelled the question.

Lee's posture drooped, and he covered his face with his hands.

"You're telling me that you've been five hours from your *kinner*, and you never felt compelled to visit us? Did you ever *think* of us? Did you ever *worry* about us?" Her voice shook as more tears trailed down her face.

Lee sniffed and wiped at his eyes with the back of his hands. "I've thought of you and your *bruder* every hour of every day for the past nineteen years."

"I find that very hard to believe." She snorted and folded her arms over her chest.

"I was lost and confused, and I'm not proud of what I did."

"So why are you here now? What do you want from us?"

"I'm better now, and I want to be your *daed* again—if . . . if you'll give me a chance." Lee took a trembling breath. "I'm remarried and *mei fraa* is expecting."

White-hot fury boiled just under her skin. "You've *replaced* us? Do we not matter to you?" Her voice creaked.

"Of course you and your *bruder* matter to me. I'm back now to make amends. I would be honored to have you and Tobias in my life again—if you'd be willing." He reached for her, and she took two steps back out of his reach.

Her body shook with her anger and heartache. "You walked away from your *sohn* who wasn't even a year old yet!" She pointed to her chest. "*I* took care of him. I believed it was my job to be his parent, and I was only five years old. For a long time, I believed it was my fault you left. I was certain that if I had been a better *dochder*, if I'd helped you more, and if I'd done a better job cleaning up my toys, then you would have stayed with us!"

A fresh crush of tears leaked from her eyes. "You have no idea what you did to us. So if you think you can just walk back in here and be our *dat*, then you are sadly mistaken. It will take more than a few words to undo what you've done to us!" A sob stole her words, and she covered her face with her hands.

Aenti Dorothy burst into the room and pulled Savannah into her arms. "It's okay," she murmured to Savannah, holding her close. "Calm down now, *mei liewe*. You're getting yourself too worked up."

Savannah took deep breaths, trying to get ahold of her emotions.

"She's been through enough for one day," *Aenti* Dorothy told Lee. "You should leave."

Savannah sniffed and wiped her eyes and nose again. "No. He needs to stay and answer my questions."

Lee wiped his eyes as well. "I want to answer your questions if you'll give me a chance to."

"It's breaking my heart to see you this upset, Savannah. Are you sure you're going to be okay if he stays and talks to you?" *Aenti* Dorothy asked, her dark eyes full of concern.

Savannah took a shuddering breath and nodded.

"And I would like to see Tobias." Lee paused, and his eyes sparkled with fresh tears. "How is he?"

"He's fine," Savannah said. "He works for a roofer, who is my ... *mei freind*."

"When will he be home?"

"I expect him soon since it's storming." Dorothy started for the door that led to the store. "Come inside. We'll close the store early, make *kaffi*, and wait for him."

Lee stood. "*Danki*. I know I don't deserve your forgiveness, but I want to ask for it—no, *beg* for it."

Savannah stared at this stranger who once was her father— the man who had held her on his lap during church services, who had read her stories at night, who had played with blocks with her on the floor—and her body continued to tremble with fury, confusion, and anguish.

Help me forgive him, Lord.

When Korey arrived home, he walked into the family room, where Crystal sat on the sofa. "Korey!" she exclaimed. "You're a mess."

He snickered and looked down at his shirt and trousers, which were soaked from the rain. "Yeah, we got caught in a downpour. How was your appointment?"

"It went well. The doctor told me to rest."

"Is that all the doctor said?"

Crystal nodded. "*Ya*, she said that I look *gut*, and I should feel better soon."

"Could I make you some tea?"

"That would be lovely." She pointed to his chest. "But you might want to get changed first."

"*Ya*, that's a *gut* idea."

She pointed to the window. "It looks like the storm has let up a bit."

"It has. The thunder and lightning have stopped, and the rain has slowed down some. I'll be right back." He jogged upstairs and changed and then hurried back down to the kitchen and made her some tea.

When Korey carried the mug into the family room, he set it on the end table beside his stepmother and then sank down onto the wing chair across from her.

"This is very thoughtful. *Danki*, Korey," she said.

"*Gern gschehne.*" He grinned. "But I have an ulterior motive."

"Okay. What is it?" She took a sip of tea.

"I need some more advice." Then he shared the truth about his relationship with Savannah, explaining how it was all pretend to keep their friends and family members from nagging them about dating. "I've been playing along with the façade, but I need to tell someone the truth, and I trust you." He rubbed the bridge of his nose. "I care for Savannah, and I can't play along with the fake relationship anymore. I want more. In fact, my heart craves more."

"Oh my goodness." Crystal's eyes widened. "I had absolutely no idea that your relationship wasn't real. Your *dat* and I honestly were thrilled that you had fallen in love, and we were convinced that you would be engaged by next spring."

"Really?"

"*Ya*, really." Crystal seemed to study him. "How do you feel about her?"

"I love her."

"And she loves you." Crystal smiled.

He ran his hands over the arm of the chair. "I think she cares for me, but I don't know if she truly loves me." *But I hope she does.* He huffed out a deep breath. "What do you think I should do?"

"Well, first of all, I'm honored that you're asking for my advice."

He gave her a sheepish smile. "I'm grateful for your help with this."

"Secondly, if you truly love her, then you need to tell her how you feel. If you believe that she's the one God has chosen for your future, then you need to make it right. Be honest with her and ask God to guide your words. Tell her that you love her and you want to start over as a real couple, not a pretend couple."

"Okay." Korey nodded as excitement and anxiety warred inside of him.

Crystal gave him a warm smile. "Korey, if she loves you, and I believe she does, then she will be relieved that you're finally telling her how you truly feel. She'll be ready to take your hand and look toward the future with you. I'm sure of it."

"*Danki.* I'll go see her after supper and tell her how I feel." Korey stood while his nerve endings continued to tingle. "I'd like to make dinner for you."

"I appreciate that so much. I defrosted some chicken. The cookbook is on the kitchen counter. I was going to fry it."

"I can handle it. I'll make some noodles and vegetables too."

Korey set to work preparing supper while contemplating what he would say to Savannah and how he would convince her that he loved her and wanted to try to give their relationship a chance—a *real* chance this time.

Korey prayed she would agree to start over and consider a future with him.

CHAPTER 23

THE DELICIOUS AROMA OF THE PIZZA CASSEROLE WAFTED OVER the kitchen while Savannah stared across the kitchen table at her father, her thoughts spinning like a weather vane in gale-force winds.

His words—no, his *excuses*—were merely background noise as she fought to extinguish the raging bewilderment, agony, and acrimony that boiled in her chest. While the thunder and lightning had ceased, the rain beat a steady cadence on the roof above them.

Her gaze moved to the propane oven, and she thought about her casserole, which continued to bake. When she had assembled the casserole last night, she hadn't imagined that her father would be sitting at the table tonight, awaiting a taste of the new recipe.

No, last night, her heart had instead been full of happy thoughts of Korey and how she was going to tell him that she loved him. Korey had been the foremost thought in her mind, and her excitement about their possible future together had kept a bright smile on her face.

But now, as the casserole baked, she had a new conundrum— her father. She couldn't bring herself to refer to him as her father. In her mind, he was simply Lee, the man who was her biological father but had been no father to her at all since she'd been five years old. Now her life had been turned upside down and she felt as if she were a boat adrift, lost in a sea of confusion.

Savannah had never dreamed that she would ever see Lee again, but here he was, sitting across from her, sharing the grief he had struggled with since he had walked out of her and Toby's lives nineteen years ago.

She gripped the table and clenched her jaw as she studied him. Every muscle in her body tensed as she contemplated jumping up from the table and retreating to her room for the remainder of the evening. But, at the same time, she couldn't move. She was cemented in place, eager to hear what he had to say, no matter how lame his excuses for abandoning her and Toby were.

"Savannah? Savannah?"

"Huh?" Savannah jumped with a start, and her eyes fell on her aunt sitting at the far end of the table. "I'm sorry. What did you need?"

Aenti Dorothy pointed toward the counter. "The timer."

It was then that Savannah heard the oven timer buzzing.

"Oh!" Savannah leapt up from her chair.

Aenti Dorothy held up her hands to stop Savannah. "I'll get the casserole out of the oven, but I wanted to check with you first. Is it done? Or does it need more time?"

"I'll get it!" Savannah raced across the kitchen, grateful for an excuse to exert some of her pent-up energy.

She fetched the casserole from the oven and set it on the stove. Then she moved to the cabinet and began retrieving dishes.

When she felt a hand on her back, she jumped with a start once again.

"Savannah." *Aenti's* voice was close to her ear. "Go sit, and I'll set the table."

Turning to face her aunt, Savannah shook her head. "No. I need to keep busy or I'm going to lose my composure."

Savannah looked toward the table, where Lee talked on and on about his farm and *Onkel* Eddie watched him, his face stony and arms crossed over his wide chest.

Aenti Dorothy rubbed her back. "Let's set the table together. Toby should be home soon."

Savannah cringed as she imagined her younger brother coming in and finding Lee there. She was certain he would crumble under the weight of his own grief after losing both of his parents only to find out that their father had been alive and well in Pennsylvania for the past ten years. This news would certainly break Toby's fragile heart.

Lord, please calm Toby and keep him strong when he faces this unexpected visitor.

"Supper smells *appeditlich*, Savannah," Lee said as she delivered the plates to the table.

She ignored him and returned with drinking glasses while *Aenti* Dorothy took care of the utensils. The back door opened just as Savannah set the casserole dish in the center of the table.

Savannah remained by her chair and held on to the back. Toby entered the room and glanced around. His gray shirt and black trousers were damp, and he pushed his hand through his soaked, dark hair.

"We got off early because of that storm," Toby said as he took a step. Then he stopped and blinked as his eyes darted around the room. "What's going on?"

Lee stood, and his gray eyes shimmered with tears. "Tobias?"

"I go by Toby." He walked over to Lee and held out his hand. "Who are you?"

Lee sniffed and wiped his eyes.

Savannah sucked in a breath.

"Am I missing something here?" Toby asked, his words halting.

Lee sniffed and wiped his eyes with a paper napkin. "Tobias, I'm Lee Zook, your *daed*."

Toby's face flashed with disbelief and then shock before he took a few steps back away from Lee. Then he faced Savannah. "Is this some kind of joke?"

"No, Toby." Savannah rushed over to him and reached for his arm, but Toby pulled it away. "It's not a joke."

Toby stared at her. "Did you know he was coming?"

"No, I had no idea. He just showed up at the store this afternoon. I was just as surprised as you are."

Toby's jaw tightened. "*Why* is he here?" His voice was strained.

"Please give me a minute to explain." Lee took a step toward Toby. "I would like the opportunity tell you why I had to leave."

Savannah gave a wry laugh. "You *had* to leave?"

Toby's hands shook and his face crumpled. "I know why you had to leave. It was because you hate me."

"Hate you?" Lee shook his head as he looked shocked. "No, that's not true. I don't hate you or Savannah. I could *never* hate *mei kinner*, Toby. That's just not possible."

Toby pointed to his chest. "Tell the truth. You hate *me* because if I hadn't been born, then *Mamm* would be alive." He pointed at Savannah. "Then you, *Mamm*, and Vannah would have been the perfect little family. But I came along and ruined it. That's why you couldn't stand the sight of me, and that's why you left. Tell the truth! That's why you left!"

A sob escaped Toby's throat, and Savannah felt her heart

shatter. She reached for her brother's arm, but Toby stumbled back, crashing into the china cabinet, which rattled.

Aenti Dorothy sidled up to Toby and opened her arms. He leaned down, and she pulled him against her. Savannah wiped her own tears while she watched her brother cry. She hugged her arms against her chest as grief sliced her into a million pieces.

"That's enough," *Onkel* Eddie said, standing at the end of the table. "Lee, you have caused enough stress today, and I can't sit here and take any more of it. It should be clear to you what your selfishness has done to these two young people. You're not fit to be called their *daed* after you abandoned them after *mei schweschder* passed away!" He shook his finger at Lee. "You never once called us and asked how they were. You just moved on and left these two innocents in the dust. You ought to be ashamed of yourself!"

Lee hung his head. "I am ashamed, Eddie. I've always been ashamed of what I did to both Savannah and Tobias." Then he looked up with contrition lining his face. "And I owe you and Dorothy so much. *Danki* for being the parents that *mei kinner* needed. I could never repay you for what you've done."

Toby stepped out of *Aenti* Dorothy's embrace and wiped his eyes and nose with a tissue.

"We love them as our own," *Aenti* Dorothy said, her dark eyes misting over with tears. "They are our *kinner*." She touched Toby's cheek and then looked lovingly at Savannah.

"I'm grateful for you both, Eddie and Dorothy. *Danki* for being the parents that *mei kinner* needed," Lee said. "And I'm so very sorry for how I left in the middle of the night with no explanation. I was struggling and begging God to lead me to the answers I was seeking. I was lost."

"Why didn't you tell us what you were going through?" *Onkel*

Eddie demanded. "We're your family. We would have helped you, Lee. You should have known that. And we were grieving too. We could have all helped each other through that terrible time."

"I know," Lee said. "I was wrong to leave. I was just broken and lost, and I regret all of my mistakes."

Savannah cleared her throat. "You didn't even say goodbye. You just left us. I was so confused and *bedauerlich*. I missed you so much. I spent years believing I had done something wrong."

Toby sniffed as he folded his arms over his wide chest.

"None of this was your fault, Savannah." Lee turned toward Toby. "You did nothing wrong, Tobias. God chose to take your *mamm*. You didn't cause her death."

Toby blinked as his expression softened.

"Now tell us why you're here, and then leave so we can get back to our lives," *Onkel* Eddie insisted. "Savannah and Toby were doing just fine until you showed up here today. What is it you want?"

Lee rubbed his cheek and pulled a deep breath in through his nose. "I confessed to my congregation, and I've vowed to right my wrongs. I want to be a better man, a better husband, and a better *daed*. I want to be the *daed* that I should have been beginning the day Savannah was born."

"What are you saying?" Toby croaked.

"What I'm saying, Tobias, is that I would be honored to start new with you both. I would love to have the opportunity to show you both what you mean to me and make up for lost time. I'm asking you both—no, *begging* you—to give me a chance to be your *daed*. I would love to have the chance to make up for my mistakes. I would love to be able to start a new relationship together. That's what I'm trying to say, Tobias."

"Please call me Toby," he insisted.

Lee cleared his throat. "I'm sorry—Toby."

"Why should we trust you?" Savannah asked, her words rough.

Lee frowned. "That is a *gut* question, Savannah. I know I can't convince you to trust me, but I hope that you'll trust God. I feel God led me here to find you, and I feel God telling me to be the father I was called to be. With God's help, I believe we can be a family—if you'll both give me a chance."

Savannah's thoughts spun like a cyclone as she stared at her father. She pivoted to face Toby, and he studied her, his expression full of confusion. Savannah rested her hand on her forehead and tried to make sense of what her father had just said.

All her life she had dreamed of her father coming for her, and now that the day had finally come, she had no idea what to do.

And then a thought hit her—she had become so distracted with her fake relationship with Korey that she had lost sight of her true purpose, which was taking care of Toby's well-being. Now, as her father sat in front of her offering her and Toby a true family, she had to get her priorities in order. It was time to push all thoughts of Korey out of her mind. Instead, she needed to figure out if her father was genuine as well as what was best for Toby.

But how could she push Korey out of her mind when she loved him?

Help me, Lord.

By the time Korey's father and younger brother arrived home after making a supply run and running a few other errands, Korey had the table set and a meal of fried chicken, noodles, green beans, and rolls sitting on the table.

"You actually made this, Kore?" Jayden asked, suspicion flickering over his face.

Korey nodded. "*Ya*, why?"

"If you had so much talent, then why didn't you actually cook a meal all of those times it was your turn to cook instead of always serving us hot dogs?"

Korey shrugged. "No one questioned me, so I got off easy, I suppose."

Dat hooted with laughter while Jayden shook his head.

"Let's enjoy this impressive meal Korey made for us," Crystal said as she sat at the table. "I appreciate your help, Korey."

"I'm happy to do it for you." Korey glanced around the table and smiled. He was grateful for his family, and he was especially thankful that they had welcomed him home after his past mistakes.

They discussed work during supper, and when they were done, Korey helped Jayden and *Dat* carry the dishes to the counter.

"I'll do the dishes since you cooked," Jayden said. "*Allegedly.*"

Korey winced. "Allegedly?"

"It was way too *gut* for you to have prepared it. I think Crystal really made it and decided to give you credit," Jayden teased.

Crystal wagged a finger at Jayden as *Dat* guided her toward the family room. "Your *bruder* truly made supper. I'm sure of it. I was in the *schtupp* resting while he worked."

"I suppose I'll believe it if you say so." Jayden smiled at Korey. "It was really *gut*."

Korey rubbed his hands together. "Do you mind doing the dishes alone?"

"No. Why?"

"I'm going to see Savannah." *And tell her how I feel about her!* Excitement filled his gut at the thought of telling her he cared for her and wanted a future with her.

Jayden grinned. "Have fun."

"Thanks." Korey hurried out the back door, his heart soaring as he imagined seeing Savannah and telling her that he loved her. He prayed she felt the same way.

The light rain pelleted the windshield of Korey's buggy as he guided his horse up to Savannah's house. His hands began to sweat, and his blood thundered through his veins as he looked up at the house.

Closing his eyes, he sent a quick prayer up to God:

Lord, guide my words and give me the courage to tell Savannah how much she means to me.

Then he wiped the palms of his hands down his trousers before climbing out of the buggy. After tying his horse to the fence post, he loped through the rain to the back porch steps. Memories of sitting on the porch with Savannah filled his mind, and he smiled.

Korey couldn't wait to tell her how he felt and ask her if he could officially be her boyfriend. Then he would visit her here more often, and they would sit on the porch for hours, sharing their deepest secrets, holding hands, dreaming out their future together, and maybe even stealing kisses. But would Savannah ever feel that way about him? Would she consider truly being his girlfriend? That idea took hold of his mind, and excitement fizzed through his veins.

Korey's steps felt light as he approached the doorway. Then he rested his hands on his hips, bowed his head, and closed his eyes, taking a moment to gather his courage and his thoughts.

Once he convinced himself he was ready to bare his soul to the woman he loved, he reached up and knocked on the door.

Korey glanced around the porch and waited, his impatient foot tapping on the wooden floor. Drizzle continued to drum the porch roof, and the scent of rain filled his nostrils.

When no one appeared, he leaned toward the storm door and listened. Muffled voices sounded from inside the house. He knocked again, striking the door a little harder this time.

After a few moments, deliberate footsteps plodded toward the door.

Korey ran his hands down his green shirt as anxiety doused him like the rain had earlier in the day. Maybe he should have put on a nicer shirt?

The door opened with a squeak, and Savannah stood on the other side. Her pretty face was clouded with a frown, and her eyes were red and puffy as if she'd been crying.

Worry sluiced through him. "Savannah! Are you—"

"I'm sorry, but this isn't a *gut* time." She started to close the storm door in his face.

Korey's foot shot out, blocking the door before it closed. "Wait. Please." He held up his hands to stop her from leaving. "Can we please talk for a few minutes?"

"I just—" She glanced behind her and then back at him, her brow wrinkled and her eyes impatient. "What do you want?"

"You look upset. What's going on?"

An unreadable expression flashed over her face, and the mask of anger seemed to fall away, revealing something that looked like confusion or possibly even anguish. "*Mei dat,* I mean, Lee Zook, is here."

"Your *dat*?" Korey pulled the storm door open wide. "Your *daed*? He's here?" He pointed to the floor.

She nodded. *"Ya."*

"Are you okay?" Korey reached for her hand.

She sniffed and shook her head. "I-I don't know."

"Do you want to talk about it?" He pointed to the glider. "We can sit there, and you can tell me how you feel about seeing him again. You've helped me so much with my family, and I want to do the same for you."

Savannah's eyes dropped. "No, this is a family matter." She looked up again slowly. "What do you want?"

"I wanted to see you. I missed you."

"I don't have time to talk right now. I need to be with my family." She reached for the door handle, and he blocked her hand. "Korey, please don't do this right now. I need to go. I need you to move away from the door." She ground out the words.

"Savannah, please just listen. I care about you and I want to help you. Please talk to—"

She cut off his words. "I don't need this fake relationship anymore. I need to concentrate on my family."

"It was never fake to me, Savannah."

She stilled and swallowed.

"I care for you deeply. I've realized that I cared for you all along, but I—"

"Move away from the door." Her words were measured, and her expression was fierce. "I told you that I need to go."

Korey's shoulders wilted and his confidence shriveled as he took a step away from the storm door. He was losing her, but he couldn't give up just yet. "Savannah, please just give me a minute. Please. I'm begging you."

"Goodbye, Korey," she said before closing the storm door and then the main door in his face.

As he stood on the porch, Korey scrubbed his hands down his face while a mixture of heartache, despondency, worry, and anger tormented him.

He traced the doorknob with his finger as he considered barging into the house and begging Savannah to listen to him, but she had made it clear that she was over him and their relationship.

Korey leaned on the railing and stared out toward the barn as sadness lodged in his throat. This was exactly what he had feared. He had opened his heart to a *maedel* and she had stomped on it.

Then he spun and faced the house. He had seen the pain and confusion in Savannah's beautiful eyes. She clearly was suffering due to her father's return. If he had only been honest with his feelings for her sooner, he could have helped her through this tough time.

If she had known weeks ago how much he cared for her, he could have been her support, someone to hold her hand and dry her tears while she tried to work through the myriad of feelings her father had caused her not only by abandoning her and Toby but by reappearing nineteen years later.

But Korey had waited too long, and now he'd lost Savannah. Cold reality washed over him. He had lost her—*forever.*

How would he ever forgive himself or recover from this tremendous loss and heartbreak?

CHAPTER 24

SAVANNAH SHUT THE DOOR AND SAGGED AGAINST IT. CLOSING her eyes, she worked to stop her body from vibrating and her sobs from breaking free as Korey's words echoed in her mind: *"It was never fake to me, Savannah. I care for you deeply. I've realized that I cared for you all along."*

She folded her arms over her chest as if to shield her heart from his words. Korey cared about her, and he insisted he had all along. This was what she'd yearned to hear. These words should have been a sweet hymn to her soul, but they weren't. Instead, they were too much for her to bear. She couldn't take any more confusion today!

Trying to untangle her feelings for her father was already too much. After years of wondering what she could have done to convince her father to stay, he was back in her life, telling her that he cared for her and offering her a nuclear family with a mother, father, and more siblings.

But how could she possibly trust him after all this time? And where did her obligation to Toby fit in with all of these new developments? She had to do what was best for her brother, even if that meant giving up Korey.

Help me, Lord.

Savannah worked to keep her emotions in check as she returned to the table, where her aunt, uncle, brother, and Lee sat. The room was silent except for the sound of forks scraping plates.

Scanning the table, she found her aunt, uncle, and father all eating the casserole, their eyes trained on their supper. Savannah peered across the table to her brother. With his shoulders slumped, Toby stared down at his portion of casserole while moving his fork absently around on the plate. His face was creased with a frown, and anguish radiated off him in waves.

Savannah lifted her fork and stabbed her casserole, then stilled. Her mind continued to reel, taunting her with memories of Korey's handsome face clouded with a frown, his voice begging her to talk to him, his words telling her that he cared for her. She longed to dash back out to the porch, take his hand, and pull him down onto the glider so that they could talk.

Had she made a mistake when she'd sent him away? But she had to put her family—specifically Toby—first right now. Regret bubbled up in her chest and her eyes started to sting.

"Who was at the door, Savannah?" *Onkel* Eddie asked.

Savannah shook her head and cleared her throat. "No one," she muttered.

"No one?" *Aenti* Dorothy set her fork beside her plate and lifted her glass of water.

Savannah met her gaze. "It was Korey."

"Who's Korey?" Lee asked.

Savannah held on to her fork and debated her response. *He's the man I love, the man whose heart I just broke, the man I'll never see again.* "He's . . . he's a *freind.*"

Aenti Dorothy gave her a questioning look, and Savannah shook her head. Her aunt frowned in response, and Savannah looked away.

"Oh." Lee nodded slowly. "Tell me more about your life here in Bird-in-Hand. Are you active in youth group?"

Savannah picked up her glass, which shook in her trembling hand. *"Ya."* She took a long drink, but the cool liquid did nothing to douse her anxiety.

"I'm so *froh* to hear that. Do you like working at the store?" Lee asked.

"Uh-huh."

"Gut." Lee turned to her brother. "What about you, Toby? Tell me about your job. Have you always wanted to become a roofer? How do you like the work?"

Toby looked up at Lee and hesitated before his expression warmed. "I actually love the work. I've always wanted to work in construction, but I never thought I would be *gut* enough."

"Why would you think that?" Lee's expression seemed to cloud with confusion.

Toby moved his fork around on his plate. "I struggled at school, so I thought I would have to keep working at the store for the rest of my life. But I taught myself how to work with wood, and a friend invited me to work on his roofing crew."

"That's fantastic, Toby. It's important to find work you enjoy." Lee looked almost proud.

Savannah snorted. Where was their father when Toby was struggling with reading and math as well as with bullies at school?

Lee met her gaze. "What is it, Savannah?"

"It's a little late for you to show an interest in our lives now, isn't it?" she snapped.

Lee looked crestfallen as his posture withered and he glanced down at his half-eaten meal.

When he met Savannah's gaze again, Lee folded his hands on the gray tablecloth. "Savannah, I know that I hurt you and Toby deeply—more deeply than I could ever comprehend—but I would like the chance to prove to you that I never stopped loving either of you. You were always on my mind."

"If we were so important to you, then why didn't you reach out to see how we were?" Savannah tapped her finger on the table. "Why didn't you visit? Why didn't you come and get us when you settled on your farm in New Wilmington?"

"He's here now, Vannah," Toby exclaimed. "Give him a chance."

"Your *schweschder* is right, Toby." Lee sniffed as his eyes filled again, and Savannah's stomach clenched. "I wanted to, but I was a wreck."

"So were we!" Savannah exclaimed. "I cried for you and *Mamm* every night, but you never came."

Onkel Eddie reached over and touched Savannah's hand. "Shhh, *mei liewe*, it's okay."

"No, it's not okay." Savannah shook her head. "He's been gone for nineteen years."

Lee wiped his eyes with a paper napkin. "You're right, and I'm sorry. I'll spend the rest of my life apologizing and begging for your forgiveness. I just hope and pray that you and Toby can find it in your hearts to forgive me and give me a chance to be the *daed* I need to be to you. The *daed* I *want* to be for you both."

The back door suddenly clicked shut and Dean walked into the kitchen.

Lee gasped. "Oh my goodness. Is this Levi?"

"No," *Onkel* Eddie said. "This is Dean."

Lee stood and held out his hand to Savannah's cousin. "I'm so blessed to meet you, Dean. I'm your *Onkel* Lee."

"Uh. Okay." Dean shook his hand. His brows drew together as his gaze bounced to his parents and then to Savannah. "Hello."

Savannah stood. "I'm going to find something for dessert," she muttered before picking up her dish and hurrying into the kitchen in the hopes of sorting through the thoughts clogging her mind.

She needed a minute to try to make sense of everything that had happened. Her father had returned, and she had most likely lost Korey forever.

How would her heart ever recover?

Korey spent the ride home thinking about Savannah and trying to come up with a plan to encourage her to talk to him. If he could only convince her that his intentions were true and that he loved her and wanted to be her friend, her confidant, her boyfriend. But she had shut him out.

He contemplated their pretend relationship and tried to figure out what he should have done differently. If only he'd told her that he loved her sooner! But would she have rejected him then?

And then there was the conundrum of her father. What did he want? Why was he back after nineteen years? And how were Savannah and Toby handling it?

The questions haunted him as he led his horse to the barn. If only he'd insisted she stay out on the porch with him and talk to him. Maybe then he could have helped her. But she had shut the door in his face. She had instructed him to leave. Yet his heart was still back on that porch, hoping she would come back to him and allow him to console her.

But he'd given up too easily. He groaned aloud as his frustration boiled over.

After stowing his horse in the stall, Korey turned and kicked the wall with all his might while letting out a loud grunt. Then, yelping, Korey hopped around and muttered to himself as pain radiated from his toes up his leg.

"Is everything all right, Kore?"

Spinning toward the barn doors, he found his older brother watching him with a concerned expression while holding a lantern. "No, nothing is."

"Do you want to talk about it?" Tyler's expression was open and eager.

Korey scowled and held his breath while his toes continued to throb. He studied his older brother, debating how much to share.

And then the truth hit Korey like a smack in the face—he needed Tyler. In fact, he craved his older brother's advice more than ever, and he was grateful that Tyler was there. "*Ya*, I would like to talk about it."

"*Gut.*" Tyler breathed the word, looking relieved. "I'm listening."

"It's about Savannah."

"Oh." Tyler frowned. "Did you break up?"

"We actually weren't really dating."

Tyler gave him a confused expression. "You had told everyone that you were dating Savannah, but now you're telling me that you weren't dating. I'm confused."

Korey blew out a puff of air before explaining to Tyler everything, starting with when Savannah suggested that they pretend to date. Then he shared how he went to Savannah's house and had hoped to confess to her that he loved her, but she told him that her father had shown up, and she instructed Korey to leave.

"I wanted to stay there and encourage her to share how she felt about her father, but she shut down on me. And then she slammed the door in my face." Korey sank down onto an upside-down bucket and set his lantern by his feet.

Tyler picked up another bucket, flipped it over, and sat across from Korey. "I'm so sorry. This is a tough situation."

"I'm so worried about her. She hasn't seen her *dat* since he walked out on her and Toby shortly after Toby was born. She must be overwrought. I want to be there for her like she's been there for me." He drummed his fingers on the plastic bucket. "I don't know what to do. I'm at a complete loss."

Tyler studied him.

"Go ahead and say what you're thinking, Ty."

"Well, I can tell you really love her."

Korey lifted an eyebrow. "That's all you have to say?"

"No." Tyler shook his head. "I'm just really *froh* to see you in love."

Korey scoffed. "So, I'm in love, and the *maedel* I love won't talk to me, and you're happy?"

"That's not what I mean." Tyler held up his hands. "I'm just saying that I'm glad you've found someone, and I think it's all going to work out."

"But she won't talk to me. You heard that part of the story, right?"

Tyler chuckled. "*Ya*, I heard it, but you're forgetting an important detail."

"What?" Korey gave him a palms-up.

"I've seen how you and Savannah look at each other in church, and Crystal has shared with Michelle how *froh* you two were when Savannah brought supper over one night. It's obvious that Savannah loves you too, Kore."

"How can you be so sure?"

"If she didn't care for you and the entire relationship was a sham, would she have gone out of her way to make you supper?"

Korey considered that question, then shook his head. "No, I don't suppose she would have."

"Believe me when I tell you that those feelings don't just disappear overnight. Right now she's probably in shock that her *dat* showed up and is trying to process what that all means. She'll be ready to talk to you and discuss your relationship after she has a plan in place for what to do about her *dat*."

"That makes sense." Korey traced the edge of the bucket with his fingers. "What do you think I should do?"

"I think you should give her a day or two to try to cope with her father's appearance and then go see her and tell her that you care for her. Tell her that you're not going to give up on her. Tell her that no matter what, you're there for her."

The staccato sound of his fingers rapping the bucket filled the silence as Korey contemplated his older brother's advice. "Do you think that will work?"

"Do you love her, Kore?"

"*Ya*, I already said that."

"Do you want a future with her?"

Korey swallowed and then nodded. "I think so. I've never felt this way about anyone. I can't get her off my mind. I think about her and worry about her constantly. I truly love her."

"*Ya*, I can relate." Tyler gave him a knowing smile. "I know what that's like. And if that's how you feel, then you need to tell her, but you should give her a little bit of time to process her *daed's* return. That is a lot for her and Toby to handle."

They both stood, and Korey gave Tyler a quick hug.

"*Danki*, Ty. I mean it. I appreciate you."

Tyler patted Korey's back. "I've missed you."

"I've missed you too," Korey told him as they walked toward the barn exit together, each of them holding a lantern to light their way. "How's Michelle feeling?"

Tyler rubbed his hands together. "She's ready for this *boppli* to arrive. I am too."

"I've been meaning to ask you. Does Michelle still paint farm scenes on old milk cans and sell them at that little gift shop?"

"*Ya*, she does. She takes a few to that store in Bird-in-Hand every couple of weeks. Since she's busy with other things, she doesn't paint as much as she'd like to, but I encourage her to make time. Painting makes her so *froh*. She won't have as much time when the *boppli* arrives, but I'll try to keep encouraging her and helping her find the time to paint."

"That's great." Korey smiled as they walked toward their father's porch. The air smelled fresh and clean after the rain.

"It's so *gut* to see you two talking again finally." Jayden jogged down the stairs and hurried over to them, his flashlight beam bouncing off the ground. "It's about time you two got along."

Korey turned to Tyler and shook his hand. "*Danki* for the talk."

"Anytime." Tyler smacked Jayden's arm. "You'd better get some sleep. We have work early in the morning. The rain really set us behind."

"No kidding," Korey deadpanned. "My crew is behind too."

"You know we'll get caught up. It will all be okay," Jayden said.

Korey smiled. He could always count on Jayden to remain positive, no matter the issue. "You're right. It will all be okay."

"That's the attitude. Never doubt God." Tyler began walking backward. *"Gut nacht."*

Korey and Jayden waved to their older brother as he started on the path toward his house before they ambled toward the porch.

"What were you and Ty discussing?" Jayden asked as they started up the stairs.

The house was dark and quiet, evidence that their *dat* and Crystal had gone to bed.

"It's a long story," Korey said.

Jayden grinned. "That means you need to tell me quickly."

"Let's go upstairs."

They padded up to the second floor and then stopped in front of Jayden's room, where Korey shared the story he had told Tyler. Jayden listened, his eyes wide.

When Korey finished, Jayden shook his head. "Huh. That's a lot."

"I know."

"But I think Tyler's advice is right. Give Savannah time to come to terms with her father's return and then tell her how you feel again. Don't give up on her." Jayden smiled. "I don't think you have anything to worry about."

"What do you mean?"

Jayden chuckled. "She loves you, Kore. It's so obvious every time you two are together. You should have recognized it in her face the day we handled that bully for Toby. Savannah is in love with you, and I don't think she'll stop loving you just because her *daed* showed up and turned her life upside down. You need to be patient, which I know is something you've always struggled with."

"That's true." Korey lifted his lantern. "I'll see you in the morning."

"Try to get some sleep," Jayden said before disappearing into his room and closing his door.

When Korey climbed into bed, he closed his eyes and rested his arm on his forehead, and then he sent up a prayer:

Lord, help me be a comfort to Savannah and help me show her that my love for her is true.

CHAPTER 25

LATER THAT EVENING, SAVANNAH KNOCKED LIGHTLY ON THE door leading to the bedroom Toby and Dean shared. After having cookies for dessert, *Onkel* Eddie had suggested that Savannah and Toby go upstairs while he and *Aenti* Dorothy had a talk with Lee. Savannah's hands trembled and she held her breath, waiting for an invitation to enter her brother's room. After a few moments of silence, she knocked again.

"*Ya?*" Toby's muffled voice asked from inside the room.

Turning the knob, she pushed open the door. She stepped inside the room and peered toward Toby's bed, where he sat on the edge.

"Are you okay?"

He nodded. "*Ya*. I'm stunned, but I'm okay."

She pulled out his desk chair and sat. Then she folded her hands in her lap and kept her eyes focused on his window, studying the dark clouds that clogged the sky, while memories of her mother filled her mind. She contemplated what life would have been like if her mother had lived.

Would they have been a happy family of four? Or would God have blessed her parents with more children—more siblings for Toby and Savannah to enjoy?

But that wasn't meant to be. Instead, God had called her mother home.

Savannah picked up a pillow that had fallen on the floor, and she hugged it to her chest. She recalled how Korey had tried to convince her to stay on the porch with him and talk about her feelings toward her father. Once again, she regretted her decision to send him away. Perhaps talking to him would have eased some of the turmoil that continued to plague her.

Then she shook her head. Korey had arrived too late.

For a moment, she mulled over what Korey had said to her. He had specifically come over to tell her how he cared for her, and it felt so out of the blue, so out of character for him. And, to make it even more confusing, she had planned to tell him how she felt as well.

What would have happened if she had told him how she felt before her father had appeared? Would they have already been a couple? But if that were the case, then where would Toby fit into this confusing situation?

"Vannah? Vannah!"

"Huh?" Her gaze locked on her brother's as he stared at her. "I'm sorry. Did you say something?"

"I asked if you were okay."

"I'm . . . I'm all right."

"No, you're not. Tell me what's wrong."

She sniffed. "Korey came over here to talk to me earlier. I was surprised by what he said." She held the pillow in her lap and smoothed her hands over the cool white pillowcase. "He wanted me to know that he cared for me."

"Okay . . ." He blinked, looking confused. "Didn't you already know that since you're dating him?"

She shook her head. "No, we weren't really dating. It was all pretend." Then she explained their relationship and why they had set up the ruse.

"That doesn't make any sense to me. It's so obvious that you two belong together. Why would you have to pretend?"

"We wanted to keep our *freinden* off our backs, so we decided to pretend to date. But the truth is that I care about him, and he came over here to tell me that he cares for me too."

"So what's the problem then if he cares for you and you care for him?"

She stared out the window again.

"Vannah, what happened? Did you two work it out and decide to date for real?"

She shook her head. "No. I asked him to leave, and then I closed the door. I can't be distracted by Korey right now. I need to figure out what to do about . . . about Lee."

"What does our *dat* have to do with you dating Korey?"

"I don't know what's best for us now that Lee has shown up. I need to figure out this situation before I can even think about Korey. You're the most important person in my life, and I need to take care of you before I can think of myself."

"Savannah," Toby began slowly, "I'm twenty now. I don't need you to be *mei mamm* anymore."

She tried to swallow past the knot of grief in her throat. "It's not that simple."

"It is, and now that *Dat* is here, maybe we can start over with him. We'll finally have our *daed* in our lives, but that doesn't mean you can't be with Korey too."

"It's not that simple, Toby."

"It should be. If you love Korey and he loves you, then what is left to figure out?"

"Having Lee here changes everything. I don't know what he means when he says he wants to be a family." She shook her head and felt her eyes narrow. "He just needs to go back to where he came from. We don't need him in our lives."

"But he's our *dat*." Toby's eyes seemed to plead with her. "How can you reject him?"

Savannah felt her face twist into a deep scowl. "No, he's *not*. *Onkel* Eddie is our *dat*. He's the man who raised us. Where was Lee when we fell down and skinned our knees? Where was Lee when you went fishing with *Onkel* Eddie, Dean, and Levi? Where was Lee when the bullies were harassing you at school?"

"But he's here now." Toby sniffed and wiped his eyes with the back of his hand. "He finally came back for us."

She snorted. "It's too late."

"You shouldn't say that. This is what we've both prayed for our entire lives, haven't we? I know it's what I've prayed for."

A tapping on the doorframe drew Savannah's attention to the doorway, where Dean stood, his expression tentative.

"Is it all right if I come in?" her cousin asked.

"*Ya.*" Savannah stood.

"Is Lee still here?" Toby asked, looking hopeful.

"*Ya.* When I came back in from taking care of the horses, I heard *mei dat* and him having a heated discussion." Dean sank down on his bed, which creaked under his weight.

Toby faced him. "What are they talking about?"

"*Mei dat* is giving your *dat* a piece of his mind."

"He's not our *dat*," Savannah grumbled.

Toby leaned forward, resting his elbows on his knees. "What did your *dat* say to him?"

"He told Lee that he is hurting you both by just showing up here after nineteen years. *Dat* gave him a lecture about how selfish he's been and how he needs to consider your feelings. *Dat* also told him that he should have reached out ahead of time instead of surprising everyone. *Mamm* told Lee that he should have called years ago to see how you both were doing." Dean's expression warmed. "Are you two okay?"

"I don't know." Savannah shrugged.

"When I headed for the stairs, I heard *Dat* tell Lee that he'd gotten you both distraught enough for one day. He asked him to leave."

Panic seemed to etch Toby's face. "Is he going back to New Wilmington?"

"No." Dean shook his head. "He has a hotel room in town. He asked if he could come back tomorrow to visit with you both."

Relief seemed to overtake Toby's face. "Oh *gut*. I want to talk to him some more."

"What else is there left to say?" Savannah demanded. "He hurt us both, Toby. Why would you want to get to know him?"

"Because he's our father, the only parent we have left."

"He left us, Toby!" She raised her voice. "That's it, end of story. What more is there to say?"

Toby opened his mouth to reply, but their cousin stood and cut off her words.

"Savannah, just calm down." Dean's tone was even as he held up his hands, encouraging her to relax. "You're right. He did leave you, and he hurt you both deeply. But don't let his sins come between you and your *bruder*."

Dean pointed at Savannah and then Toby. "You two have always had each other, and you'll always have my parents, Levi, and me. We're all a family. Don't let Lee destroy what we've all built together."

Toby peered up at the ceiling and swallowed, his Adam's apple bobbing. He sniffed and then rubbed his eyes.

"I'm sorry, Toby." Savannah ran her hands down her wet cheeks. "*Danki*, Dean, for reminding us of what's important." Then she stood and peered out the window as her father climbed into a taxi. "He's leaving."

"I'm going to see if *Aenti* Dorothy needs help in the kitchen." She crossed to the doorway and then headed downstairs while considering all of her confusing feelings.

While she wanted her brother in her life, she also wanted Korey. But how could she work things out with Korey if she had to make sure Toby had what he needed? Her father's showing up made everything more complicated! Could she trust her father not to hurt Toby after the way he had abandoned them nineteen years ago?

By the time she reached the bottom step, Savannah had made a decision. She would try to let her worries and concerns percolate for the night. She'd pray and then decide about how to handle Lee in the morning.

With God's help, she'd get through this.

The aroma of pancakes and coffee hovered over the kitchen as Savannah stared down at her small stack of blueberry pancakes the following morning. Thoughts of Korey spun through her mind, and her heart clutched as she recalled how Korey had discussed pancakes with Toby the first time he had come into the store.

She closed her eyes as the words he'd declared to her on the porch echoed in her mind once again: *"It was never fake to me, Savannah. I care for you deeply. I've realized that I cared for you all along."*

"Lee said he wants to come back today." *Onkel* Eddie's words broke through her thoughts. He gave a heavy sigh. "He wants to see you both and talk to you some more."

Savannah turned toward her uncle.

Aenti Dorothy touched Toby's shoulder. "You don't have to stay. If you'd rather go to work, it's okay. I'll tell him that you have nothing further to say to him."

"I want to stay." Toby's words came out in a rush. "I want to talk to him some more."

Their aunt nodded. "Okay."

"I'll leave a message for Korey and let him know I'm not going to be at work today, but I'll return on Monday." Toby smothered his stack of pancakes with syrup and then began cutting them up.

Savannah's heart did a funny little dance when Toby mentioned Korey's name, but she ignored it.

Toby looked at Savannah across the table. "Will you stay and talk to *Dat* too?"

Savannah pressed her lips together.

"Please, Vannah?"

She shook her head. "I have nothing more to say to him. I told him how I felt about him last night."

"But I want you here." Toby hesitated. "I *need* you here. We should be a united front in this. Please, Vannah. Stay for me, okay?"

Savannah faced Dean across the table, and she recalled his advice from last night.

"You two have always had each other, and you'll always have my parents, Levi, and me. We're all a family. Don't let Lee destroy what we've all built together."

Then she released a long breath and felt her expression fall. "Of course I'll stay for you, but don't expect me to participate in the conversation. I said my piece last night." She turned to her aunt. "Will you be able to handle the store without me?"

Aenti Dorothy smiled. "Of course, *mei liewe.*"

"Danki, Vannah," Toby said.

"I want to caution you, Toby," *Onkel* Eddie began while wiping his beard with a paper napkin. "I know that you're anxious to get to know Lee and find out why he did what he did, but I want you to be careful."

Toby swallowed a piece of pancake. "Why?"

Her uncle and aunt shared a look.

Aenti Dorothy clutched her mug of coffee with her hands. "We're just concerned that he's going to hurt you more than he already has."

"That's what I've been trying to tell him." Savannah covered her pancakes with butter.

"I've spent most of my life wondering where he was, and now he's back," Toby said. "If he's trying to make himself right with the church, then maybe his intentions are *gut.*"

"And maybe they're not," Savannah quipped.

"Hold on now." *Onkel* Eddie held up his hand. "I'm not suggesting that you ignore him, and I'm not suggesting that you welcome him back into your life with open arms. I'm merely asking you to be cautious. Your heart is fragile right now, Toby. And,

Savannah, your *aenti* and I both remember how difficult it was for you when you first moved in with us."

Aenti Dorothy sniffed. "I held you while you cried every night."

"We don't want to see you both go through more pain," her uncle said. "You've both suffered enough."

Toby's handsome face lit up with a hopeful smile. "But maybe our *dat* is here to make amends, and maybe he will finally be the father I've always prayed he could be."

Savannah pressed her lips together and silently prayed that their father wouldn't break her precious brother's heart.

CHAPTER 26

THE SKY WAS BRIGHT BLUE, AND THE HOT EARLY-AUGUST
afternoon sun beat down on Savannah's neck as she sat between
her brother and Lee on a park bench later that afternoon. Birds
chirped in the trees, and children shouted and played on an elaborate swing set and jungle gym while squirrels chased each other up
a nearby tree. The air smelled of wood chips and flowers.

"This is a nice park," Lee said, breaking the silence that
had hovered over the three of them while they'd walked from
Savannah's aunt and uncle's house to the park down the street.

Toby nodded. "*Aenti* Dorothy used to bring us here when we
were little." He pointed to the slide. "Dean and I loved that slide so
much that one day we refused to leave." He turned to Savannah and
chuckled. "Dean and I both threw a fit. Do you remember that?"

"*Ya*, I do." Savannah sighed. She couldn't bring herself to chat
with their father. It all seemed so . . . phony. It was too little too late.

"Your *mamm* used to take you to a park like this, Savannah,"
Lee said.

She turned toward him and tried to conjure up a memory of
visiting a park with her beloved mother, but nothing came to the
forefront of her mind. "Really?"

"*Ya.* I remember her telling me that you loved the swing. She would push you until her arms were sore, and then you asked her to push you more." Her father nodded.

"Where was the park?"

Her father rubbed his graying dark-brown beard. "It was close to our *haus*, but I don't recall the name of it." He angled his body toward her. "Do you remember our *haus*?"

Savannah folded her hands over her chest and tried to stop her emotions from leaking from her stinging eyes. "I do. I remember we had a large *schtupp*, and I had a wooden toy box in the corner. I kept my blocks and my dolls in it. I liked to play blocks with you on the floor. One time I knocked over your blocks, and you were laughing and then you tickled me."

Lee blinked and his eyes filled with tears. "You remember that?"

"I remember a lot."

"Do you remember your *mamm*?" Lee's tone was soft, hesitant.

"I do."

"What do you remember about her?"

"I can still envision what she looked like, how beautiful her voice was when she sang to me, and how much I loved her hugs. I recall her reading to me at night, and I can still see her laughing with you in the kitchen while she was doing the dishes." Savannah spotted Toby's anxious expression in her peripheral vision, and she sat up straight. She was ready to get to the purpose of his visit. "What did you want to talk to us about?"

Lee swallowed. "I was hoping to have the chance to apologize to you again and tell you that I want to start over with you two. I know that I've hurt you both, and there's nothing I can do to fix that, but I would love the chance to have you both back in my life. Of course, that's if you'll accept me."

Their father clasped his hands as if he were praying. "I'm here to beg for your forgiveness and also to plead with you to give me another chance."

Savannah narrowed her eyes as she studied Lee. "There has to be more to this story if you're just showing up here now nineteen years after you left us. Did your bishop say that you'll be forgiven if you visit your *kinner* and tell them how sorry you are for destroying their biological family?"

Lee winced as if Savannah had struck him.

"Calm down, Vannah." Toby placed his hand on Savannah's shoulder, but she brushed it off with her fingers.

Lee shook his head. "No, my bishop didn't instruct me to come here."

"Then who did?" Savannah's tone dared him.

"*Mei fraa.*"

Savannah popped up from the bench and wagged a finger at them both. "Now we have the truth, Toby. He's only here because his *fraa* told him to come."

A group of women and children congregated on the sidewalk near the jungle gym turned and stared over at Savannah with curious expressions.

"Sit down, Vannah. You're making a scene," Toby hissed.

"I really don't care." She pointed toward the road. "I'm going home. I'm certain *Aenti* Dorothy and *Onkel* Eddie need my help in the store."

"Please sit," Lee said, his voice calm.

Savannah studied him, as her uncle's warnings buzzed through her mind. Lee was only going to hurt them. She should have convinced Toby to go to work with Korey today instead of spending more time with their deadbeat father.

Korey.

She missed him so much her entire body ached for him.

"Please, Savannah," Lee said.

She rubbed her elbow with her opposite hand and then sank back down between her brother and father.

"What is your *fraa*'s name?" Toby asked.

Savannah swallowed a groan. She really didn't want to hear about her father's new family—the family that had replaced *Mamm*, Toby, and her.

"Liza."

Toby nodded. "Why did she tell you to come to see us?"

"She's expecting our first *kind*, and she and I would like you both to know your sibling."

"When you first met her, did you tell her that you abandoned your *kinner*?" Savannah snipped. "Did you say, 'Hi. My name is Lee, and I left *mei kinner* back in Bird-in-Hand with relatives after their *mamm* died. I just walked away from my family. Would you like to date me?'"

Lee looked down at his lap and then over at Savannah. "That's a fair question, and the answer is no, I didn't tell her right away."

"Because you knew what you did was wrong," Savannah said.

"You're right, *dochder*. I did know it was wrong. That's why I'm here to make it right."

Toby angled his body toward their father. "If you knew what you did was wrong, then why did you wait so long to come to see us?"

Lee frowned as he turned his gaze toward the children playing on the jungle gym. "I've wanted to come for years, but I was a coward. I was afraid to face you because I was ashamed. I told Liza about you when I was certain I wanted to build a life with her. I expected her to reject me, and I believe she should have. She deserves someone better than I am, but she said she still loved me. She told me that I needed to confess before the congregation and God in order to make it right."

"When was that?" Savannah asked. "Three years ago?"

Lee shook his head. "No. It was a year ago."

"When did you get married?" Toby chimed in.

"We were married last fall."

Fire burned in Savannah's belly. "So, let me get this straight. Your *fraa* told you a year ago to come and see us, and you just now showed up?"

"I told you that I'm a coward, Savannah. I have no other excuse. I accept that I was wrong, and I'm going to spend the rest of my life trying to make it up to you."

Savannah gave him a palms-up. "What do you want from us? Forgiveness? We have to forgive you because that's our way. So, you're forgiven, Lee." She waved their father off. "Now you can go back to your new *fraa*, your new *kind*, your new farm, and enjoy your brand-new life, and we'll get back to our life." Then she brushed her hands together. "Problem solved."

"That's not the only thing I want to offer you." Lee kept his voice even. "I want to be part of your lives . . . if you'll have me. I came here to invite you to come back to New Wilmington with me. Liza and I want you to be a part of our family."

He turned to Savannah. "You could help Liza, or you could get a job in a store since you like working at your *aenti* and *onkel*'s store." Then he met Toby's curious gaze. "And you could find a job on a roofing crew or doing something else you want for work. But

I would be honored to have you both with me full-time. I would love to be a family again."

To her surprise, Toby's expression lit up, and he smiled. "I'll give it some thought, but I like the idea."

"What about you, Savannah?" Lee asked. "What do you say? Will you come live with Liza and me and be a part of our family?"

Savannah stared at him as her head spun with confusion.

<hr />

"How was your day?" *Dat* asked as Korey entered the kitchen that evening.

Korey began scrubbing his hands at the sink. "Long. Toby called out saying that he had a family issue. I guess it has to do with his *dat*. I was hoping he'd come to work today so I could check on how he and Savannah are doing." During breakfast, he had told his parents about how he had gone to visit Savannah and she told him that she had to go since her father was there.

"That's a tough situation," *Dat* said as he sat in his seat at the table. "I hope it's going well."

Crystal set a platter of pork chops on the center of the table. "I've been thinking of them and praying for them today."

"Are you going to go see Savannah tonight?" Jayden asked as he carried a pitcher of water to the table.

Korey leaned back on the counter while drying his hands. "I actually have a better idea."

"Oh *ya*?" Jayden started filling their glasses.

"Since tomorrow is an off-Sunday without a church service, I'm going to pick her up for the youth gathering and ask her if we can talk on the way. Hopefully, I can encourage her to open up to me." He tossed the paper towel into the trash can. "And hopefully she'll listen when I tell her that I love her and I want her in my life for real."

Dat smiled. "I think she will, *sohn*."

"*Danki.*" Korey prayed his father was right. Tomorrow couldn't come fast enough.

Korey jogged down the stairs the following morning on his way out to pick up Savannah. When his socks hit the bottom step, he found his entire family sitting in the family room, and he stopped short.

Tyler, Michelle, and Jayden sat on the sofa while his parents were each perched on their favorite chairs.

Korey joined them in the room. "What's going on?"

"I know you have to leave soon, but would you join us for a moment?" *Dat* pointed to the empty wing chair. "Please."

Korey traipsed to the chair and sat down, nodding a hello to Michelle and Tyler. "Is everything all right, *Dat*?" he asked.

His father and Crystal shared a warm look.

"Okay," Jayden began, "you've kept us waiting long enough. Tell us why we're having this family meeting."

Tyler grinned. "*Ya*, the suspense is exasperating."

"Okay." *Dat* smiled at Crystal and threaded his fingers with hers. "We have an announcement." Then he nodded. "Go ahead, *mei liewe*."

Crystal licked her lips and then gave a sheepish smile. "Well, we promised to give you an update after my doctor's appointment."

Korey leaned forward and rested his arms on his thighs, his shoulders stiffening.

"We wanted to tell you all at once so that no one's feelings are hurt." *Dat* met Korey's gaze. "You're all important to us, and we want to make sure you all know that."

Korey's stomach dipped. "Are you *krank*, Crystal?"

"Please just tell us." Tyler looped his arm around Michelle's shoulders.

Jayden frowned. "Is everything all right?"

"*Ya*, it is." *Dat* smiled. "We're sorry for worrying you, but we wanted to be sure everything was all right before we told you. It's a miracle from God. Crystal is expecting."

Korey gasped and glanced around the room. Michelle and Tyler clapped while Jayden smiled.

"Oh my goodness!" Michelle said. "*Ya*, it's a miracle!"

Tyler hooted. "We'll have *kinner* the same age, *Dat*. Will our *kind* need to call yours *aenti* or *onkel*?"

"I'm so *froh* for you. Now I won't be the youngest anymore," Jayden said.

Joy bubbled up inside of Korey as he took in the news. It was truly a miracle from God! He couldn't have been happier for his parents and their family. "That's fantastic!"

"*Danki*. We've had some heartaches over the past couple of years, which is why we wanted to wait before we told you," *Dat* continued.

Crystal's expression was solemn as she nodded. "We had to be sure everything was going well this time. We didn't want to tell you and then have something happen."

"We understand," Michelle told her. "And we're so very *froh*."

"We want to keep it private in our family, which is what most

Amish couples do, but we wanted you to know what's going on and why Crystal hasn't been feeling well," *Dat* said. "I didn't want you all to worry."

"We understand," Korey said. "We'll definitely keep it quiet."

His siblings and Michelle agreed.

They discussed the news for a little while longer, and then Korey stood. "I'm so sorry, but I need to go." He pointed to the clock on the wall. "I want to pick up Savannah before she leaves for the youth gathering with Toby. I'm so grateful that you shared this news with us today. I'm truly *froh*."

"*Danki*, Korey," Crystal said. "I hope your conversation goes well with Savannah." She smiled. "And feel free to tell Savannah our good news if you want. I know she'll keep it to herself."

Korey nodded, and then he started for the door. "Thank you. I'll see you all later."

His family called their goodbyes to him as he crossed into the kitchen, where he stopped to grab a bagel.

When Korey stepped outside, he sent up a prayer of thanksgiving to God, and then he begged God to let him be a blessing to Savannah and also help him fix his relationship with her.

CHAPTER 27

SAVANNAH RUBBED HER HANDS DOWN HER APRON AND checked her reflection in her mirror that same morning. She frowned as she took in the dark circles under her eyes, evidence that she'd tossed and turned most of the night while praying and begging God to help her disentangle her confusing thoughts and emotions about her father and his request for her and Toby to join his new family in New Wilmington.

When a knock sounded on her door, she jumped with a start. "Who is it?"

"It's me, Vannah. May I come in?" her brother's voice sounded outside the door.

"Ya." She sank down on the chair in the corner of her room as her door opened with a squeak and Toby walked in, gently closing the door behind him. Her stomach clenched when she took in his serious expression.

Toby cleared his throat and held on to his suspenders. "Could we please talk for a minute?"

"Of course. What's on your mind?"

"Last night I did a lot of thinking and praying, and I decided that I want to go with *Dat* to New Wilmington."

Savannah blinked as her throat dried. "Why?" she croaked.

He dropped down onto the corner of her bed. "Vannah, you have memories of *Mamm* and *Dat*, but I don't. I don't remember what it's like to be a part of a nuclear family with a mother and a father."

"*Ya*, you do. We have our *aenti* and *onkel*."

"But they aren't our parents."

"Of course they are, Toby. They raised us. They've always been here for us. They took us in, and they—"

"Vannah." He held up his hand to stop her from speaking. "It's not the same, and you know it even though you won't admit it." He sighed. "I want to get to know *Dat*. I want to make memories with him, and I want to get to know our sibling."

She bit her lower lip. "You're serious about this."

"*Ya*, I am." Toby nodded. "I know that *Dat* made mistakes and he hurt us, but I believe he wants to make amends. And I know that his *fraa* is the one who convinced him to do it, but he's still here, begging for our forgiveness."

She sniffed. "So you're going to leave Bird-in-Hand?" Her heart jumped into her throat at the thought of losing her precious brother.

"I am, but you don't have to go with me. It's okay if you want to stay here."

"Of course I'll go with you."

Toby eyed her. "But what about Korey?"

"You're *mei bruder*, and I need to be wherever you are." *And I have to make sure you're okay. It's my job.*

He shook his head. "No, you don't. It's okay if you stay here."

"I want to go with you." But even as she said the words, her heart started to splinter at the idea of leaving a future with Korey behind.

285

Korey knocked on Savannah's back door and then rocked back on his heels while he considered what he would say to her to convince her that he loved her. Worry threaded through him as he jammed his hands in his trouser pockets and hoped she hadn't already left for the youth gathering

The door opened, and Dean stuck his head out. "Korey. Hey."

"Hi. I was hoping to talk to Savannah."

Dean grimaced. "It's not a *gut* time."

"Please, Dean." Korey clasped his hands together. "I really need to see her."

Dean hesitated and then tapped the door jamb. "Okay. Just a moment."

Korey paced on the porch, his thoughts spinning out of control as he worried that the situation with her father had gotten worse. He hoped he could be a blessing to her and help her work through this confusing time.

When the door opened and then clicked shut, he looked up as Savannah stepped onto the porch. Her blue eyes were dull and rimmed with dark circles. She looked as if she hadn't slept in days.

His heart wrenched as he stepped toward her.

She studied him. "Hey."

"Hey." He smiled despite her sad expression. "I missed you. I need to talk to you." He reached for her hands, but she shifted away from him. "Look, I'm in love with you, Savannah. I was afraid to tell you because I was afraid of losing you, but by not telling you, I lost you."

He lifted his straw hat and raked his hand through his thick hair. "I want to be with you and I need you."

Savannah shook her head. "You thought you needed me, but you've worked things out with your family. You don't need me anymore."

"That's not true."

"It is true, Korey. I was just a pretend girlfriend that helped you get acclimated into the community."

"You're more than that, Savannah, and you know it. You're my greatest confidant. I shared things with you that I've never shared with anyone before. I've never felt this way about anyone. You've helped me so much, and I think I've helped you too."

Savannah frowned. "I know. But everything has changed now. I don't think we have a future anymore." Her voice was hoarse as she placed her hand on the door handle. "Goodbye, Korey."

"Don't go!" His voice was full of panic. "Please give me a minute. I want to share some news with you."

She spun to face him.

"I just found out that Crystal is expecting a baby." He held his straw hat in his hands and turned it. "Our family is thrilled by this miracle. Crystal and *Dat* asked us all to keep it quiet, but Crystal said I could tell you. You've helped me grow up so much and appreciate my family, and I'm grateful for that."

She swallowed. "I'm *froh* for your family. That's great news."

"It is." He folded his hands, pleading with her, hoping she would stay out on the porch and talk to him, *really* talk to him. "Do you want to talk about your *dat*?"

Savannah shook her head. "No. I-I don't need your help anymore." She took a shaky breath, and her blue eyes glittered. "God sent *mei dat* back to me and Toby, and I'm . . . I'm grateful." She swallowed and then sniffed. "That's why Toby and I are moving to New Wilmington with him."

Korey froze as her words rocked him to his core. For a moment, he couldn't breathe, couldn't speak. Then he found his words once again. "You're—you're *leaving*?"

"I believe God is giving us a second chance to be a family."

He closed the distance between them and dropped his hat on the glider beside them. "How could you possibly trust him after all of these years?"

"It's our way to forgive, and Toby wants to start over with him."

Korey reached for her and then pulled his hands back. The space between them felt a million miles wide—a distance impossible to cross.

"But he abandoned you and Toby. And your life is here, Savannah." He pointed to the floor. "You can forgive your *dat* without moving away to live with him."

"But Toby wants to have our *dat* in our life."

"Then your *dat* should move here." Korey gestured around the porch. "He should make the sacrifice after leaving you and Toby."

"But he has a farm and a *fraa* in New Wilmington. His *fraa* is expecting, and he asked us to be a part of his family. Toby wants to go, so that means I have to go with him."

"Why do you have to go if Toby wants to go?"

"Because it's my job to take care of Toby." She pointed to her chest.

Korey shook his head as frustration soaked through him. "No, it isn't."

"*Ya,* it is," she insisted. "It became my job when *mei mamm* passed away and then *mei dat* left."

"Savannah, Toby is twenty years old. He's capable of making his own decisions."

"I need to be there for him." She looked down at the toes of her black shoes before looking back up at him with a fierce gaze. "I believe it's my obligation to take care of *mei bruder* for the rest of my life. I need to make sure he's *froh*."

"Please, Savannah," Korey pleaded with her, and his voice felt scratchy in his throat. "Think about what you're saying. Toby isn't a child anymore. He's a grown man. Your *mamm* would want you both to live *froh* lives. Does the idea of moving away truly make you happy?"

She hesitated.

"Your frown tells me that it doesn't."

"I'm sorry, but I have to go." She yanked the door open. "I'm sure you'll find someone else. All of the *maed* talk about how handsome the Bontrager *bruders* are. You won't have any trouble finding another girlfriend—a *real* one." Her words felt like a punch to his gut.

He reached out and touched her elbow. "I don't want any other *maedel* but you. Don't go. Don't leave me. Let's make this work. Let's break new ground in our relationship and build a future together. I love you, Savannah. You're the love of my life. I'm sure of it." He placed his hand on his chest, covering his heart. "I know it in here that God wants us to be together."

"I'm suddenly the love of your life when I tell you that it's over?" Her eyes filled with tears, but her words pierced him like an arrow.

"I told you that I've been in love with you for a while, but I was afraid to admit it. Let Toby go if he truly wants to be with your *dat* while you stay here with me. We can visit your *dat* and Toby a couple of times per year."

He took her hand in his. "Listen to me, Savannah. If you stay here with me, I'll never let you down. I promise you."

"No." Savannah yanked her hand out of his grasp. "Family is a gift from God, and I plan to cherish mine while I still can. That means I need to go to New Wilmington with Toby and *mei dat.*"

Korey's hope deflated like a balloon as he searched for words to convince her to stay. "You can't possibly tell me that you don't feel a connection with me. What about all of those times we talked in my buggy? Or the times we sat on my porch and this porch and talked? Or when we walked to the back of the pasture and I poured out my heart to you?" He pointed toward where they had sat. "Didn't that mean anything to you, Savannah?"

"I'm going to New Wilmington, and that's it. You need to accept that it's over." Tears trickled down her cheeks. "Goodbye, Korey."

Savannah entered the house and shut the door behind her.

Korey dropped onto the glider and hung his head in his hands as the world around him crumbled.

He'd lost Savannah, the love of his life, and he had no idea what to do to fix it.

Savannah leaned her head against the door and covered her face with her hands as her tears slid down her cheeks. Saying goodbye to Korey had ripped her soul to shreds.

Then his sweet declaration of love echoed in her mind:

"Let's break new ground in our relationship and build a future together. I love you, Savannah. You're the love of my life."

Witnessing the pain and anguish reflected on his handsome face had been too much to bear, but she had to be wherever Toby chose to live. After all, it was her duty as his older sister.

Savannah worked to get ahold of her emotions and then stood up straight. Pulling a tissue from her pocket, she blotted her cheeks and nose and gathered all of the strength she could muster. She was strong. Her heart would eventually heal, and she would get over Korey.

Right now, however, she had to focus on her brother. Losing her focus on him and allowing her fake relationship to become important was what had led her astray to begin with.

She was going to travel down the path she felt that God had sent her on—which meant she had to follow her brother and make sure he was happy.

"What did Korey want?" Dean asked.

Savannah swiveled toward where Dean and Toby stood watching her, concern lining their faces.

"He just wanted to talk." She focused on her brother. "Toby, you need to let Korey know that you're leaving."

Toby nodded. "I know."

When she felt her eyes fill again, she hurried past them and up the stairs toward her room, where she would allow her tears to break free in private.

The back door clicked open, and Korey's heart lifted. Had Savannah returned to tell him that she loved him and had decided to stay in Bird-in-Hand?

When he turned to face the door, his shoulders drooped as Toby stepped toward him, his expression unreadable. Korey swallowed back his disappointment. "Toby."

"Hi, Korey." Toby cleared his throat as he came to stand beside the glider. "I wanted to thank you for the incredible chance you've given me to work on your roofing crew. I've really enjoyed and appreciated it. You're the first person outside of my family who has believed in me, and you helped me learn to believe in myself."

Toby leaned back against the railing behind him. "*Mei dat* invited me to move to New Wilmington with him, so I'm going to look for a new roofing job there. I'll use the skills you've taught me to find a new job, and I even feel confident enough to fill out a job application. I owe it all to you."

Korey nodded as sadness filled him. "I didn't do anything, Toby. You're the one with the skills."

"You've been a wonderful *freind* to me, and I'll always be grateful. In fact, you've been the best *freind* I've ever had." Toby held out his hand to Korey. "I thought I should go ahead and let you know now so that you can find someone to replace me. I think *mei dat* wants to head back to New Wilmington soon."

As Korey shook Toby's hand, he tried to keep his anguish at bay. "And Savannah is going with you, right?" He held his breath, even though he already knew the heartbreaking answer to the question.

"*Ya.* I'm trying to convince her to stay, but she's determined to go with me."

Korey hoped he could keep his despondency hidden behind a mask of indifference despite his breaking heart. "I wish you the best, Toby. I'll miss you both." *More than you'll ever know.*

"We'll miss you too."

Korey pushed himself up from the glider and placed his hat on his head. He needed to get on the road before his emotions got the best of him in front of Toby. "I hope you have a restful Sunday."

"You too, Korey."

While Toby disappeared into the house, Korey trudged toward his waiting horse and buggy. He felt the weight of his grief sitting heavily on his chest, squeezing at his lungs and crushing his heart.

He had never expected his conversation with Savannah to go the way it had. He had believed that by the time he left her house she would be his girlfriend and they would be planning a future—or at least talking about where their future might lead.

But instead, he was leaving alone. He'd left his hopes, dreams, and heart on the porch with her. In fact, he had lost the love of his life along with his best friend, and he would never be the same.

Why, God? Why?

The sound of tires crunching along the rock driveway drew Korey's attention to a car motoring toward the house. He stood by his horse as the car came to a stop and an Amish man climbed out of the back seat.

When the man started walking toward the house, Korey noticed that he had dark-brown hair, and the shape of his nose and his jaw resembled Toby's.

Lee Zook.

Korey's chest constricted, and his curiosity propelled him toward the porch. "Excuse me," he called.

The man stopped and pivoted toward him. He gave Korey a hesitant smile. *"Wie geht's?"*

"Are you Savannah and Toby's *dat*?"

"Ya. I'm Lee Zook. Nice to meet you." Lee held out his hand to Korey, but when Korey didn't shake it, Lee cleared his throat and gave him an awkward smile. "And you are . . . ?"

Korey studied him, his eyes narrowing. "Korey Bontrager. Promise me you won't break their hearts again."

Lee's smile froze on his lips.

"Promise me, Lee."

"I promise."

"*Danki.*" Korey spun on his heel and strutted back to his buggy, leaving Savannah's father behind.

Along with Korey's broken spirit.

A choir of frogs croaked in the distance while lightning bugs sparkled around the porch. The sunset bathed the sky in vibrant colors, and cicadas sang their nightly song.

Savannah hugged her arms to her chest and tried her best to calm her racing heart. She had spent the afternoon visiting with Toby, her father, her aunt, and her uncle while Dean had gone to the youth gathering.

Although Savannah had tried to listen while her father discussed his life in New Wilmington, her heart was conflicted. No matter how hard she'd tried all afternoon, she couldn't dislodge the pain in Korey's eyes from her thoughts. His voice kept echoing in her mind:

"*I told you that I've been in love with you for a while, but I was afraid to admit it. Let Toby go if he truly wants to be with your dat while you stay here with me. We can visit your dat and Toby a couple of times per year . . . If you stay here with me, I'll never let you down. I promise you.*"

"Toby, Savannah, I don't want you to do anything that *you* don't want to," *Dat* said, turning toward where her brother sat on the glider beside *Dat*'s rocking chair. "The last thing I want to do is cause you more pain. Now, I need you to be honest with me. Are you sure you want to come to New Wilmington with me?"

Her brother nodded with emphasis. "*Ya*, I'm positive I want to go. I want to have you in my life. I'm confident that I will find another job as a roofer." Toby angled his body toward Savannah, sitting on a rocking chair beside him. "What about you, Vannah?"

Savannah sat up straight, squaring her shoulders. "I'll go with you."

Toby studied her. "I promise you that I'll be fine without you. You don't need to feel obligated to go with me. Are you sure you want to go with us?"

"*Ya*, I'm positive. We're a family, and we shouldn't be separated." Her voice was thin and reedy despite her attempts at appearing confident. She turned to her father. "Toby and I have always been there for each other, and that won't ever change."

Lee nodded. "That's *gut*. I'm glad you had each other. It was my prayer that you stayed close."

"Of course we stayed close." Savannah frowned at Lee. "We only had each other." She turned her attention to the fireflies dancing over her uncle's pasture as more thoughts of Korey flittered through her mind. He had promised her a future with him! How would her heart ever heal after she left him behind? She squeezed her arms to her chest, hoping to shield her battered heart.

"I'm so grateful God brought you back to us, *Dat*." Toby's voice suddenly broke through Savannah's mental tirade. "I want to know my new sibling and my stepmother. Maybe we can all visit *Aenti* Dorothy, *Onkel* Eddie, and our cousins as a family once a year."

Dat nodded. "I like that idea."

Savannah swallowed hard and looked out toward the store. She would miss working there. Would she find a job working in

New Wilmington? Or would she help her stepmother in the house after her sibling was born?

"I'll purchase three bus tickets, and we can leave on Tuesday," *Dat* said.

Savannah's mouth opened and closed as reality crashed down on her. "Tuesday?"

"Is that too soon?" *Dat*'s gray eyes searched hers.

She blinked and swallowed back her apprehension.

"No, no," Toby jumped in. "I've already told Korey that I'm leaving and suggested he find someone else to replace me. That should give me enough time to pack and get ready."

"Perfect." *Dat* stood. "I'm going to call for a ride and head back to the hotel for the night. I'll buy the tickets tomorrow and then come to see you both again. Okay?"

Toby jumped up from the rocker. "*Ya. Gut.* I'll get the key for the store so you can use the phone."

As Toby dashed into the house to collect the key, a feeling of foreboding overtook Savannah. Soon she was going to leave her home for good, and her heart would never be the same.

CHAPTER 28

LATER THAT EVENING, KOREY PLODDED INTO HIS HOUSE AND shuffled into the family room where his parents sat, each reading a book. He flopped down on the sofa across from them and rubbed his eyes.

He had spent the afternoon sitting on a park bench, watching ducks play in a pond while he contemplated everything—losing Savannah, reconciling with his family, and his unborn brother or sister.

Savannah's words had haunted him throughout the afternoon, and he'd come to the conclusion that he would never get over losing her. While he'd begged God to help him win her back, he doubted that it was possible. He'd seen how stubborn Savannah was when she'd made up her mind, which meant she was going to go to New Wilmington and leave him behind, no matter how much he pleaded with her to stay.

Dat and Crystal studied him with concern.

His father set down his book on the end table beside him. "You look upset. Are you okay, Korey?"

Crystal closed her book and placed it on her lap.

Korey sniffed and found his voice. "I spent the day at a park thinking about everything, and I've evaluated my life. I'm sorry for how I've acted during the past few years. I've been immature, selfish, thoughtless, and cruel. And I'm also sorry that you've had to deal with me. I know that I made both of your lives difficult when you first met, started dating, and then decided to get married, and I'll regret that for the rest of my life."

"Korey," *Dat* began. "You don't need to apologize. It was a tough time for you."

"No, *Dat*. There's no excuse for how I behaved." Korey licked his lips as he gathered his thoughts. "When I was in Ohio, I befriended an elderly man named Sherman, who lived next door to me in Sugarcreek. He said something to me that was so profound and inspiring that it changed my life. In fact, he's the reason why I came home."

"What did he say?" Crystal asked.

"When I told him that I came to Ohio to get away from Tyler, Sherman told me to repent and work things out with my family because he regretted that he didn't reconcile with his *bruder* before he passed away. He told me, 'You're hiding from your problems here. Family is God's gift to us. Don't forsake your family.'"

"Korey," *Dat* said, his dark eyes filling with tears, "you're being much too hard on yourself."

Korey shook his head. "No, I'm not. I'm so sorry for forsaking you all. I see how *froh* you two are, and I'm grateful to be a part of this family. This baby is a blessing, and I want to be a part of your life. I'm so grateful God sent you happiness, *Dat*."

Crystal and *Dat* shared a smile.

"*Danki*, Korey, and we're grateful for you," Crystal said, and *Dat* nodded. "But you said you spent the day in a park. Was Savannah with you?"

Korey shook his head. "No, she wasn't. I lost her today, and I don't know what to do. I'll never get over losing her." His voice broke, and he dipped his chin, focusing on his trousers.

"*Ach* no," *Dat* said. "What happened?"

Korey explained how he confessed his feelings for her but that she insisted she was going to move to New Wilmington with her *bruder* and father.

"You can change her mind," Crystal said. "I know she loves you."

Korey wiped his eyes. "I'm sure it's too late because she's just as stubborn as I am."

"Don't give up hope, *sohn*," *Dat* said.

Korey rested his right ankle on his left knee. "I was afraid of falling in love and getting hurt, and it happened. I'll never feel this way about anyone else. So I guess I'm just going to be alone."

"I don't believe that for a second," Crystal told him. "You need to pray and let God work it out for you."

Dat nodded. "I agree. Rely on your faith."

"I'll try." But as Korey said the words, a cold block of sadness formed in his chest. He was certain he'd lost Savannah forever.

"I'm so glad you could all come to visit this afternoon," Savannah said the following day as she glanced around the family room at her four friends—Macy, Gail, Jodie, and Willa. "I wanted to tell you all something important."

Macy yelped. "Oh! You're engaged!"

"I knew it." Gail snapped her fingers. "I could tell you and Korey were deeply in love."

Willa squealed. "When is the wedding?"

"I hope it's not the same day as mine," Jodie snipped.

Savannah held up her hands. "Hold on. I'm not engaged. It's something completely different." She took a deep breath. "*Mei daed* surprised us last week. He just showed up at the store on Friday. It was completely out of the blue."

All of her friends gasped in unison.

Macy came to sit with Savannah on the sofa and placed her hand on Savannah's arm. "Are you okay?"

"Ah . . . well." Savannah touched the ties on her prayer covering. "It's been . . . well, we've been doing a lot of talking, and he wants a new start with me and Toby." She paused. "He and his *fraa* have a farm in New Wilmington, and they're expecting a *boppli*." She hesitated, and Macy rubbed her arm. "He invited Toby and me to move to New Wilmington with him."

Macy's eyes widened. "Are you going?"

Savannah nodded as her eyes stung.

"No!" Willa exclaimed.

"What about Korey?" Macy asked. "You two are so *froh* together."

Savannah shook her head. "It was never real between us." Then she explained how she had hatched the plan for them to pretend to date.

"I fell in love with Korey, but by the time he told me that he truly cared for me too, *mei dat* had come back and I realized that I needed to focus on Toby and not my own relationship. Now I'm moving to New Wilmington, so it doesn't matter. Korey is going to be here, and I'm going to be in New Wilmington with my family. This is how it's supposed to be. I need to stay with Toby and make sure he's okay. I have to be wherever *mei bruder* is." Savannah said the words as if her heart didn't matter, but her lungs constricted as if a giant rubber band were wrapped around them. For a moment, she couldn't breathe.

Her friends shared confused expressions, and then they all started talking at once.

"If you and Korey love each other, then why wouldn't you give that love a chance?" Jodie asked.

Macy wiped at her eyes. "You can't leave us, Savannah! Why can't your *dat* come visit you and Toby? And you can visit him too. You don't have to move."

"Where has your *dat* been this entire time? Didn't he leave when Toby was an infant?" Willa asked.

"I think your *dat* has more explaining to do before you leave the life you've built here and move in with him," Gail said. "You'll break your *aenti*'s and *onkel*'s hearts if you go. They raised you."

Jodie wagged a finger at Savannah. "I agree with Gail. Your *aenti* and *onkel* are your parents, not that stranger. Your *dat* needs to feel guilty for hiding all of these years while they were taking care of you and Toby."

"Toby wants to go to New Wilmington?" Macy asked.

"*Ya.*" Savannah sank back on the sofa as her friends' words roared through her mind like a cyclone. "He said he prayed for *Dat* to come back, and now he's here. Toby wants to be a part of our *dat*'s life since he doesn't have memories of our parents."

Willa leaned forward in the armchair beside the sofa. "Then you should let Toby go, and you can stay here with Korey and us."

"No, I need to be with Toby." Savannah sighed as she examined her short fingernails.

"But what about Korey?" Macy asked. "You care for him, and he cares for you. Why would you throw that all away?"

Savannah pushed the ribbons from her prayer cover behind her shoulders. "It wasn't meant to be between Korey and me. God brought our *daed* back for a reason. I can visit you all when I come to see *mei aenti* and *onkel*."

"But when you get married, you won't have time to visit," Jodie said.

Savannah's stomach soured at the idea of meeting another man—someone other than Korey—and then marrying him.

Gail sniffed and wiped her eyes. "When are you leaving?"

"Tomorrow," Savannah whispered.

"*Ach* no! That's too soon." Macy took Savannah's hand in hers. "We're going to miss you so much."

Their friends agreed.

"Let's make something sweet to eat while we talk." Gail stood. "It will be our last time baking together."

Willa hopped up and followed her toward the kitchen. "*Gut* idea."

"How about brownies or a cake?" Jodie trailed after them.

Macy pulled Savannah in for a hug. "What am I going to do without you?"

Savannah held on to her best friend and fought back her tears. She was going to leave her heart in Bird-in-Hand.

Savannah folded her aprons and added them to her suitcase. Sitting on the edge of her bed, she pulled a tissue from the box on her nightstand and wiped her eyes and nose. Then she stared at her half-full suitcase before she scanned her room, the room that had been hers since she was five years old.

This house was her home, the place where she'd grown up, and she was going to leave it. Forever.

Her already shattered heart began to dissolve. She tried to shake off the anguish, but it just continued to expand in her belly.

If moving to New Wilmington to be with Toby and her father was the right thing to do, then why did the idea of leaving hurt so much?

A soft knock drew Savannah's attention to her aunt standing in her doorway. "May I come in?" *Aenti* Dorothy asked.

"Of course." Savannah sniffed and tried her best to smile.

"How's packing going?"

"Slowly."

Her aunt peeked in her suitcase. "Is there anything I can do to help?"

"No, *danki*." Savannah wiped away fresh tears.

Aenti Dorothy touched Savannah's cheek and gave her a warm smile before sitting down beside her. "You know, Savannah," she began, "you can have a relationship with your *dat* and Toby without moving away. You can stay here and write them letters. You can call them a couple of times every month. You can even visit them once or twice a year. You don't have to rearrange your life in order to be a part of theirs."

Savannah nodded and fidgeted with the zipper on her suitcase. "What about Korey?"

"I told him that I need to be with *mei bruder*." Savannah kept her focus on the zipper.

"And how did Korey take that news?"

Savannah closed her eyes as memories pressed in on her. A vision of his pained expression filled her mind. "He was crushed. He tried to convince me to stay. He said he wants a future with me.

He said that if I stayed with him, he would go with me to visit New Wilmington every year." Her voice caught and then recovered. "He said I'm the love of his life." Her words were barely a whisper.

"Please look at me."

Savannah blinked up at her.

"You don't have to go." Then *Aenti* Dorothy touched Savannah's hand. "Pray about it, okay? Ask God to guide your heart toward the right decision for you. Then follow your heart."

Savannah leaned over and hugged her aunt, pulling her close. "*Danki,*" she whispered. "I'm so grateful you're *mei mamm.*"

"Oh, sweetheart. You know I love you."

"I love you too," Savannah said as she buried her face in her aunt's shoulder.

The cicadas serenaded Korey, and the lightning bugs set off their nightly fireworks display while he rocked on the porch swing later that evening. He had spent the day silently begging God to bring Savannah back to him and heal his heart, but he still felt broken.

More than once this evening he had considered hitching up his horse and heading over to Savannah's house to once again beg her to stay, but he recalled the fierceness in her eyes when she'd told him it was too late. She had made it clear that she had chosen a life in New Wilmington over a future with him in Bird-in-Hand.

Now all he could do was wait for God to piece his heart back together. He closed his eyes and kneaded his fingers on his temple.

Help me, Lord.

When he opened his eyes, Korey spotted a flashlight beam bouncing down the rock path that led from the stable to Tyler's house. He sat up straight in the swing and rubbed his hands down his thighs as a tall shadow drew closer to the porch.

"Want some company?" his older brother asked.

Korey felt a glimmer of relief. *"Ya."*

Tyler climbed the porch steps and sat on a rocker beside him. "How are you doing?"

Korey eyed him with suspicion. "Why do you ask?"

Tyler sighed. "Jay told me what happened. He said that you two talked when he got home last night. I'm sorry." He pushed the chair into motion. "I know how it feels when you're sure you've lost everything. There's no pain like it. All I can tell you is to keep your eyes on Jesus."

"I appreciate that." Korey stared out toward the barn and considered his words. Then he turned toward his older brother. "I'm sorry for forsaking you."

Tyler chuckled. "What?"

"I don't think I told you what inspired me to come home." Korey explained how he had met Sherman and the piece of advice that the elderly man had imparted to him. "I'm sorry I was a *dummkopp* for so long."

Tyler grinned. "Well, Kore, you've been a *dummkopp* your entire life, but I still love you, little *bruder.*"

Korey laughed, and the release warmed his soul for a moment. "I'm glad you and Michelle are *froh.* I just hope I can find that with someone, and I'd like that someone to be Savannah."

"Don't give up your faith in God."

"I won't." Air swished out of Korey's lungs. He was so grateful for his older brother.

CHAPTER 29

THE FOLLOWING MORNING SAVANNAH SAT ON THE PORCH beside her suitcase and looked out toward the driveway. She inhaled the humid early-August air and the scent of her aunt's colorful flowers, which wafted over from the nearby garden. The sky was bright blue and cloudless as birds sang in the nearby trees.

She had spent the night praying and asking God to guide her heart to the right decision, but she still felt conflicted. While she still believed it was her duty to follow her brother to New Wilmington, her heart ached at the thought of leaving Bird-in-Hand.

The door opened with a click, and Toby stepped out onto the porch and set his suitcase next to hers. "We need to talk, Vannah."

She looked up at him. "What do you mean?"

"You've looked miserable ever since you said you'd go with me to New Wilmington, and every time I've told you that you didn't need to go, you've argued with me." Toby sank down onto the glider beside her rocker. "I need you to listen to me now before *Dat* gets here."

She nodded. "I'm listening."

"Vannah, you practically raised me, and I'm grateful for that. You were always there for me—helping me with my reading and

306

math, standing up to bullies for me, putting Band-Aids on my scrapes when *Aenti* was busy at the store. I love and appreciate you, Vannah, but I'm a grown man now."

She shook her head. "Toby, it's my job to—

"No, it's not," he interrupted her. "It was never your job to raise me, and you've always done more than your share of mothering me, but it's time to stop. I want to go to New Wilmington and get to know our *daed*. Because of you and Korey, I'm confident that I'll find another job as a roofer, and I finally believe that I'm capable of living my own life."

Toby pointed toward her chest. "Now it's your time to build a life of your own, and you should build it with Korey. You belong here, Vannah. You need to think about your future. I'll always be your *bruder*, and I promise that we'll see each other, call each other, and maybe even write each other. You won't stop being a part of my life, even if your life is here and mine is in New Wilmington."

She took a shuddering breath as his words filtered through her mind.

"You need to go after Korey, Vannah. It's obvious that you belong together. Tell him how much he means to you before it's too late."

Savannah blinked as confusion overtook her mind like a dense fog. Could her brother be right? Did she belong with Korey instead of with Toby? Was it time for her to build her own life?

A large SUV taxi motored into the driveway, and Toby stood. "Tell *Dat* goodbye and then go see Korey. I know where he's working today."

She shook her head despite her doubts. "No, I'm going with you."

"Vannah," Toby groaned her name. "You know I'm right. Stop being so stubborn!"

Savannah ignored him and shouldered her purse before hefting her suitcase down the porch steps. When she stepped out onto the driveway, the hot sun kissed her cheeks. She pulled out the handle on her suitcase, and it bumped along the rock driveway behind her.

When Savannah glanced back at the house where she'd grown up, her heart squeezed. Was her brother right? How could she leave all of this behind? And Korey!

The SUV stopped, and her father climbed out of the back seat. He rushed over and pulled her in for a warm hug. She closed her eyes and breathed in his familiar scent. It had been nineteen years since he'd hugged her, but she still recalled the fragrance of his soap. *Dat* hugged Toby next, and Toby held on to him as if his life depended on it. The sweet scene tugged at Savannah's heartstrings.

"*Gude mariye*," *Dat* said as he took Savannah's suitcase. "It's a *schee* day."

The taxi driver popped the tailgate open, and *Dat* set their suitcases inside it beside his.

Then *Dat* clapped his hands. "Well, let's get you two home to New Wilmington."

She blinked. *Home?* Her brother's words twirled through her mind. Perhaps her home was here just as Toby had said.

Dat opened the back door and made a sweeping gesture toward the SUV. "Well, are you two ready to start your new life?"

When she felt a hand on her shoulder, Savannah looked over at her brother as his expression filled with concern.

"Think about what I said," Toby whispered next to her ear. "It's not too late to change your mind. *Dat* will understand."

Savannah lifted her chin. "I need to go," she said, her voice gravelly.

Shaking his head, Toby frowned and then hopped in before sliding over to the far end of the large bench seat.

Savannah climbed into the back seat and slid to the middle before *Dat* sat beside her. Her father's face beamed with a bright smile while she fought back tears.

As the SUV backed out of the driveway, she studied the store and imagined her aunt and uncle helping customers and stocking shelves. She had hugged them close and told them goodbye this morning, promising to call, write, and visit.

Savannah closed her eyes as Toby's words continued to echo through her mind.

"Who's Korey Bontrager?"

She jumped with a start as she looked at her father, shocked by his question. "He's a . . . *mei freind*. Why?"

"I met him Sunday. He was leaving your *onkel's haus* when I arrived. We had a very short conversation."

She touched the stitching on her plain black purse. "What did he say to you?"

"He asked who I was, and then he made me promise not to break your heart. He was serious about it too."

A squeak escaped her throat before she caught a sob. She covered her face with her hands as her tears continued to fall.

A bottomless quicksand of sadness grabbed her and started to pull her under as the truth hit her: Toby was right. Savannah couldn't leave Korey. She couldn't leave her home— her *true* home.

Toby rubbed her shoulder. "It's okay," he whispered. "It's going to be okay."

"Savannah?" *Dat's* voice was close to her ear. "Savannah? Honey? What did I say to upset you?"

She pulled a handful of tissues from her apron pocket and mopped up her face. Then she met her father's confused gaze. "Please take me home."

"What?"

"I'm sorry, *Dat*, but I can't go with you. Take me home now. Please." She looked at Toby. "You're right. I need to let you go to New Wilmington without me. I belong here, and you belong with *Dat*."

Toby grinned. "I'm so glad you're finally admitting I'm right."

Dat's gray eyes searched Savannah's. "What am I missing here?"

"Toby has been trying to tell me something, and I just realized he's right." She sniffed. "Toby wants to go with you, but I felt like I had to go in order to watch over him. But I understand now that I don't need to go. My home is here. I'll come visit you or you can come visit me, but I can't move to New Wilmington with you. I'm sorry."

Dat nodded and rubbed her shoulder. "I understand. It's okay." Then he leaned forward. "I'm sorry, sir, but we need to go back."

As the SUV motored down the road toward her house, a plan came together in Savannah's mind. She knew exactly what she had to do, and her heart suddenly started to come back to life.

Korey pushed his sunglasses farther up on his nose while he stood on the roof of the antique mall where he and his crew worked. Cars rumbled past on the street below while the sound of banging hammers echoed through the air.

The sun was brutal today, beating down on the back of his

neck. He lifted his straw hat and swiped the back of his arm across his forehead while he gazed over to where the two members of his crew diligently worked.

Korey had tried to concentrate on his work, but he couldn't stop thinking about Savannah and Toby. He wondered if they had left Bird-in-Hand yet. Were they on their way to their new home? Would Savannah ever think of him, or had she already erased him from her mind?

He had prayed repeatedly that she would call him or come over to his house to tell him that she had a change of heart. He had hoped that somehow she would realize that they were meant to be together, but he never heard from her.

Korey's insides turned and dropped as that reality hit him hard—he had lost her forever. But he did his best to swallow back his despondency as he tried in vain to work. He'd managed to hammer his thumb three times already, and it wasn't even lunchtime.

When a taxi steered into the parking lot behind the antique mall, Korey glanced up and then returned his focus to his hammer. After a few moments, he felt as if someone was watching him.

He peeked up again and did a double take when he spotted Savannah standing by the taxi, waving both of her arms in the air. He jumped up to his feet, his pulse thumping wildly as he felt a spark of hope.

"Savannah?" he called.

She beckoned him to come down.

Excitement twined in Korey's chest as he scooted over to the ladder and climbed down. Then he darted across the parking lot to her, hope igniting his soul.

His steps slowed when he realized that she could have just stopped by to say goodbye on her way to the bus station. But he didn't see her father and brother in the taxi. Instead, she had come alone.

Korey rubbed his sweaty palms down his trouser legs as he approached her. His words were caught in his throat as he took in her beautiful face.

"Hi," she said, and she seemed sheepish.

"Hi." Korey's heart pounded against his rib cage. "What are you doing here?"

"I need to tell you something."

He held his breath. *Please don't tell me goodbye again!*

"Okay," she muttered. "I practiced this on the way over, but now I'm so *naerfich* . . ."

He reached for her hand and was surprised when she allowed him to hold it. "Just take your time, Savannah."

"Korey, I'm sorry for pushing you away. I'm sorry for not believing you when you said you loved me. The truth is that when Toby said he wanted to move to New Wilmington with our *dat*, I was so blinded by the belief that I was supposed to look out for Toby that I completely missed what was right in front of me, and that's a future with you. Toby has been trying to tell me that it wasn't my job to mother him, and you even told me that too. But I was too stubborn to believe either of you."

He threaded his fingers with hers as his throat thickened.

She reached up and pushed his sunglasses up on his head.

"What are you doing?" he asked with a chuckle.

"I want to see those *schee* milk-chocolate-brown eyes when I tell you what I have to say."

"You're the one who's *schee*, Savannah. You're the most beautiful *maedel* I've ever known."

She looked surprised and then cleared her throat. "The truth is, Korey, that I love you," she continued. "In fact, you have shown me what love is. You're my best *freind*, my confidant. And I can't ever thank you enough for what you've done for Toby. You've shown him that he is *schmaert*, and you've proven to him that he's just as capable as our cousins. Because of you, he's ready to start a new life and a new job."

She smiled as she cupped her free hand to his cheek. "I thought that God was guiding me to New Wilmington with Toby, but I realized I wasn't listening to what he was trying to tell me. This morning Toby talked to me again, and he reminded me that he's a man now and he's ready to live his own life. When we were on our way to the bus station, I finally realized he was right. That was when I understood that God has been trying to guide me to stay right here with you, and this is where I want to be."

He leaned into her touch as her words soothed his soul. Was he dreaming?

Her smile faded. "Please say something, Korey."

"I really want to kiss you right now. May I?"

She gave a little laugh. "Well, you *are* my real boyfriend, so yes, please kiss me."

"I'm your real boyfriend, huh?"

"*Ya*, you are. In fact, I think you have been all along."

"I'm so *froh* to hear that." Then he placed his finger under her chin, leaned down, and brushed his lips against hers. The feel of her lips against his was as soft as he'd imagined, and it set his blood ablaze. If a kiss could melt his bones, this one would.

When he broke the kiss, the heat in her eyes sent a tingle of desire shimmying through him. "I believe you're my future, Savannah, and I want to start planning our future right now."

"I'd like that," she said.

"Marry me, Savannah," he told her. "Do me the honor of being *mei fraa*. Let's build a *haus* on *mei dat*'s land and raise a family."

She beamed, her beautiful face seeming to glow. "I'd love to, but you need to ask *mei onkel* first."

"I'll ask him tonight." He trailed a finger down her cheek. "*Ich liebe dich*, Savannah Zook."

"*Ich liebe dich*, Korey Bontrager."

Then he pulled her into his arms and kissed her until she was breathless.

SEVEN MONTHS LATER

The early March sky was bright blue while happy birds ate at the feeder in Crystal's garden. Savannah pulled her sweater against her body before threading her fingers with Korey's while they walked down the path leading from his parents' house to theirs.

She smiled as she contemplated the whirlwind of events since Korey had proposed to her seven months earlier. Both of their families had been delighted and helped them build a house on his father's property while they started planning a wedding.

They had been married in her aunt and uncle's barn in November, with Macy as her attendant and Jayden as his. She was grateful that her brother, father, and stepmother had come from New Wilmington to celebrate the nuptials with them.

Then Savannah and Korey had started their new life together in the three-bedroom house that sat next door to Tyler's. She loved their house, and she enjoyed being a part of Korey's family.

Their family had grown as well. Michelle delivered a healthy baby girl in September, and she and Tyler named her Connie Elaine, after their mothers. Crystal welcomed a baby girl named Kristena May in January.

Liza, Savannah's stepmother, also delivered a baby boy, Stephen Lee, in February. Savannah talked to Toby, Liza, and *Dat* every other week, and she hoped to visit them soon. Savannah was also delighted to hear that Toby had found a roofing job he loved, started dating a couple of months ago, and was happy. Life was just about perfect.

Savannah sighed as she leaned against her husband while they climbed their front porch steps.

Korey smiled down at her. "That sounded like a *froh* sigh."

She reached up and touched his cheek. She loved how his beard had started to grow in. It had made him somehow even handsomer than he already was. "I need to tell you something."

"I've been thinking," he said at the same time, then laughed. "I'm sorry. You first."

"No, you."

"Okay." He took her hand while they stood on the porch together. "I was thinking that we should go see Toby in May."

"I would love that. I'm so excited to meet my new baby *bruder.*"

"Perfect." He rested his hands on her hips. "We'll make a plan, and Jay can run my roofing crew when we go. Now it's your turn to talk. Let me guess what you were about to say." He tapped his bearded chin. "You wanted to tell me that you love me."

She laughed and tapped his shoulder. "You already know that."

"*Ya*, that's true." He grinned. "Then tell me something I don't know."

Savannah touched her abdomen. "Well, I haven't been to the doctor yet, but I believe we're going to have a baby of our own."

His milk-chocolate-colored eyes widened, and he took her hands in his. "Savannah! Are you sure?"

She nodded.

Laughter burst from Korey's lips as he picked her up and twirled her around.

Savannah giggled and held on to him.

Then he set her down and pulled her close. She rested her head against his chest and breathed in his familiar, comfortable scent.

"I want to go to the doctor with you," he said.

She lifted her head. "Of course you will." Then she smiled. "*Ich liebe dich*, Korey."

"*Ich liebe dich*, Savannah." Then he leaned down and kissed her, and she smiled against his sweet lips as the wings from a thousand butterflies flapped in her chest.

She couldn't wait to see what God had in store for their little family.

ACKNOWLEDGMENTS

As always, I'm thankful for my loving family, including my mother, Lola Goebelbecker; my husband, Joe; and my sons, Zac and Matt. I'm blessed to have such an awesome and amazing family who puts up with me when I'm stressed out on a book deadline.

Thank you to my mother, as well as my dear friends Maggie Halpin and DeeDee Vazquetelles, who graciously read the draft of this book to check for typos.

Maggie, I can't believe this is the last book of mine that you proofread for me. Words can't describe how much I'll miss our discussions about writing and our giggles over my typos. You told me that you believed in Korey and related to his experience as a middle child. Every time I think of Korey, I always remember you and how much your encouragement for his story meant to me. I'll forever carry your friendship and love in my heart. I'll always miss you, sweet friend. Thank you for the precious memories.

I'm also grateful to my special Amish friend, who patiently answers my endless stream of questions.

Thank you to my wonderful church family at Morning Star Lutheran in Matthews, North Carolina, for your encouragement, prayers, love, and friendship. You all mean so much to my family and me.

Thank you to Zac Weikal and the fabulous members of my Bookworm Bunch! I'm grateful for your friendship and your excitement about my books. You all are amazing!

To my agent, Natasha Kern—I can't thank you enough for your guidance, advice, and friendship. You are a tremendous blessing in my life.

Thank you to my wonderful editor, Laura Wheeler, for your friendship and guidance. Thank you for all you've done to help me improve this book. I appreciate how you've pushed me and inspired me to dig deeper to improve both my writing and this book. I'm excited to work with you, and I look forward to our future projects together.

Special thanks to editor Becky Philpott for polishing the story and connecting the dots. I'm grateful that we are working together again!

I'm grateful to each and every person at HarperCollins Christian Publishing who helped make this book a reality.

To my readers—thank you for choosing my novels. My books are a blessing in my life for many reasons, including the special friendships I've formed with my readers. Thank you for your email messages, Facebook notes, and letters.

Thank you most of all to God for giving me the inspiration and the words to glorify you. I'm grateful and humbled you've chosen this path for me.

DISCUSSION QUESTIONS

1. Korey returns to Bird-in-Hand after spending fourteen months away. He had left after having a falling out with his older brother. Do you agree with his choice to leave his family? Or do you think he should have stayed and worked things out with Tyler?

2. Toby has low self-esteem because he has always struggled with reading and math and he was bullied in school. He compares himself to his cousins and believes he will never be successful working as a carpenter or in another trade. Can you relate to how he feels? Have you ever compared yourself to someone else? If so, how did you overcome those feelings of inadequacy?

3. Lee Zook, Savannah and Toby's father, left his children with his brother-in-law after his wife died. He was so distraught that he couldn't handle raising his children alone. What is your opinion on how he handled his grief? Do you think he was justified in returning to Bird-in-Hand and asking for a relationship with his children after nineteen years?

4. Korey befriended an elderly man in Sugarcreek, Ohio, who inspired him to return to Bird-in-Hand and work out his problems with his family. Have you ever been estranged from a family member? If so, were you able to reconcile your differences?

5. Savannah is angry when her father returns to Bird-in-Hand after abandoning her and her brother nineteen years ago. As her father explains why he left, however, Toby quickly feels a connection with him, and he longs to get to know him better. Do you think Toby forgave his father too soon? Or do you think Toby is right to long for a relationship with him?

6. Savannah believes she needs to move to New Wilmington to keep watch over her brother. Do you believe she is obligated to always look out for Toby since their mother passed away and their father left them? Why or why not? Have you ever felt it was your job to take care of another family member? If so, how did that situation turn out for you and your family member?

7. Tyler works hard to earn Korey's forgiveness, going as far as to beg Korey to talk to him. In the end, Korey apologizes to Tyler to mend their relationship. If you were in Tyler's shoes, would you have worked as hard as he did to fix your relationship with your sibling? Why or why not?

8. Jayden acts as the peacemaker of the Bontrager family, always trying to encourage his brothers to get along. Did you ever have that role in your family? If so, how did you handle it?

9. Crystal forgives Korey for treating her disrespectfully

in the past, and throughout the story, she becomes a wonderful confidant for him. How do you think Crystal felt when Korey apologized? Could you relate to her role as a stepparent?

10. Savannah realizes throughout the book that Bird-in-Hand is her home. She decides not to move to New Wilmington to be with her brother. Do you agree with her choice to stay in Bird-in-Hand and start a life with Korey? Why or why not?